Anne Herries lives in Cambridgeshire, where she is fond of watching wildlife, and spoils the birds and squirrels that are frequent visitors to her garden. Anne loves to write about the beauty of nature, and sometimes puts a little into her books—although they are mostly about love and romance. She writes for her own enjoyment, and to give pleasure to her readers. She is a winner of the Romantic Novelists' Association Romance Prize.

Previous novels by the same author:

MARRYING CAPTAIN JACK
THE UNKNOWN HEIR
THE HOMELESS HEIRESS
THE RAKE'S REBELLIOUS LADY
A COUNTRY MISS IN HANOVER SQUARE*
AN INNOCENT DEBUTANTE IN HANOVER SQUARE*
THE MISTRESS OF HANOVER SQUARE*
FORBIDDEN LADY†
THE LORD'S FORCED BRIDE†
THE PIRATE'S WILLING CAPTIVE†

*A Season in Town trilogy
†The Melford Dynasty

And in the Regency series
The Steepwood Scandal:

LORD RAVENSDEN'S MARRIAGE
COUNTERFEIT EARL

And in *The Hellfire Mysteries*:

AN IMPROPER COMPAN
A WEALTHY WIDOW
A WORTHY GENTLEMA

Chapter One

Stefan, Lord de Montfort, looked down at the body of the woman lying at the feet of her murderer. She had betrayed Stefan, lured him here to meet his death, but instead she lay dead, slain by the man who had once more plotted to destroy Stefan.

'You are a vile murderer,' Stefan accused, his eyes hard as he met those of his enemy. He was a strong man, broad in the shoulder and powerful, which is why his enemy had plotted to entrap him rather than meet him in open combat. 'She did all that you asked and yet you killed her…' He looked about him, seeking a weapon. He had not brought his sword to the chamber of a lady he thought innocent and so was unarmed.

'You are her murderer,' Sir Hugh said, an evil smile on his mouth. 'For I intend to see you dead, and she had to be silenced. She had served her purpose. Besides, she fell on my sword—which, as you know, was meant for you.'

'You are a cold devil,' Stefan said. He was trapped

in this house, for Sir Hugh was not alone. Stefan should never have been fool enough to come here alone and unarmed, but the lady Madeline had begged for his help. He saw the open window and knew that it might be his only way of escape. Yet even as he moved cautiously towards it, Sir Hugh lunged at him with his sword, just catching him with a slight slash to his thigh. Stefan dodged back, picking up a wooden stool and using it as a shield to fend off his attacker. Sir Hugh laughed like the demon he was, aware that Stefan was trapped and that he must win this time. 'I should have finished you the last time we met.' Sir Hugh bore a scar at his temple that was testimony to the last clash between them many years previously.

'This time I have the advantage…' Sir Hugh cried, triumph in his eyes. 'I have hated you since we were lads and you gave me this…' He motioned to the scar. 'Your brother was an arrogant brat and he gave me good sport before I killed him, but you—'

He broke off as the door crashed open and a large man came in. He was dressed in the clothes of a man of the east, his face horribly scarred, a turban on his head, and a wicked-looking scimitar in one hand, a sword in the other.

'It is as I thought, my lord, she trapped you,' Hassan said and threw the sword towards Stefan, who caught it neatly by the hilt. Even before he did so, Sir Hugh flung himself at the newcomer, slashing at him with his great sword and roaring his anger.

'Saracen dog! You should have died long ago!'

Hassan counter-attacked, his deadly blade flashing out in an arc and catching the other man's sword. With a twist of his wrist he sent the sword skimming across the floor and in the next instant his blade cut Sir Hugh across the body, a deep deadly wound that sent him sprawling to the ground, his lifeblood gushing out in a stream. For some minutes, he twitched, an expression of disbelief in his eyes, and then he lay still.

'That devil will bother us no more,' Hassan said, a look of satisfaction in his eyes. 'He has tortured and murdered for the last time, my lord.'

'Yes,' Stefan agreed. 'You have done what I should have done long ago, Hassan—but now we must leave for his men are coming....'

Stefan advanced to the door, sword in hand. The sounds of fighting would have reached the ears of Sir Hugh Grantham's men. They would need to fight their way out, side by side, as they had many times before this day, comrades and brothers, their swords for hire to any that would pay them.

Anne Melford stopped to watch the mummers on the village green. The men were a fine sight as they danced, the bells they wore on leather straps about their legs jingling merrily as they jigged to the fiddler's tune. The summer fair had come to Melford and Lady Melford had promised her daughter that they would buy cloth for new gowns, as was their custom. Normally, that thought would be pleasing, but Anne frowned as she turned away from the celebrations. Since her sister Catherine's wedding three years earlier, Anne had grown restless at home. Sometimes she despaired of it ever being her turn to visit the court and find a husband. Her parents had talked of it the previous year, but then her young brother had fallen ill and the visit had been postponed. At sixteen years of age it would have been usual for Anne to at least be betrothed by now and she had thought of her marriage constantly for years.

At one time she had believed herself in love with Will Shearer. She had feared Catherine might wed him, but Anne's sister had fallen in love with Andrew, Earl of Gifford. Anne occasionally visited her sister and brother-in-law and envied them their happiness. She was no longer sure who she wished to marry, for she knew that Will had recently married his mistress, a woman not of his own class. His marriage had made his mother very angry, and at first Anne had been terribly hurt because she had truly believed that he would love her one day. However, her distress had given way to a feeling of emptiness and uncertainty that grew with the passing of time. Perhaps her mother had decided that it would be best if she remained at home. It might be that she would never marry…

As she crossed the village green, Anne caught sight of two men approaching on horseback. It was not an unusual sight, except that one of them was dressed rather oddly in loose flowing robes over his leggings. His head was covered by some kind of cloth, the bottom half of his face hidden. She could see his black eyes and his nose, and noticed that his skin was the colour of polished walnut, as were the hands that held the reins of his horse. The second man was dressed as befitted a nobleman, though not in the English style, and, as Anne moved her curious gaze to him, she saw a fierce, proud, handsome face with eyes as blue as a summer sky. She noticed a dark brown stain on his silken hose and wondered if it were dried blood.

He had become aware of her interest and his gaze narrowed, icy cold and challenging. Anne was startled.

What could she possibly have done to make him look at her that way? She felt that he was hostile and shivered, feeling nervous as she hurried on her way. She sensed that the men were strangers to her village and wondered what brought them to this quiet valley in the Marches that lay on the borders of England and Wales.

She was not sure what nationality the men were; one had much lighter skin than the other, but both had a foreign air about them and she did not think that either was English. She wondered if they were Saracens, because one looked as if he came from the East, but what would men like that be doing here? Her father, Lord Robert Melford, sometimes traded with men from other lands, but she did not think they had come from her father's estate. She would judge that they had travelled some distance for there was dust on their boots, and the dark man's clothes had been spattered with brown marks that Anne took to be mud—or was it blood?

She thought about the strangers for a few minutes as she made her way through the meadows to her home. The grass was long and sprinkled with wild flowers—it had been left to grow wild and would be cropped for hay later in the year. However, as she entered the court-yard of her father's manor house she saw that several men on horseback had just arrived, and one of them was her elder brother Harry—or Sir Harry as he was known since King Henry had knighted him after Prince Arthur's wedding. Sadly, the prince had died only a few months after his marriage. The King's heir was now Prince Henry and there had been some talk of him marrying his brother's widow.

Anne's feeling of boredom vanished as she saw her brother. Harry was some years older than Anne, was

Catherine's twin, and was often at court or on some business for the King. He had not visited for more than six months and Anne's feeling of boredom vanished as she saw him.

'Harry! Harry!' Anne cried, gathering her skirt in one hand so that she could run faster, heedless of the fact that she was revealing a pair of pretty ankles.

Anne was in fact a very pretty young woman. Her hair always turned lighter in the sunshine, and it was presently the colour of ripe corn, lighter than Harry's dark auburn and their mother's red tresses. Anne's eyes were a greenish blue, but often became a deeper green when she was angry, at least her brothers told her so, because they said she had eyes like a cat. Slim, fiery and always eager for life, she had a temper that she was at pains to hide for her mother's sake.

'Anne!' Harry turned towards her with a smile on his lips. He had matured these past years and was now a powerful man, strong and influential at court, too busy to think often of his home and family. 'You grow more lovely each time I see you.'

'You hardly ever come home,' Anne accused, but with a smile on her lips because she was glad to see him. 'You are too busy with your fine friends at court. Mother said only yesterday that she despairs of you ever settling down.'

'Then perhaps she will be pleased with my news,' Harry said and grinned. 'It is my intention to take a wife quite soon. We shall live at court for a time, but once we have children my lady may wish to live on my estate—and Father will be pleased to learn that I have secured land no more than thirty leagues from Shrewsbury.'

'Close enough for us to visit you often,' Anne said and sighed. 'I am glad you are to wed at last, Harry, but I wish I was betrothed.'

Harry chuckled at his sister's impatience. 'What a woeful picture you are, Anne. You are still young enough, never fear. I dare say Father will take you to court before another year is out.'

Anne slipped her arm through his, smiling at him as they went into the house. His men were seeing to the horses and the baggage cart. These days Harry travelled with a train of at least ten men-at-arms and the servants necessary to fetch and carry for them.

'Sometimes I feel as if I shall be a maid all my life,' Anne said and pulled a face. 'But tell me, brother, what is the lady's name and where does she live?'

'She is Mademoiselle Claire St Orleans,' Harry said and gazed down at her, for she reached only as far as his shoulder. Above six foot in height and broad shouldered, Harry was a giant amongst men and very attractive. 'In truth, I do not know that she will take me. We have met but three times. Once at court, when she attended a masque with her father, and twice in Paris when I was on business for the King. She lives in the Loire valley and it is there that I must journey if I am to ask for her hand in marriage.'

'She is French?' Anne was surprised and curious. She wondered what her parents would think about Harry marrying a French lady. 'And of noble birth?'

'Her father is a comte,' Harry told her. 'She is very beautiful, Anne. Her hair is similar in colour to yours, but her eyes are blue. She has a soft, gentle nature and I love her. I have taken my time in deciding whether or not to ask Claire to be my wife, because she would have to leave her home and come to England to live. I am not sure that she will wish to give up so much for my sake.'

'If she loves you, she will not think it a sacrifice,' Anne told him. 'I would be willing to go anywhere with the man I loved.'

'Claire is not like you,' Harry said. 'You are braver... even reckless, as I remember from your childhood.'

'She would not have to be brave to marry you,' Anne said and laughed. 'If I had a few minutes alone with her, I would soon dispel any fear she might have about becoming your wife...'

Harry nodded, making no answer, but he was thoughtful as they went into the parlour where the sound of voices told them the family was gathered.

'We should rest,' Hassan said, glancing at his companion, who had endured his pain without complaint, but looked exhausted. 'That wound needs to be dressed. It has bled again, my lord.'

Stefan scowled at him. A more faithful friend than Hassan was not to be found in all the kingdoms of Christendom, though he be a Saracen and an unbeliever. They had fought shoulder to shoulder as mercenaries for ten years or more, bound by blood and friendship since Stefan had rescued Hassan from the slaver who had beaten and tortured him.

'I have known worse,' he growled, cursing the foolish moment that had led him to trust a lying woman. Undoubtedly, he owed his life to Hassan's timely intervention. 'Women are the devil incarnate, Hassan. Remind me of that next time I am minded to answer a woman's plea for help.'

Hassan grinned, his teeth white against the walnut tones of his skin. Looking at the top half of his face, none could guess at the fearful scars to the lower part… scars inflicted by Sir Hugh many years ago when he had for a short time been the man's slave.

'Devils in truth, my friend,' Hassan agreed. 'But sweeter than honey amongst the silken cushions of thy couch.'

Stefan's eyes narrowed as he thought of the beautiful woman who had enticed him to her chamber with tales of a cruel uncle. He had not known then that the man she spoke of as holding her to ransom was Sir Hugh and that she had conspired with him to capture a man it seemed they both hated. He knew there were reasons enough for Sir Hugh's hatred, but could not guess at the reason for Madeline's need to wreak revenge on him. It was doubtful if he would ever discover it now since she lay dead on the floor of her chamber, slain by the man who had enlisted her help. Yet he had played a part in her death, for he had thrown her towards Sir Hugh as he sought to escape the man who meant to kill him. He thought that he would never forget her scream as Sir Hugh's sword sliced into her stomach. Even though she had tried to trap him, he would never intentionally harm a woman, and her violent death would lay heavy on his conscience.

'Sweeter than honey, sharper than a serpent's tooth,' Stefan agreed. 'Thanks to you, Sir Hugh will not trouble us again, but he has a cousin…' Hassan nodded—they both knew that it was probably Lord Cowper who had ordered Stefan's death. 'Sir Hugh's death will add one more reason to the list he has for wanting me dead.'

'It is a pity that the English King would not grant you

a hearing, my lord,' Hassan said as Stefan dismounted. 'Had he done so, you might have revealed Cowper for the murdering devil he has become.'

'When my father disowned me, I swore I would never return to England's shores,' Stefan said. 'I left vowing never to forgive him for believing Cowper's lies. My father trusted him and now Cowper has all that was my father's and he lies rotting in the churchyard. I have his title, for none can take that from me, but his lands are lost, stolen by trickery and deceit. Had I returned years ago, I might have saved my father from the evil trick that was played on him in his declining years. As his mind descended into blackness they took everything he had, though they have deeds and letters to prove the land was sold and the money lost in foolish ventures. Answer me this—whose was the hand that guided an old man's as he squandered his birthright?'

'Lord Cowper gained too much influence over your father,' Hassan said. 'We have the testimony of Lord de Montfort's steward, who was later dismissed for some wrongdoing and left to starve.'

'Edmund would never have stolen even half a loaf from my father,' Stefan said. 'But Cowper is a clever man. He found it easy to convince my father that I had murdered my brother in cold blood. I found Gervase lying in the forest with his hands bound and his throat cut. I know it was either Sir Hugh or Cowper himself who murdered my brother, but because Gervase and I had quarrelled violently that very morning, my father chose to believe I was guilty. He disowned me, told me to leave England or he would hand me over to the King for justice. If he would believe that of his eldest son, how much easier was it to convince him that his steward had been robbing him for years?'

A nerve was flicking at Stefan's temple. The injustice that had been done him when he was a young man still rankled deep inside him. He had taken his sword and a horse when he rode away from his home at the edge of the great forest of Sherwood, finding a ship bound for France. From there he had travelled to many lands, hiring his sword to any merchant or prince that would take him. He had grown rich on the spoils of war, and it was not for money that he had returned to England. His hope of reconciliation with his father had ended with the news of his death, and the discovery that Lord Cowper now owned everything that ought by rights to have been Stefan's.

His request for an audience with King Henry had been denied. His reputation as a mercenary had gone before him and his claims were dismissed without due hearing. His father had disowned him and Cowper had the deeds to the land and house, signed and witnessed by a man of impeccable character—Sir Hugh Grantham. How King Henry would have felt if he had learnt that during his years on a so-called pilgrimage to the Holy Land, Sir Hugh had murdered, raped and lived as a slaver, growing rich on his ill-gotten goods, would never be known for the words would never now be heard. Even more damning might be the suspicion that Sir Hugh was in the pay of Spain and therefore an enemy of England. Since the death of Queen Isabella, relations between England and Spain were not as warm as they had once been.

Stefan knew that his accusations of murder and trick-ery would fall on deaf ears once he was refused a private audience with Henry of England. Indeed, the English estate meant little to him, for he now owned a beautiful chateau and extensive lands in Normandy, much of which had been granted to him by the French king in return for a large payment of gold and silver. It was the bitterness of knowing that his father had died neglected and mistreated, and the way he had been driven from his birthright by wicked lies that gnawed at Stefan's guts and made him thirst for revenge.

Stefan was thoughtful as he dismounted. One of his enemies was now dead, but the other remained, as vicious as a poison adder and twice as dangerous. It would not be so easy to get to Lord Cowper, for he stayed within the confines of his manor house, protected by an army of servants and armed men, afraid of the vengeance that threatened while Stefan lived and breathed. His attempts to have his enemy murdered would only become more determined now that Sir Hugh was dead.

Stefan squatted down on the earth, his back to a tree as Hassan examined the wound, applying salves that had been made by skilled men of Arabia. A fierce fight had ensued during their escape from the house, during which Stefan had received a wound to his side, which pained him far more than the scratch to his thigh inflicted by Sir Hugh.

'You will do for a few hours,' Hassan said as he bound him tightly, 'but the wound should be tended by a physician.'

'I would trust none in this country; the physicians here are ignorant and hidebound by conventions,' Stefan muttered, gritting his teeth against the pain. 'We must go home to France, Hassan. I cannot fight in this condition.

We need more men and we must be careful. The law here protects Cowper. I want him to pay for his crimes, but I have to find a way to prove his guilt. I must have incontrovertible proof and I must find someone who stands high in the King's favour to present it—or at least to help me gain a hearing at court.'

'Aye, but first we must make our way to the coast and find a ship,' Hassan said. 'You will rest better at home in Normandy. Once you are healed, we can find a way to take revenge for what has been done here.'

'I want justice for my father's shade,' Stefan said. 'Otherwise his face will haunt my dreams. Sir Hugh is dead, and I believe it was he who murdered my brother, but it is Cowper that has my father's lands.' His eyes were as cold as the North Sea. 'I swear by all I hold dear that he shall pay with his life one day…'

Anne heard her father's voice as she paused outside his chambers. She knew that Harry was with him and they had been talking for a long time. Lord Melford would be delighted with the news that his son had decided to marry, but would he be as pleased with the revelation that the bride was French?

Anne knocked at the door and was invited to enter. Her father looked at her as she did so, his brows lifting. 'Your mother has sent you to fetch us to table, I dare say?'

'Yes, Father. Mother says that supper is ready, and she wants to talk to Harry.'

'In other words, I have kept you too long to myself, Hal,' his father told him with a smile. 'We must not keep Lady Melford waiting another second. She will want to hear all you can tell her about the lovely lady you intend to ask to wed you.'

Anne realised that her father was happy with the marriage. He did not mind that the lady Claire St Orleans was French, and that pleased Anne, for she would not have wished her brother to be disappointed.

Lord Melford's eyes came to rest on his daughter. 'As for you, miss, your brother has made a request of me that I am minded to grant, but we must ask your mother first. She may not agree that you should go with Harry to fetch the lady Claire home to us.'

'Go with Harry?' Anne's pulses leaped with excitement as she looked at her brother. 'Do you mean it? May I truly come to France with you?'

'Father has given his permission if Mother agrees,' Harry told her and grinned. 'I thought it might be a good thing if Claire met someone from my family, someone who thinks well of me and will reassure her that I am to be trusted. Otherwise she might refuse me.'

'Oh, Harry, thank you,' Anne cried, her excitement bubbling over. 'I should like that so very much.'

'Well, we must ask your mother first,' Lord Melford said, but with an indulgent look. 'Had circumstances not interfered, you would have been taken to court at least once before this, Anne. It may do you good to see something of the world outside this house and our village. We have excellent neighbours, but few young men of your age. It is possible that you may meet someone in Harry's company. On your return from France, you will go with him to London, and make your long-delayed appearance there. Lady Melford and I will come up to join you. We shall all return here for the wedding.'

Anne's smile lit up her eyes. It was all she had longed

for—an adventure that would take her somewhere far away from her home. To visit London had once been the extent of her dreams, but France conjured such pictures in her mind, though she had little to go on except for stories that Harry sometimes told her about the French court. He was one of King Henry's trusted courtiers and had visited several countries in his Majesty's service. She knew that he spoke both French and Spanish fluently, so perhaps it was not surprising that his choice had fallen on a French lady.

'It is so good of you to take me, Harry,' she told him excitedly. 'You are the very best of brothers!'

'I hope you will tell Claire that,' Harry said. 'I have gifts for both you and Mother in my saddlebags. It is as well that the fair is coming tomorrow, for you will need a new gown before we leave, Anne.'

'When are we to leave?' Anne asked.

'In three days,' her brother replied. 'I have a month before I need to return to court. I know that Henry has further work for me soon, but he has granted me leave to visit my home and to fetch my bride home…if she will have me. I shall need to spend time at Claire's home, and if we marry I shall wish some time alone with her before I return to my duties, so the sooner we start our journey, the better.'

'How could she refuse you?' Anne asked. She was surprised and thrilled that her brother wanted her to accompany him. 'When I tell her how kind and generous you are, she will be happy to wed you.'

It was as they returned home from the fair that afternoon that the news came to Melford of a terrible murder in Shrewsbury.

'Lady Madeline Forester and her uncle, Sir Hugh Grantham, were brutally slain,' Lord Melford told his family when they gathered that evening. 'Sir Hugh's men tried to stop the murderers escaping and they wounded one, but unfortunately the rogues escaped.'

'That is awful,' Melissa said, her eyes dark with shock as she looked at her husband. 'When did this terrible thing happen?'

'It must be two days gone,' Rob replied.

'And do they know the names of these evil men?'

'The messenger did not say. Apparently one was dark-skinned, perhaps a Saracen, from the east certainly, and the other might have been Spanish or French. He did not look English, I am told, but that might mean anything.'

'I did not care for Sir Hugh,' Melissa, said frowning slightly. 'But the lady Madeline was pleasant enough, though I have met her but once. Her elder sister died tragically by her own hand some years ago I believe. There was some story of her having been with child.'

'She was to be betrothed to Gervase de Montfort,' Rob said. 'Few knew of the arrangement, for I believe it was not spoken of—and he was murdered. Some say by his own brother, though I have always wondered if there was some mystery there. However, Stefan de Montfort left England and the scandal was hushed up. He would be Lord de Montfort since his father's death, of course, though there is nothing left of the estate. Lord Cowper purchased it when the old man lost his fortune.'

'That is a sad story, Father,' Anne said and shivered. 'And now the lady Madeleine has been murdered and her uncle with her…who could do such a terrible thing?'

'It may have been robbers,' Rob replied. 'I do not

know of anyone living locally that answers the description of the men involved. Perhaps they were just passing through. I doubt that it would have been local men.'

Anne remembered the two strangers she had seen on the day of Harry's arrival. She wondered if she ought to mention them to her father but decided against it. Even if they were the men who had murdered the lady Madeline and her uncle, they would be long gone by now, and she could not be certain that they had been anywhere near Shrewsbury…though they had seemed to come from that direction. She decided to say nothing. If the travellers had passed through it was best if they went unheeded and were never seen again, for if they had brutally murdered a lady and a knight, they would murder anyone else who got in their way.

The seamstresses had sat up all night to finish Anne's new gown, which was made of a dark emerald green silk and became her well. She would not wear it on the journey but keep it for when they arrived at the Comte's chateau in France. It was packed into her trunk with all her very best things and was on the baggage cart, which had started out some hours earlier so as to be at the arranged meeting place by the time they arrived.

Anne hugged her mother excitedly, thanking her for allowing her to accompany Harry to fetch his bride home. It was such an adventure, for she would go to court when she returned to England and who knew what might happen then? She might even meet a handsome young man in France!

'Be mindful of your brother and remember your manners,' Melissa said as she kissed Anne's cheek. 'You are sometimes inclined to be hasty, dearest, though I know you have a good heart.'

'I promise I shall do all that you would wish,' Anne said, her lovely face serious. She had never been parted from her mother in her life and realised that she would miss her and her young brother. 'I shall do nothing that would make either you or Father ashamed of me.'

'I know that you have oft thought of marriage, but be careful where you give your heart,' Melissa said. 'I was fortunate to find your father, and Catherine is happy with Andrew. I would wish for you to be as fortunate in your marriage, my love.'

'I shall heed your warning, dearest Mother,' Anne promised. 'I thought once that my heart was given, and that he would ask me to marry him one day—but it was not to be and I shall be careful in future.'

Anne's groom came forward then to help her mount her palfrey. She realised that Harry was waiting and she broke away from her mother. Her eyes were moist as she waved goodbye to them; parting was harder than she had anticipated. However, after they had been riding for a few hours the shadows passed and her excitement began to mount once more.

That night they stopped at an inn that Harry had frequented before and the rooms were the best the host had to offer. Anne's maid had accompanied them and she slept on a truckle bed beside the bed where Anne lay, the sound of her snores keeping her mistress awake for a while.

When Anne awoke her maid was still snoring gently. Anne slipped from the bed and looked out of the window.

She was in time to see two men on horseback; they were leaving and had obviously stayed overnight, though she had seen nothing of them—it had been late when they arrived and she had gone straight to her chamber. There was something familiar about the travellers, but it was not until some minutes later that she remembered the strangers who had come to her village. The man who looked as if he might be from the East—and the man who had looked at her so coldly!

Were they wicked murderers? Anne shuddered as it occurred to her that they might all have been slain as they slept, but then common sense returned. She was still alive and as far as she knew no one else had been attacked during the night. The travellers might be quite innocent and it was a good thing that she had not spoken to anyone about her suspicions.

They continued their journey after they had broken their fast in the inn parlour. All seemed peaceful and the host was as cheerful and friendly as the previous night. Clearly no evil deeds had been done here and Anne put the two men out of her mind. She was too interested in looking about her on the road for she had never been this way before.

When they reached the port on the third day, Anne was glad to see the inn where they would stop for the night. She was not used to so much riding, and, though she would not have confessed it to her brother, her back ached and she was weary. The hour was too late to see much, but the tall masts of a ship were visible in the small harbour. Despite her weariness as she sought her bed that night, Anne was once again excited. She had never been on a ship before and she felt that it would be a true adventure.

'If you feel a little ill at first, you must not mind it,' Harry told her before they parted that night. 'Many people are seasick, Anne, but if we have good weather it should not be too bad. It is only if the sea becomes really rough that the effects are truly unpleasant.'

'I hope I do not feel sick, because I want to spend as much time on deck as I can,' Anne told her brother, eyes bright with enthusiasm. 'I have never been to the sea, Harry, but I love the smell of it already. I cannot wait for the morning.'

'Well, we must break our fast at six, for the tide leaves at seven.' Harry smiled at her. 'Sleep well, sister. Never fear that I shall fail to wake you.'

Anne thanked him, then left straight for bed. She fell asleep quickly, for she was tired.

She was awake at dawn and dressed when he came to knock at her door. She opened it to him and smiled, eager to begin the next part of their journey. Surely being carried over the sea in a ship must be less tiring than riding a horse for so many leagues?

Watching all the people going on board was interesting. The cargo was being loaded as they arrived, bales of good English wool that would be sold in France and traded for lace, French wines and other goods. Anne was reluctant to go below to their cabin, but Harry insisted it would be safer for her until they were underway. The ship's crew was busy and passengers would only be a nuisance until they had cleared the harbour.

Anne went down to the cabin she had been allocated for the voyage. It seemed small and airless and she felt restless until the ship began to move and Harry told her that she could come up on deck.

'Sailors are sometimes superstitious about women on board,' Harry told her as they stood on deck and watched the shores of England receding into the distance. 'I thought it best you should stay below until we were under sail, because with all the activity on deck accidents can happen. Mother would never forgive me if you were hurt, Anne.'

'Why should anything happen?' Anne asked and laughed, because she was feeling so pleased with life. The sea was calm and the sky above their heads was a beautiful azure blue. 'It was so good of you to bring me, Harry. I love being at sea. Everything is so exciting!'

'We are fortunate in the weather,' Harry said and glanced up at the sky. 'I heard one of the sailors say he expected a storm before nightfall, but I cannot believe it when the sky is so blue.'

'A storm?' Anne asked and shook her head. 'I am sure he is mistaken, Harry. It is a lovely summer day— how could there be a storm?'

Anne wondered how it was possible for the weather to change so fast. One minute the skies had been clear blue, and then clouds started to drift across the sky; small and fluffy at first, they gradually became one mass of grey. As the afternoon wore on the wind began to rise and the sea became much rougher, the waves rising higher and higher so that by the time the light faded the ship was being tossed about like a child's toy in a giant's hand.

Most of the passengers had gone below to their cabins, and Anne had seen several of them being sick over the side of the ship. She wondered if it would affect her, but she seemed to be immune to the sickness that others were suffering.

'Do you not think you would be better below?' Harry asked when the storm worsened and the spray came right over the sides of the ship.

Anne shook her head. The wind whipped her hair about her face and she could taste the salt spray on her lips, but she found the storm exhilarating. She looked beautiful, a recklessness about her that made her brother laugh.

'I would prefer to stay here if I may,' she said. 'It is so stuffy and cramped in my cabin, Harry. I think I should be sick if I had to stay there. I should like to remain on board for as long as possible.'

Harry looked at her doubtfully. 'I am not sure it is wise,' he said as a huge wave came rushing towards the ship. He grabbed his sister and held her as the water came over the side of the ship, knocking it sideways so that some cargo that had been lashed down with ropes broke free and began to slide towards them. 'We should go below…' He pulled Anne clear of the loose cargo, but one of the ropes caught him, knocking him to the ground. He went sliding towards the side of the ship. Anne screamed and ran after him, thinking he would be swept overboard.

'Harry…' she cried. 'Harry…'

Harry grabbed an iron hook that was used for securing ropes and held on to it as yet another mountainous wave came towards them. The ship was thrown to one side, listing heavily as it took water on board. Anne was caught mid-deck and the force of the wave knocked her off her feet. She was swept across the deck by the water that rushed over the ship, knocking her head against something hard and falling into blackness as the water claimed her.

'Anne… Oh, my God, Anne,' Harry cried as he struggled to his feet. He shouted for help as he ran to the side where he had last seen his sister, peering into the darkness. There were wooden crates and other debris from the ship floating in the water, for the storm had taken one of their masts. 'Anne…Anne…' Harry peered over the side in desperation, searching for a sight of her. 'Help! Man overboard!'

Most of the sailors were too busy fighting the storm as it played havoc with their vessel to heed his cry, but one young sailor came to join him at the rails.

'I saw her go,' he told Harry. 'The force of the water took her over and she must have hit her head. She probably went down, and if she didn't we'll never find her in this. She is lost…lost to the sea…'

'No! She can't be lost,' Harry said. 'We have to find her. We have to get her back. She is my sister. My parents will never forgive me…' He gave a cry of despair and put his foot on the rail as if he would jump into the sea after Anne. 'I have to find her.'

'Stop him!' the young sailor cried. 'It's no use, sir. She's gone…you'll never find her.' He grabbed hold of Harry, struggling to stop him from throwing his life away by jumping in after his sister. 'Help me…' he cried and a couple of sailors came to his assistance. Seeing that Harry was out of his mind with worry and would not be subdued, one of them grabbed a baton and struck him on the back of the head so that he slumped to the deck. 'What did you do that for?' the young sailor asked.

'He'll be better below deck until the storm is done.

There's nothing to be done for the wench now. He should have taken her below before the storm reached its height. We haven't time to bother with this now or we'll all end up at the bottom of the ocean. The girl is lost—forget her and get about your work or you'll feel the bosun's lash!'

The storm had gone as if it had never been. Driven south by the furious winds, the French ship, Lady Maribelle, had headed for shelter as soon as it struck and ridden out the worst of the weather. Now it was putting out to sea again, making its way up the coast to Normandy. Hassan was on deck, staring out towards the coastline. He was one of the first to see the debris tossed by the still-choppy water. He shaded his eyes with a hand, because after a storm like the one the previous night it was not unexpected that a ship might have been capsized and sunk. He shouted to one of the crew and pointed, and others came crowding to the side of the Lady Maribelle, staring at what was possibly the wreckage of a ship. It was obvious that some cargo had been lost and part of a mast.

'What is that?' Stefan asked as he caught sight of what looked like a half-clothed body. 'Man overboard! There is someone caught in the debris.'

Excited voices echoed his discovery and the decision was made to put a boat over the side. They all knew that whoever was in the sea was more likely to be dead than alive, but every man jack aboard was more than willing to help in the recovery. They lived by the sea and sometimes died by it, and if there was a small chance that the man in the water was alive they would do their best for him, because one day it might be one of them.

Hassan and Stefan joined the volunteers. Six more of the crew went with them as the boat was lowered and cast off. It took only a few minutes to reach the debris, and as they drew close silence fell over the men, as it became apparent that the body was that of a young woman. The sea had torn much of her clothing away from her, and only a thin shift covered the bottom half of her body, her breasts exposed to their eyes and the elements.

Stefan leaned over the side of the boat, slipping into the water to grab hold of the body. Her limbs had become entangled with the ropes attached to the mast and it was this that had kept her afloat. He cut her free with his knife and then dragged her back to the boat, where eager hands reached out to haul her on board.

'Is she dead?' one of the sailors asked. 'Poor lass.'

'I'm not sure,' Stefan said. 'I think one of her hands twitched as I cut her free. Hassan, give her your cloak, please. Cover her for decency's sake, whether she be alive or dead.'

Hassan did as Stefan asked, wrapping the thick, soft material about her. As he did so her eyelids flickered and her lips moved, though no sound came out.

'Allah be praised,' Hassan cried. ''Tis a miracle that the waters did not claim her.'

'Had it been winter, she could not have survived the night in these waters,' Stefan said. 'We must get her back on board as swiftly as possible, for she may yet die if we do not bring back some warmth to her body.'

The sailors made a murmur of agreement. Women were often considered to be unlucky on board ship, but no one grudged the poor lass her chance at life.

'The Seagull, that be the name of the ship that was

lost,' one of the sailors said as he caught sight of some writing on one of the chests. 'I cannot see any other survivors nor yet more bodies. Mayhap they were swept further down by the tide.'

'We'll keep an eye out,' one of the sailors said. 'But the woman comes first. She clings to life, but only God can save her now.'

Stefan looked at Hassan, shaking his head as he saw the unspoken protest. Sailors were simple folk and superstitious enough without making them suspicious. If Hassan told them that the woman would live if she were properly cared for, they might think him a dealer in the black arts, especially because of his looks.

'I shall care for her,' Stefan said. They would not deny him—he was a nobleman and respected in the country he had made his own. 'I saw her first and I claimed her from the sea, therefore she is my responsibility. If she still lives when we reach shore, I shall take her to my home. If she recovers, she will need help to return to her home, wherever that may be.'

Stefan was helped to carry the young woman's body up the rope ladder, and more hands reached down to lift her on to the deck. Some of the sailors crossed themselves as they looked down at her. Wrapped in Hassan's cloak, it was possible only to see her face and her hair, which was a dark blonde and soaked with salt water. Her skin was pale, her lips blue and yet her eyelids flickered and her lips moved slightly, proving that she was still alive.

''Tis a miracle…'

'Or the devil's work,' one sailor said and crossed himself again. 'How is it possible that she survived a night like that in the sea?'

'She was caught by ropes and the broken mast kept her head above water,' Stefan said. He bent down and gathered the unconscious woman into his arms. 'I shall take her to my cabin until we make land.'

Below in the cabin, which was the best on board, Stefan laid the woman on his bed. He looked at Hassan over his shoulder as he followed him into the room.

'We must get her out of what remains of her clothing and wrap her in as many blankets as we have. I have some strong brandy wine in my sea chest. When we have her dry and warm, we shall give her some. Once we are home, Ali will help her—but she may not survive the journey.'

'It is fortunate that we found her in time,' Hassan said. 'Allah must have meant it, for otherwise we should have passed her by. He has given her to us, my lord. From now on her life is in our hands.'

'As Allah wills it?' Stefan shot him a suspicious look. 'Yet you would have denied them earlier, for I saw it in your face.'

'They are ignorant fools, for they would do nothing to help her. Allah has sent her to us, but her fate is in our hands; if we did nothing, left her to live or die as God wills it, as they would given the chance, she would die.'

Stefan's face was harsh as he bent over the young woman. He rubbed her skin with a drying cloth until she felt dry to the touch and some warmth started to come back to her body, and then he wrapped her in every blanket and cloak he could find. He would not argue with Hassan on the subject of religion, for he did not believe in God. Once he had been Christian, but now he had his own faith, which was to give justice for justice and hurt for hurt. He had been forced to live by the sword and he knew that in time he would die by it. There was no room for softness or religion in his life. However, he was not a cruel man and he did not take life without good cause. He had pulled this young woman from the sea more alive than dead, and he would do all he could to make her live.

Harry came to himself to find a young sailor bending over him. He groaned because his head ached. For a moment he could not think what had happened to him, and he stared at the sailor blankly.

'What happened to me?'

'Someone hit you as we struggled to stop you jumping into the sea last night,' the sailor said. 'You would have gone after her, sir, and it was hopeless. She must have gone down like a stone when she hit the water, for there was no sign of her.'

'Anne!' Memory came flooding back. Harry sat up in alarm, his aching head forgotten as a deeper pain took hold. 'My sister…she was swept overboard by a huge wave and I could not help her. What have I done? My father will blame me and he will be justified; I should have taken better care of her. She wanted to stay on deck while the storm raged, because she thought it exciting, but I should have made her go below. She is lost and I am at fault…'

'No one could have seen it coming,' the sailor said. 'We rode the storm out because we headed inshore and sheltered for the night, but for a while it was touch and go whether the ship went down. Had your sister been below she would then have gone down with the vessel, as many others would. You were as safe on deck as anywhere until those freak waves hit us. If that had not happened, your sister would not have been swept overboard.'

Harry shook his head. He felt stunned, racked with guilt and despair at the thought of his younger sister going to a watery grave. He wished that the sailors had not stopped him going into the sea. At least he could have searched for her, made certain that there was no hope of her being found alive.

Harry wished that he had not thought of bringing Anne with him. He had forgotten how dangerous the sea could be for the unwary. But the waves had been so huge. Harry had never experienced anything like it himself, though he had been to sea many times. Who could have imagined that a summer storm could come from nowhere and be so fierce? It was a miracle that the ship had survived! He knew that if he had not been lucky enough to catch hold of that iron ring himself he, too, would have been swept into the raging sea.

He would rather it had been him than his lovely sister! Harry had not been as close to Anne as to his twin Catherine, but he had loved her—he still loved her and mourned her. He was not sure how he would find the strength to go on with his purpose. How could he court Claire when his heart was so heavy?

Harry had written to her father and was honour bound to complete his journey to the Comte's chateau. Yet if there was even a slight chance that Anne might have survived he would leave no stone unturned to find her. Occasionally, sailors were pulled alive from the wreckage of a ship, but Anne was a frail girl. It was unlikely that she could survive a night in the cold waters of the Channel.

If there were any chance that Anne had been plucked from the sea, dead or alive, he owed it to her and his family to discover it. He would set agents to search from port to port. He held little hope that she would be found alive, but, if her body had chanced to be washed on shore, he could at least make sure that she was decently buried.

Harry's grief lay over him like a dark cloud. He knew that the news would also sorely grieve his parents, and he was not certain whether it would be best to write at once and send the letter back to England with the ship or wait.

Perhaps it would be best to wait for a while. If her body could be found, he might at least offer some comfort that she had been properly buried. However, it was more likely that she was lost at sea and nothing remained. No doubt their family would want to mourn her and hold a service of remembrance, but that was for the future. Harry would leave no stone unturned in the hope of news of Anne, though he knew it must be a hopeless cause.

Chapter Two

'Is there any change?' Stefan asked of the physician as he entered the bedchamber where the young woman lay in the great wooden bed. They had brought her to Chateau de Montifiori ten days earlier. For eight days the fever had raged as her skin heated and she tossed restlessly on the pillows; her long hair was matted by sweat and salt, for they had not dared to wash it. Ali Ben Hammed had suggested cutting it at one time, but Stefan had resisted, despite the physician's insistence that her hair was taking her strength. However, on the ninth day the fever had waned and the girl seemed less restless. As yet she had not opened her eyes. Stefan walked to the bed and laid his hand on her forehead. Her temperature seemed normal. He looked at the Arab physician, a man skilled in the arts of medicine, and a friend of some nine years since he had rescued him from Sir Hugh Grantham, who had ordered his execution at the stake. Had Stefan not intervened, Ali would have been burned to death. He looked at the physician. 'Why does she not wake? She no longer has a fever.'

'I cannot tell,' Ali replied, his face wizened by the hot sun of his native land and the passing of years. 'I know that sometimes the mind lies dormant so that the body may heal. I believe that she is past the worst, my lord, though when she will awake I know not. She may not remember anything when she does, for the trauma she has experienced will be hard to bear, especially if she has lost loved ones.'

'She would not have been travelling alone,' Stefan said. 'If the vessel was sunk, it is likely that all the others perished. It was mere chance that she was caught by the ropes to that mast and survived the perils of the ocean.'

'As Allah wills,' Ali said, steepling his hands and bending his head. 'It was meant to be that you should find her, my lord. If you save a life, that life is yours. You are bound to her and must protect her henceforth.'

Stefan frowned. 'If she ever wakes, and can tell me her name and her family, I shall see her restored to them,' he said. 'You should know that there is no room in my life for a woman…especially one like this. Her hair will be beautiful once it is washed free of the salt and sweat, and her hands are soft. She has never done manual work.'

'A lady,' Ali agreed, nodding wisely. 'Do you not wonder why Allah brought her to you, my lord? These things are for a purpose. She has some place in your life, otherwise it would not have been so ordained.'

'I would not offend you or Hassan,' Stefan said, his features set in harsh lines. 'But I have no God and I see no purpose for a woman in my life. I have lived by the sword and shall doubtless die by it. Lord Cowper is responsible for my father's untimely death, and for the life I have led. I have sworn vengeance and when I am ready I shall return to England and take back what is mine. By the end of this year either he or I will lie in the earth. This I owe to my father's shade!'

'Your wound is not yet completely healed,' Ali said, ignoring this speech for the most part. He knew as well as anyone that Stefan had suffered too much injustice, and that he had reason enough to be bitter. Yet he had never allowed this to interfere with his compassion for others. Ali was not the only one to have benefited; Stefan de Montfort had rescued and taken in more than one casualty of life. 'It would be foolish to confront your enemy while you are at a disadvantage, would it not, my lord?'

'And?' Stefan's gaze narrowed.

'Who knows?' Ali asked, deliberately obtuse. 'The girl is here and she needs your help. I do not believe you would desert her.'

'Once she knows who she is, I shall return her to her family. As that is probably in England, she may accompany me when I return to confront Lord Cowper.'

'In the meantime, it is best that you rest, my lord,' Ali said. 'The young woman must also rest. Perhaps in time you may learn the reason she was sent to you.'

'It was chance,' Stefan said, 'and the tides.'

'Ah, chance and the tides.' Ali smiled as he turned away. 'Who but Allah controls the tides…'

Stefan was no longer listening. A low moaning sound came from behind him. He turned and looked at the bed. The woman was stirring, her eyelids fluttering. He bent over her, stroking the damp hair back from her forehead with hands that were surprisingly gentle for such a man.

'Do not fear, mademoiselle,' he said softly, the timbre of his voice deep and caressing. 'You are quite safe here. You have been very ill, but you will soon be better now.'

The woman opened her eyes, which he saw were a deep blue-green, like the changing waters of the Mediterranean Sea on a sunlit day. She stared at him for a moment, looking bewildered. Her hand reached towards him and her lips moved, then her hand dropped and she closed her eyes once more. He had the oddest feeling that he had seen her before, though he could not place her in his memory.

'What is wrong?' Stefan asked of the physician. 'Is she better or not? Her skin feels cool…and she opened her eyes for a moment.'

'She is sleeping because she is exhausted,' Ali said as he looked down at her. 'She will live, my lord, but her recovery may be slow—and she will need your help.'

Stefan looked down at the woman. He had saved her from the sea and brought her to his home for Ali to nurse. She was beautiful, it was true, but he had seen lovely women before; he had taken those he desired to his bed but none had touched the inner core he guarded. This one was no different. She had tugged at something deep inside him as she lay hovering between life and death, but once she was well he would help her to find safety and then forget her.

'We are sorry to learn of your tragic loss,' Comte St Orleans said as he welcomed Harry to his home in Normandy. 'Your late arrival made us wonder if something had happened and when your letter came my daughter was much affected by the tragedy.'

'I thank you for your kind words, sir,' Harry said and glanced at the young woman standing just behind her father. She was as beautiful as always and his heart caught with love, and yet his grief was still so raw and so terrible that he could not summon a smile for her. 'I was delayed, for I have employed agents to search for any sign of Anne. I know there is little hope of her being found alive—we could see no sign of her in the water. However, if her body were found, I could at least tell our family that she rests in peace.'

Claire came forward, a look of such sorrow and sweetness on her face that Harry caught his breath. She was all he could ever desire in a wife, and he loved her so! 'We are happy to have you here while the search continues, are we not, Father? And if there is anything we may do to help you, we should wish to be of service.'

'Your kindness overwhelms me,' Harry said and took her hand. He held it briefly, but made no attempt to kiss it, as he would have had they met under other circumstances. The gallantry and experience of a handsome courtier had fled before the tide of grief that possessed him, and he could be no more than the man he was at heart. 'I fear it is an impossible task, but I have asked that any news should come to me here for the next few weeks, and I shall avail myself of your kind offer, mademoiselle.'

'You must refresh yourself and rest after your journey,' the Comte said, nodding his approval. He had not been certain that the young man they had met at the English court would do for his precious daughter, but now he saw that the polished manners of a popular courtier hid an honest heart, and one that grieved sincerely. It would be interesting to see what developed between the two over the next weeks, for the Comte would not influence his daughter one way or the other. Claire was free to decide for herself. 'I shall also send out messengers for I may know more of the tides than you, Sir Harry. Between us, we should be able to find news of your sister if there is any to find...'

'I pray that one of us is successful,' Harry said. 'Anne is my younger sister and I feel responsible for what happened to her.'

Claire rested her hand on his arm. 'The sea is a cruel mistress, sir. You must grieve for your sister, but the blame does not lie with you.'

She opened her eyes, whimpering as the light hurt them. Her body felt so sore and painful, as if she had been punched and kicked, and her head ached. She put up a hand to touch her face and then her hair. It was matted, tangled and stiff, as if it had not been washed for a long time. She did not like the feel of it that way and shuddered, because something was terribly wrong, though for the moment she had no idea what it was. She tried to sit up, but fell back as the dizziness overcame her. She was too weak and she cried out for help.

'So, you are awake at last,' a man's voice said and someone came to the bed. The sun had darkened his skin and his eyes were black like little jet beads. However, there was something reassuring about him. 'Do not fear me, little one. You have been ill for a long time and I have tended you. Soon you will be better, but for the moment you must rest. A serving woman will bring you some nourishing soup. You must try to eat it because it will help build your strength.'

'May I have some water?' she asked.

'Yes, of course.'

The man went to a small walnut chest-on-stand at the far side of the room, filled a cup with water from a pewter ewer and brought it back to her. He supported her as she took a few sips, but the effort exhausted her and she fell back against the pillows once more.

'As I said, you must rest. Your strength will come back soon.'

'Who are you?' the woman asked. 'And where am I?'

'My name is Ali. I am a physician and this is the Chateau de Montifiori. We are both guests of Lord de Montfort.'

The woman frowned. She closed her eyes for a moment, and her hands worked restlessly on the covers, then she opened her eyes and looked at him once more.

'I do not know you. I do not know Lord de Montfort...' A little wail of despair issued from her lips. 'I do not know who I am or where I came from...'

'You were on a ship bound for France from England and the ship sank in a storm,' Ali told her. 'I do not know your name, little one—but it will come back to you in time.'

'Will it?' The woman's eyes were fearful as she looked at him. 'If the ship sank, how did I come here?'

'Lord de Montfort pulled you from the water. He saved your life and he brought you here. He placed you in my care and I have used my arts to make you well. When you are better, you will be returned to your family.'

'Were my family on the ship? Were they saved too?'

'You were the only one found. Some ropes had

secured you to the ship's mast and it was for this reason that you survived. It was Allah's will.'

'Allah…' The woman wrinkled her brow as she tried to understand what he was saying. 'Is Allah not the god of the infidel Saracens?'

'You must be a Christian, for only a Christian would speak thus of Allah,' Ali told her and smiled, clearly amused. 'We are followers of the beloved prophet Mohamed, and our faith is shared by many peoples of the east. Christians follow the prophet Jesus, but there is only one true god and that is Allah. However, I am a physician and I do not judge others by their beliefs.'

She looked at him. 'I do not understand any of this,' she said and yawned because she felt so weary. 'I know that I have been taught to believe in Jesus Christ the Son of God…'

'I shall not attempt to convert you,' Ali told her. 'Religion has caused too many wars and too many deaths. I believe as I believe, but my life is dedicated to saving life. You shall keep your faith and I mine. We shall not quarrel because of it.'

'Please do not be angry with me. I did not mean to call you a Saracen infidel.' She looked distressed. 'You are kind…'

Ali smiled once more. 'I am not offended, little one. I am an Arab and have been used to insults far worse than any you could think of, mistress. However, there are others within this house that might find such words offensive. It would be best if you kept your thoughts on these matters to yourself while you stay here.'

'I think you are a very wise man,' she said. 'Please, may I sleep now?'

'Sleep for as long as you wish, but I shall have a

serving woman bring you some soup as soon as you wake again, for you need food.'

'Thank you…and thank you for saving my life.'

'It was Lord Montfort who saved you from the sea,' Ali said. He watched as the woman slept. She was through the worst of her ordeal, but now she must learn to live again. Her mind had blocked out the terror of being taken by the sea, and with it had gone her identity, but he felt certain it would return once she had fully recovered. However, should it not, she would be alone in the world. Perhaps it was part of Allah's plan that she had forgotten her past.

'As Allah wills,' he said piously and went from the chamber, to pass on the good news to Stefan de Montfort. He had haunted her chamber for days, though he had pretended to a casual interest in her recovery. Ali smiled as he wondered what the future might bring. He hoped that the man he loved as a brother might find peace at last.

'Swallow a little more if you can,' the serving woman said. 'It will make you strong, lady, and you need to recover your strength.'

The woman looked at the serving girl. 'How long have you lived in this house, Sulina? Why are you here, for I do not think you born to this land? If we are in France?' Her eyes became dark with distress. 'I do not even know where I am…but the word France comes to mind.'

'You are in Normandy, at the home of the Lord de Montfort,' Sulina said. 'I am here because my uncle sold me into slavery after my parents died of a fever. I was but thirteen years of age and my first master used me ill, but then Stefan de Montfort bought me. He set me free, but when he gave up the wars and came here to live I chose to come with him. He allows me to serve him and I am content to be his servant. Here I am treated with kindness and respect. In my homeland I should be shunned and cast out by my family; they might stone me to death, for I am unclean in their eyes.'

'That is sad for you, but Lord de Montfort seems kind and generous, though I have never seen him.'

'He can be and often is,' Sulina agreed. 'But when he is angry he is fearful. I should not wish to be his enemy.' She hesitated, then, 'Stefan de Montfort is not an easy man to understand…'

'And yet you love him, do you not?'

'I admire him…I would love him if he looked at me in that way but he does not.' Sulina was startled as the patient put back the covers and swung her legs over the bed. 'You should not try to get up yet, my lady. Ali said you must rest for some days.'

'I feel restless,' the woman replied. 'I need to walk, to wash myself and my hair.'

'It is my job to bathe you and to wash your hair once you feel better,' Sulina told her. 'I shall wash your hair and your body, my lady, but once you are well you may use the bathing pool.'

'What is a bathing pool? I have not heard of such a thing. I believe I have bathed in a wooden tub…' She wrinkled her brow as she tried to remember, but failed. Sometimes she saw flashes, pictures in her mind, but they were all jumbled up and she could not understand what they meant.

'In my country we often use a bathing pool,' Sulina told her. 'My lord has adopted some of our customs…

at least those he approves of, and he approves of being clean.'

'I am not clean. I can smell the stink on myself.'

'I shall help you, my lady, but you are not well enough to walk or to use the bathing pool yet.'

'No...' She sighed and fell back on the bed. 'I would be happy for you to bathe me, Sulina. I am too weak to do it yet.'

'Lie still, then, lady, and let me tend you. I think your hair will be pretty once it is clean.'

She opened her eyes as she sensed someone near her. At first she thought it must be Sulina, but the subtle perfume she smelled did not belong to the serving woman. She had fallen asleep after eating the food Sulina brought her, for she was still weak. It was night now and the only light was a small candle, which gave off a dim light. A shadow moved towards her and she saw that it was a man...a stranger! She shrank back as he approached the bed, her instinct to be afraid. Who was he and why had he come to her in the dead of night?

'Who are you?' She swallowed hard, her heart racing wildly.

The shadowy figure paused, and then moved forwards slowly so that the light fell across his face. 'I am Stefan de Montfort,' he said in a deep, gentle voice she felt was familiar to her. Surely she had heard it before? Yet she did not know him. 'I was out hunting when you came to your senses. We need fresh meat and it was a long day. I have but this minute returned. Forgive me that I did not come to you before, lady.'

She pushed herself up against the pillows, holding the covers to her naked breasts. Stefan de Montfort was a large man, powerful and impressive, a little frightening. He was not smiling as he looked at her. She wondered if he was angry with her, but did not know in what way she might have offended him.

'I have been well cared for,' she whispered. 'I have been told that you saved my life, sir.'

'I pulled you from the sea, but it is Ali who hath made you well again.' His expression was almost stern as he gazed down at her, her hair freshly washed and spreading over the pillows in soft waves of corn-coloured silk. She was, as he had suspected, very beautiful now that she was awake. 'Ali tells me that you do not know your name or from whence you came?'

'I can remember nothing…at least, I know things, but I do not know who I am, where I came from or where I was going.'

'That is unfortunate—I had hoped to return you to your family as soon as you were well enough to travel.' He looked thoughtful, almost stern. 'Well, it cannot be helped. I shall make inquiries about a vessel that sank and see if your family is trying to trace you.'

'Supposing I have no family…supposing they were lost as the ship went down?'

'We shall face that if the time comes. My house is large and you will find a place here for the moment, but you are not a prisoner and may leave whenever you wish.'

'You are kind, sir.'

'Kind?' A harsh laugh escaped him. 'I would not describe myself in that manner…' His gaze narrowed. 'You should have a name. Since we do not know your true name we must discover one that suits you… What would you call yourself? Maria, Elizabeth, Roseanne…'

His brows rose as her hand moved towards him. 'You have remembered something?'

'I am not sure, but Roseanne…no, Anne. I like the name Anne. It seems familiar to me, though I cannot remember where I heard it or if it was my name.'

'But you like it, therefore it shall be your name. Anne—yes, it is a good name for you, lady. It suits you. I shall call you Anne.'

She closed her eyes for a moment, struggling to recall something, but the curtain in her mind remained in position. At the mention of the name Anne she had almost seen something…a face…faces and a house, but they had faded in seconds.

Tears caught at her throat, but she fought them. 'Ali says that I shall remember one day. Do you think it is true, my lord?'

She gazed at him as he stood there, a powerful man, feet apart, arms crossed. He was dressed in a nobleman's gown of some deep blue cloth braided with rich gold, his dark blond hair touching his shoulders, his face tanned by the sun. He was not exactly handsome, but striking, his features carved, almost harsh.

'Ali understands many things that affect the body, but I do not think anyone truly understands the mind,' Stefan answered honestly. 'How can we know what makes one man clever and another stupid? You are an intelligent woman. Everything about you tells me that you come from a good home and family, and you speak English better than French. In time we may discover who you are or your memory may return. Until then you must make yourself at home here, Anne.'

'But what shall I do if I never remember?' Her eyes were wide and dark with fear.

'Then your life begins here,' Stefan told her. 'When I was a young man, about your own age, I was forced to leave all that I knew and loved. I found a new life and a new identity as a mercenary. My life was stolen from me, as the sea has robbed you of yours. I shall help you, Anne—and somehow you will find the courage to become yourself once more.' His harsh features softened slightly and she saw a man who was very different. She wanted to be comforted by his words, but it was so strange not to remember her own name.

It was frightening to think that she might never know who she was, never remember her mother or father...or if she had sisters and brothers. The future seemed dark, terrifying, and yet she sensed that she was safe here in this house. Sulina and Ali had told her that Stefan de Montfort had sheltered others who needed a home and a protector. He had said that she must think of it as a new beginning...that her life began here. A part of her mind protested, because she wanted to know who she was and where she came from, and yet another part of her felt reassured by his words.

'Will I be a servant like Sulina?'

'Sulina chooses to serve me,' he replied. 'Others also choose to serve, but they are free to leave as they please. You will be a guest. You are a lady, Anne, a woman of gentle birth. Everyone in this house will treat you as such.' His voice had at that moment a deep, rich timbre, its softness like velvet, reassuring and comforting.

'Thank you. I do not mind working if I can be of help...perhaps sewing. I am not as clever with my needle as Catherine, of course, but—' Anne broke off and stared at him.

'You have remembered something?' Stefan's eyebrows rose, his eyes narrowed and intent.

Anne hesitated, then shook her head. 'I remember there was once someone called Catherine and she helped me with my sewing, but it was a long time ago...'

'Was Catherine your mother?'

'I do not know,' Anne replied and looked bewildered. 'How can I know that Catherine was a better needlewoman than me, but not know who she is?'

'I do not know,' Stefan said. He turned as the door opened and someone came in and he saw the physician. 'She is awake and we have decided that her name is to be Anne—at least for the moment.'

Ali came forwards so that Anne could see his face. 'I see you are well, lady. I shall not disturb you—unless you have need of me? You are not in pain?'

'I am quite well, thank you.'

'I shall leave you to rest, lady.'

'And I shall go too, Anne,' Stefan said. 'It is not fitting that I should be in your room. I came only to see for myself that you were well. I shall not see you again until you are able to join us in the hall downstairs. Goodnight, lady. Do not fret too much. You are safe here and in time you will remember all you should.' He turned to Ali. 'Come, my friend, share a cup of wine with me. I have something I wish to discuss with you.'

Anne lay back against the pillows as the two men went out together. She closed her eyes, struggling to remember something...anything that would tell her who and what she was. A tear slid from the corner of her eye, but she dashed it away with her hand. She would not weep tears of self-pity. Lord de Montfort had told her she was safe here and for some reason she believed him.

She must be content to stay here until she remembered who she was. The name Catherine was at the back of her mind. She tried to put a face to the name and failed, but something told her that Catherine had once been important in her life.

'Do you believe that she has truly lost her memory?' Stefan asked of the physician. 'She picked the name Anne for herself. It seemed to please her. I think it may well be her own name.'

'It is possible, my lord. Her memory may come back in little strands like the mists in a forest, weaving between the trees, revealing clear spaces where the canopy is broken, and concealing the rest.'

'You do not think that she is pretending that she cannot recall her name?'

'Why would she do that, my lord?'

Stefan shook his head, feeling an ache in his side, a constant reminder of the last woman that had tried to trap him. 'No, I am too suspicious. I plucked her from the sea. An enemy could not have sent her. She is innocent and I am unkind to doubt her.'

'I believe her distress is genuine, my lord. She will begin to remember things slowly, a little at a time, and then perhaps it will all come to her—or it may not. The mind is a strange thing...'

'Yet she remembered that Catherine taught her how to sew—and that she was not as good at her work as the other woman.'

'She did not know who Catherine was?'

'Possibly her mother or someone she knew well.'

Ali nodded. 'I do not think she would think of her mother as Catherine. It seems as if the woman was important to her, but perhaps not of prime importance in her life. If she remembered a lover or her mother the rest might come, but until then it may be that she remembers only fragments of her life.'

'We must give her time,' Stefan said. 'My wound broke open again as we hunted this morning and has bled. I believe I need some of your salves, old friend.'

'You should still be resting.'

'We needed meat for the pot,' Stefan said. 'We took a wild boar and two hinds today, besides some game that my peregrine brought down. We shall eat well enough for the next few weeks.'

Ali nodded. He knew from experience that it was a thankless task to tell Lord de Montfort to rest. He would push himself to the limit, and his wound would heal in time, as it always had. The forests about the chateau teemed with game, and hunting was a way of life for the lord. Stefan took his position seriously and was well respected and liked by his tenants and retainers alike.

Most of them looked forwards to the day when their lord would settle down and take a wife, but those who knew him best understood that he would not allow himself any peace until his brother and father's murderers were brought to justice.

'Is there any way we can help her to regain her memory?'

Ali looked at his lord's face. There was a hint of impatience in his eyes, an odd expression on his face. 'I think it must be left to time, my lord. She will find her own way if left to herself.'

Stefan nodded. Anne was beautiful and a part of him wanted to keep her here at the chateau, but another felt it would be best to send her on her way as soon as possible, before she had time to work her way under his guard. Something about her drew him like a moth to a flame. While she lay unconscious he had spent time sitting by her bed, but from now on he would keep out of her way as much as possible. He had no time for a gentle, lovely woman—or love! He must remember that he had made a vow to take revenge for his father's murder!

'Excuses!' Lord Cowper scowled as the man told him what he already knew. Stefan de Montfort and that hell-hound of a Saracen he counted a friend had succeeded in leaving England alive and were no doubt safe at his chateau in France. 'My instructions were that he was not to be allowed to leave England alive! Am I served by dolts and incompetents? How was he able to get away?'

'Your plan failed, my lord. The Saracen suspected a trap and came looking for him. We think Sir Hugh killed the Lady Madeline, as you planned to incriminate Lord de Montfort, and then the Saracen arrived and killed him with one slash of his wicked blade.'

'Where were the rest of you?'

'We tried to stop them escaping,' the servant said and flinched as his master struck him in the face. 'Lord de Montfort was wounded in the side, but he is a strong man and with the Saracen at his side they fought their way out.'

'Curse him!' Lord Cowper snarled. 'We should have killed him years ago instead of his brother, but the younger son was the father's favourite and he would not have believed ill of him. The years Stefan de Montfort spent as a mercenary have made him as wily as a fox and sharper than a serpent.'

Lord Cowper paced the room. He knew that once his enemy had recovered his strength he would come after him, and this time he would not be denied. His only chance was to strike first.

'We must go to Normandy,' he said, making up his mind. 'He will be more relaxed on his own land. We shall watch and wait, and when the time comes we shall kill him.'

'As you wish, my lord.' Fritz did not attempt to point out that the Chateau de Montifiori was well guarded and that it might be safer to stay here and let the enemy come to them. Lord Cowper was a man of uncertain temper and anyone who thwarted his will would meet a sticky end. It was only that he was one of the few able to actually recognise Lord de Montfort that had saved his life this time. Some of the others involved in the fiasco had not been as lucky and were already beneath the earth.

Cowper rounded on him, eyes bulging, flaming with fury. He was an ugly man with a bull neck and a mottled colour that spoke of a life of indulgence. He struck Fritz again, making him stagger back.

'Of course it is as I wish. You failed me once, oaf. Do it again and I'll hang you and all the other dolts who betrayed me. Tell the men to prepare. We leave in the morning.'

Fritz backed away, bowing to the master he disliked. If it were not for his sister, Helene, and his mother, nothing would keep him in this creature's service, even though he knew that he was Cowper's bastard. The lord had forced himself on Fritz's mother but never acknowledged that the child she bore was his. However, Fritz's sister was Cowper's mistress. He treated her well enough, giving her rich clothes and jewels, but she was his slave. If Fritz disobeyed his master, Helene would suffer and his mother and stepfather would be turned from their home. Fritz knew that his sister was held by a similar threat, and he suspected that she hated her master as much as he did.

'One day,' he muttered beneath his breath. 'One day he will go too far…' A quick knife thrust in the belly might be enough, but fear held Fritz's hand. If he made a mistake and Cowper didn't die, others besides himself would suffer.

'When may I get up?' Anne asked as the physician came to see her. She was restless, anxious to be up and about, because lying here alone only made her more aware of the dark places in her mind.

'You should rest for another few days,' Ali told her and smiled. 'It is good that you are feeling better, lady, but you have been very ill and you are not yet strong.'

'I think I could come down,' Anne said. 'It is lonely lying here alone. I think about who I am and what happened to me…and it frightens me.'

'You need something to occupy your mind,' Ali told her. 'Do you think you could read a book—or would you prefer some sewing?'

'I should love to read,' Anne said with a sigh. 'But books are so expensive…'

'Nevertheless, Lord de Montfort has many,' Ali said and smiled at her. 'I shall ask him if you may borrow one to help pass the time—would you like a Bible or a book of fables?'

'Is there such a thing?' Anne's interest was caught. 'I should love to read a story. A story such as the storyteller told at Christmastide.' She remembered that Christmas had been a happy time for her as a child, but she could not recall the people who had made it so.

'Then I shall speak to Lord de Montfort and ask him,' Ali told her. 'In the meantime I shall bring you something to help you sleep.'

'You are all so kind…' She sighed and lay back against the pillows. Everyone was kind to her, but she wished she knew who she was and whence she came.

Stefan looked down at the woman's face as she lay sleeping. He did not know what drew him to her chamber at this hour, except that she haunted his thoughts waking or sleeping. He had forced himself to stay away from her for some days, but he was not satisfied to hear the women say she was doing well, and had come to see for himself, and to bring the book of legends and fables she had requested. He placed the leather-covered volume on the chest-on-stand beside her bed. How lovely she looked with her hair spread on the pillow! The sight of her touched something deep inside him.

She was deeply asleep, though now and then she cried out, and he leaned closer to catch the words.

'Mother…' she whimpered. 'Mother…'

Stefan was tempted to stroke her hair as he had while she was ill, but the scent of her wafted into his nostrils, setting up a fierce craving for something he did not recognise and he drew back. If he woke her, he might be tempted to do more than simply touch her.

Cursing himself for a fool, he turned and left her. He should not have come. Yet she drew him to her again and again, making him aware that his life was empty, had long been empty of all the things that he had desired as a young man.

Foolish dreams! He frowned as he strode away from the house to the garden and the pool where he bathed whenever he was restless. He had given up all hope when he left England, banished from home and all that he loved. It would be stupid to let a young woman make him dissatisfied with the life he had chosen for himself, for if he gave in to the disturbing feelings she roused in him, he would become soft and lose his resolve!

'You look so sad,' Claire said as they walked together in the grounds of her father's estate. 'I am sorry that nothing has been heard of your poor sister, but it was unlikely that she would be found alive.'

Harry looked down at her lovely face. Her eyes were soft with concern for him, and he felt that she was sincere in all she said. He knew that she was right. Anne was gone, lost to the sea. He had grieved for her for the past three weeks, and in another week he must return to England and the court. Before that he would ask Claire if she was willing to return with him as his wife.

'I know that I should put my sorrow behind me,' Harry said, regret in his face. 'I came here to ask you to be my wife, Claire, and I have not had the heart to do it. Tomorrow I must leave, because I want to visit my parents before I return to court. I had hoped you would accompany me as my wife, but I have not courted you or told you of my feelings…'

Claire smiled at him gently. 'I knew why you came,' she said, 'and I have understood why you have not spoken. In the circumstances it could not be otherwise. I respect you, Harry—and your grief for Anne has shown me that you feel deeply. When we met at court I thought you might be too proud and careless to make me a good husband, but sharing your sorrow has brought us closer. If you were to ask me to marry you, Harry, you might be pleased with my answer.'

Harry looked at her uncertainly, then went down on his knee before her. 'I love you beyond my life, Claire. I would do anything for you and protect you with my life. If you could bring yourself to accept my offer, I should be happy to wed you.'

'Yes, Harry, I shall marry you,' Claire told him with a smile. 'Delay your journey two days so that we may be betrothed and I shall accompany you to your home. Once your parents are over their grief, I shall wed you.'

'You are as generous and good as you are lovely,' Harry said and stood up. He drew her to him, bending his head to kiss her lips. 'But will your father allow you to come with me—and shall you brave it, my love? The sea is always dangerous, Claire. After what happened to my sister, I am reluctant to expose you to such a journey.'

'Anne was unfortunate,' Claire said and held his hand. 'No one could have expected such freak waves... and she should have gone below deck when you begged her to. Never fear that I shall not obey you, my love.'

Harry smiled down at her, touching her cheek with his fingertips. 'You have courage, Claire, and I would die rather than let anything happen to you. I would have gone into the sea for Anne had they not struck me from behind, but nothing would stop me if it were you.' He bent his head and kissed her once more. 'If your father permits, we shall be betrothed and then I shall take you to my parents.'

Claire held her hand out to him. 'We must find

my father and speak to him, for there is no time to be lost.'

'I know that seeing you will help to ease my mother's unhappiness,' Harry said. 'She will grieve long and hard for her daughter, but she will welcome my wife with open arms.'

'I look forward to meeting her,' Claire told him. 'Look, Father is coming to meet us.' She looked at her father's face and then at Harry. 'I believe he has some news, Harry. Perhaps he has heard something at last…'

'If Anne's body has been found at least I can make sure that she has a decent burial.' Holding Claire's hand, he went to meet the Comte. 'Sir, we have been seeking you.'

'And I have been seeking you,' the Comte told him. 'The news I bring is better than we might have hoped, though it is not certain.'

'Sir…' Harry stared at him, an icy tingle starting at the nape of his neck. 'You have heard news of Anne?'

'I cannot be certain it was your sister, but my agent has been told of a young woman plucked from the wreckage of a ship at about the point the debris from your ship might have drifted to by the next morning.'

'Plucked from the sea?' Harry stared at him and let go of Claire's hand. 'Are you saying…? No, it cannot be.'

'The girl taken from the sea was still alive,' Comte St Orleans said and frowned. 'The man who gave us this information said she was unconscious and looked near death. When she was taken from the ship she had not recovered her senses, but she was still breathing.'

'God be praised!' Harry cried. 'You say she was

taken from the ship—does this informant know where she was taken?'

'I fear that he knows no more than he has told me,' the Comte said. 'You may question him yourself, but I do not think he can help you much more. If you wish to search for her you must travel to Normandy, for it was there the ship was headed, and ask for news. It is possible that someone may have heard of her.' He looked at his daughter. 'What was it you wished to tell me, Claire?'

'I think it will keep for another day,' she said and gazed up at Harry. 'You must look for Anne. I know that you love me and your promise was sincerely meant, but you would never rest if you did not try to find Anne.'

The Comte looked at Harry. 'It is settled that you are to marry?'

'With your blessing, sir. I would have taken Claire to my parents had this news not come.'

'You must look for your sister,' the Comte told him, agreeing with his daughter. 'I shall take Claire to England and we shall break the news to Lord Melford. It will be much better if your family know that you are searching for Anne, Harry. Claire and I will wait at Melford for your return, whatever the news.'

Harry's eyes dwelled on Claire's sweet face. 'You will not mind if I leave you now?'

'I love you and I know what Anne means to you,' Claire told him. 'It may come to nothing, but you have something now. Someone may know the people who took Anne. Clearly they must have meant to care for her or the ship's captain would have abandoned her to the nuns as soon as they reached land.'

Harry took her hand and kissed it. 'I love you,' he

said. 'It is hardly fair that I should leave you, having just asked you to wed me, but you are right. I must find Anne if I can, but in time I shall come to England to find you, and God willing I shall bring my sister with me...'

Anne looked at herself in the small hand mirror Sulina had brought her. Her hair was flowing loose over her shoulders, kept in place by a small cap of black velvet framed with gold threads. Her gown was also fashioned of some soft black cloth, and the hanging sleeves were embroidered with beads and gold thread. It suited her well enough, though had she chosen for herself she would have picked green or blue. However, the gown had been brought for her and was a gift from the lord of this manor. Anne was grateful for his generosity and had made no complaint when she was given the gown to wear. She knew it had not been made for her, because Sulina had altered it to fit her. Anne was not certain whether it had belonged to Lord de Montfort's mistress or was simply something he had bought from a dealer in such things.

'My lord is waiting below,' Sulina told her with a faint smile. 'He has asked every day if you were ready to go down. I think he is impatient to see you, lady.'

'He might have come to visit me and asked for himself,' Anne said, feeling slightly aggrieved that he had not done so.

'It would not have been fitting once you had recovered your senses,' Sulina told her. 'What would your family think if it became known that Lord Montfort had frequented your bedchamber while you lay recovering from your illness?'

'I do not know if I have a family,' Anne reminded her. 'But I dare say you are right. I cannot think that my mother would approve—if she is still living...' Her eyes were sad as she thought of the woman she could not remember. Something told her that her mother had loved her and that she had been happy at home.

She followed Sulina down the wide staircase to the hall below. The chateau was old, the walls built of a honey-coloured stone hung with silk tapestries, and the ceilings were high. The floors were made of wood on the upper floor, covered in places with brightly coloured rugs and carpets that had an eastern look, but on the ground floor they were tiled with marble. Most of the furniture was heavily carved, dark wood that also had an eastern look. Anne knew that this house was very different to the one she had been raised in, though she could not remember her home, but everything here was strange, unusual. She did not think it was the style that would be normally found on French soil, though she could not know that for certain. Sometimes now she saw a picture of a house set in a pleasant valley, but it was only in brief flashes and she had not mentioned it to anyone. She thought that perhaps the house had been her home, but as she did not know where it was to be found that did not help her to remember.

As she entered the large hall, which was the heart of the chateau, she saw two men standing together. They turned their heads as she approached. Anne caught her breath, for one of them had skin the colour of polished walnut and the bottom of his face was scarred dreadfully, the skin puckered and discoloured as though he had been burned, his mouth twisted to one side. His dark eyes went over her, his gaze narrowed and thoughtful.

Anne felt nothing but pity for him, because she sensed that at one time in his life he had suffered terribly.

'Ah, the lady Anne,' Stefan said, inclining his head in welcome. 'We are glad that you feel well enough to join us at last. This is Hassan, the best friend a man could have. He helped me to pull you from the sea.'

Anne dipped a curtsy to them. 'Sir, I must thank you as I have thanked others who helped me.'

'You are welcome, lady,' Hassan said. There was a slightly puzzled look in his eyes. 'Forgive me, but as you came towards us I thought that I had seen you before this day.'

Stefan stared at him. 'You do not speak of when we pulled her from the water. Can you recall where you saw Anne the first time?' He too had felt that he might have seen her, but could not recall when or where.

Hassan's eyes were on her. Anne shivered, feeling a mixture of fear and excitement as she anticipated his reply, but he shook his head and she was disappointed.

'Forgive me, but I do not remember where I saw you. There was something in the way you walked and held yourself, but the memory is not strong. At the moment it eludes me, but it may yet return.'

Stefan looked thoughtful. If he had seen her, it must have been brief and at a time when he was not taking much notice, for she was too beautiful to have slipped his mind had he ever spoken to her.

'Memory is a strange thing; it eludes us when we try to recall something and returns when we least expect it. If you have truly seen Anne before, it will come to you, Hassan.'

'Yes, perhaps,' Hassan replied. 'I should leave if I

am to reach my destination before nightfall. I wish you well, lady.'

'Thank you…' Anne watched as he walked from them. She turned to look at Lord de Montfort. 'It would be a strange coincidence if we had met before you rescued me, though I doubt it can be so, for I do not think I have been to France before this time. Everything here is strange to me.'

'You are in Normandy, and my home contains many things I have collected in other lands,' Stefan said. 'Why are you so sure that you had not been to France before this?'

'I do not know. Sometimes I seem to know things instinctively, without truly remembering, but you told me yourself that I speak English better than French.'

'Yes, that is true. Hassan might have seen you recently, for we were returning from a visit to England when we found you. He is very observant and it is possible he saw you only briefly.' Possible that he had seen her too—but where?

'I thought your ship was travelling along the French coast?'

'We were swept down the coast by the fierce winds and decided to run before them until we found a sheltered cove. Had we made land before the storm hit, we should not have been there that morning.'

'I was more fortunate than I knew,' Anne said and shivered. 'Had you not seen me…'

'You were close to death. Another hour or two…' Stefan shrugged his broad shoulders. 'Who knows why these things happen?'

'Ali would say it was as Allah wills,' Anne said and her eyes sparkled with mischief. In that moment the shadows fell away from her and she was beautiful, a spirited girl whose smile held enchantment. The change was so marked that it made Stefan catch his breath.

He laughed huskily. 'I see you have recovered your spirit, whatever else you lack, my lady.' His eyes went over her with a hint of disapproval. 'That gown does not do you justice, Anne. It was found in a chest in the storeroom and must have belonged to the late lady of the manor, but all her gowns were black, for I believe she was widowed many years. We must buy some silk and have something new made for you. I believe that a fair has come to a town near by. If you feel well enough on the morrow, we could go there together and choose something from the merchants.'

Anne was pleased that the gown had not belonged to his mistress, though she did not know why it should matter. She smiled at him, her heart beating faster as his gaze intensified. He looked so very different when his features were relaxed by humour. When he actually smiled he became a man she found fascinating, instead of the stern cold master of the chateau who frightened her a little.

'You have already been generous to me,' she said, her eyes wide and questing as she met his gaze. 'It was good of you to lend me your book, for I know such things are costly.'

'I have many books,' Stefan told her. 'You are welcome to read them while you stay here.'

'You are too good, sir. I do not know what I may do to repay your kindness.'

'I have done nothing that common decency did not command of me,' Stefan replied. 'Ali says that if you save a life you are responsible for that life. Perhaps he is right.'

'Silk is expensive…' Anne's mouth felt dry. She felt as if an invisible bond drew her to him. His gaze was stern, but sometimes his voice was like dark velvet, caressing her, soothing her. 'I have no money…nothing to offer in return.'

'Believe me, you have much to offer,' Stefan said. He moved closer, reached out, tipping her chin so that she looked up at him. 'If I were less honourable I would keep you with me, make you my mistress. You are a beautiful woman, Anne. I could happily lie with you, but honour demands that I must help you to return to your family.'

Anne's pulses raced. For a moment she could not breathe. She ached for something, but did not know what she craved. What was this feeling he had roused in her? She thrilled to his smile and the sound of his voice, and yet he scared her so much. Her eyes widened, innocent and inviting. Stefan bent his head and kissed her softly on the mouth. Her body swayed towards him, and he made a harsh sound in his throat, pulling her hard against him. His kiss intensified, his tongue seeking entrance as her lips parted beneath his, a sensation so sweet and heady sweeping through her that she was ready to swoon. She wanted it to go on and on for ever, and she wanted something more, though she knew not what she longed for. When he let her go abruptly, she almost fell.

'Forgive me,' he said. 'Your eyes invited and I took advantage of your innocence. I shall not sully that innocence with lust, for you must know now that I can never love you. All that was tender and innocent died in me a long time ago, Anne. I am not fit to be the husband of any gentle woman—and especially one like you. I should not have kissed you.'

Anne touched her fingers to her lips in wonder. Instinctively, she knew that it was the first time she had been kissed in such a way. No man had ever made her feel this way before, she was certain, and felt the invisible bond that seemed to fasten itself about her heart.

'I liked it,' she said, for there was no artifice in her. 'Why do you say you are not fit to be my husband?'

'I have lived as a mercenary for many years. Have you any idea of what that means?' Anne shook her head. 'It means that I fought for money. I killed men… and sometimes women; even children died in the cities we stormed and the ships we sent to the bottom of the ocean. I did not fight for honour or for my country, but for the gold it earned me and because of the hatred inside me. Do you understand what I am saying? I have seen things that no man should see and done things that shame me. There is blood on my hands, Anne. I do not think you would want such a man to be the father of your children.'

'But they told me…Sulina told me you rescued her and Ali…' Anne's voice shook because his words conjured up pictures of horror that made her shudder. 'They said you were a good man.'

'A few good deeds amongst the bad,' Stefan said, his coldness shattering her illusions. 'I doubt they will be enough to save me from the fires of hell. No, little one, I am not for you. I promise that you are safe from me. That kiss was a moment of weakness, nothing more. Run away now and find something to amuse yourself with,

Anne. I must speak with my steward. Tomorrow we shall visit the fair and buy silks for your new gowns.'

Anne stared after him as he walked away. Tears burned behind her eyes. Her mind was in turmoil and she did not know how she felt. When he kissed her she had experienced wonderful sensations that made her want to stay in his arms for ever, but then his harsh words made her tremble.

What kind of a man was Stefan de Montfort? His expression as he spoke of his past was so harsh, so angry, that he had frightened her. He described himself as a man who had taken life wantonly, and she saw pictures in her mind of burning cities and ships on fire, women and children screaming as the ship sank beneath the waves. He had lived by the sword, his life harsh, cruel and unforgiving.

How could she want to be the wife of such a man? And yet when he had spoken of buying her a new gown, when he had said that he could happily lie with her… when he had laughed with her about the physician…her heart had sung for joy. She felt confused, distressed, her heart pulled two ways.

Anne shook her head as she went out into the garden. The sun was shining and the air was heavy with the scent of roses and lavender. The sheltered gardens of the chateau were guarded with high walls and a thick hedge all around. It was warm and safe here and the pictures of hell and damnation Lord de Montfort had conjured up faded as she walked amongst the flowers.

She began to pick lavender stalks, smoothing the flower heads between her fingers and inhaling their scent. Now was the time to harvest some of nature's bounty before all this beauty went to waste. She would make lavender bags to place in chests of linen. It was her mother's habit every summer and a job she had always enjoyed…

In her mind, Anne saw a woman smiling at her. They were in a garden much like this, but more open, and they were picking flowers.

'We shall make some lavender essence,' the woman told her. 'There is nothing so helpful when one has a headache.'

Anne felt tears begin to trickle down her cheeks as the picture faded. She was sure the woman was her mother. They had gathered flowers and herbs together every year to make the essences that her mother used in her stillroom.

Why could she not remember her own name? Why did she not know where she belonged? Anne felt a deep longing to go home. She was afraid that, if she stayed here in the chateau, the Lord de Montfort might break her heart.

Chapter Three

Anne found it easy enough to find work once she began to look. Opening the linen chests, which were stored in one of the upstairs rooms, she discovered that much of it was in need of some care. Most was in good condition, but sheets and cloths had lain unused for years and had turned yellow. Gathering an armful, she took it downstairs and asked a startled Sulina where the washhouse was to be found.

'Such work is not for you, lady,' Sulina told her. 'The village women wash the linen, but where did you find so much?'

'These have lain unused for years,' Anne said. 'Linen should be used in rotation so that the wear is even, and the chests should be checked every year so that anything that needs it can be washed and aired.'

'But they will not be used,' Sulina said. 'These are the best linens and they are kept only for the guest rooms. The servants have their own and I do not use them, nor does Hassan or Lord de Montfort.'

'But how do they sleep?'

'I have a mattress on the floor and use only a blanket,' Sulina said. 'It is what I have been used to all my life. I could not sleep in a bed as you do. Hassan and my master have their couches. I do not think they use sheets or blankets—perhaps a cloak if the night is cold. It is the way they have become accustomed to sleeping.'

'Well, this linen should be washed or it will soon become unfit for use,' Anne said. 'Perhaps if the bed were made up in Lord de Montfort's room he would use it. He is a gentleman and must have slept that way once.'

'The washhouse is this way,' Sulina said. 'But I do not think my master intended that you should do such work.'

'You can help me,' Anne replied. 'Together we shall make light work of it. However, it will be best to leave the linen to soak for a few hours, because the yellow stains will not come out if we simply wash them.'

'Give them to me,' Sulina said with a sulky look. 'I shall put them to soak in the tubs. It is a lot of work for nothing, for as I told you they will not be used.'

'We shall see,' Anne said. 'If Lord de Montfort has guests, they may be needed.'

'He never has guests, except you,' Sulina said. 'Give me the cloth you have in your hand if you want them all put to soak.'

'This is torn. I shall use it for lavender bags. When the sheets are stored once more, the lavender will keep them fresh and sweet. I have found a sewing box; if you insist on taking the linen yourself, I may as well begin at once.'

Sulina went off with the linen, still muttering to

herself. Anne smiled as she took the torn cloth into a small parlour she had discovered at the back of the house. The windows here were larger and the view was of the garden where she had picked lavender and roses. She had used some of her harvest for bowls of potpourri, and the scent was already drifting through the house. She sat down on a wooden bench with a high, smooth back and took the sewing box she had found stored in the linen room. She was smiling, humming to herself as she began her work.

Stefan saw the Arab girl as she was hanging some linen out to dry on bushes in the kitchen gardens. It was an unusual sight for most of the washing was sent to women in the village, and he had not seen quite so much since they first came here.

'You have been busy, Sulina?'

She turned and saw him, pulling a face. 'She would insist that it all be washed, my lord. I told her it was a waste of time, but she says that linen must be washed and aired every year to keep it sweet. She is making bags with lavender to put in the chests and the house smells of it everywhere.'

'My mother made them every summer,' Stefan said, an odd expression in his eyes as he remembered a home that smelled of lavender. 'And Anne is right about the linen. I remember that my mother's maids had the same task every year.'

Stefan missed the girl's look of annoyance as he walked on into the house. He caught the smell of roses and lavender as he entered and breathed it in, a smile on his lips. He was reminded of a time when he was a child. His mother had been making lavender bags and she smelled of it as he ran to her. She lifted him into her arms and hugged him. Her skin had been soft to the touch and he had loved her. It had been a house filled with laughter and love while she lived. The change had come later after she died. Lord de Montfort had become harder, angry…bitter. He had turned against his elder son for some reason and they had drifted apart.

Hearing the sound of a woman singing, Stefan turned towards it. He realized that Anne had discovered the parlour that had belonged to the last mistress here. He had never used it, because it was too comfortable, too soft, furnished in the French style. He was more at home in the great hall or his own chambers, which he had furnished in the eastern style—a style he had adopted during his time as a mercenary.

Anne had her head bent over her work. She had not heard him coming and her face wore a dreamy expression. The smell of the lavender was strong, wafting towards him, nostalgic, haunting. Anne became aware and turned her head. She stopped singing, uncertain for a moment, and then smiled as she saw him.

'I have been making these for the linen chests,' she said. 'You have a fine house here, my lord, but it is sadly in need of a woman's touch. I have thought of several items we need from the merchants. Once we have them, the silver and pewter may be cleaned properly and the furniture polished with beeswax.'

Stefan advanced into the room. 'I saw that Sulina had been washing the linen and putting it out to dry. I remember it was always done at home when I was a child and my mother lived.'

'Not afterwards?'

'No. My father did not bother about such things. The

servants did what was necessary and no more. I had forgotten such things existed…' He picked up one of the lavender bags and fingered it, feeling the grains of lavender move beneath his fingers and catching their fragrance.

'You were born a gentleman, I think, and I have seen some lovely things as I explored the house. Many of them are strange to me. Did you buy them on your travels?'

'I acquired some, a few I bought,' Stefan agreed. 'I fought for princes and merchants, protecting them as they transported their merchandise through dangerous lands. Some paid me with goods rather than gold. When I decided to settle here, I asked the French King for permission to live in this country. He granted me this manor for gold and favours rendered.'

'Are you of English birth? I am not certain. Your name could be Norman or English, I believe?'

'My ancestors went from Normandy to England with Duke William,' Stefan said. 'They were granted lands in England for services rendered and settled there. I might have lived there yet had certain events not changed the course of my life.'

Anne put down her needle, looking at him curiously. 'Why did you become a mercenary?'

'You ask too many questions. I was forced to leave my birthright and make my own way in the world. You do not need to know more than that, lady.'

'Have I made you angry?'

He shook his head, an odd smile on his lips. 'You fill my house with the scent of lavender and then ask if I am angry. I do not know how to answer you. The perfume of lavender brings happy memories, but grief and bitterness taint them. If I am angry it is not with you, but with a world that is oft cruel and unfair.'

'Yes, life is cruel,' Anne replied, a frown creasing her smooth brow. 'Do you think it is God that makes it so or do we hurt each other…is it our nature to be cruel?'

'You have an inquiring mind,' Stefan said and laughed. 'It is not my way to ponder such things, Anne. I accept and deal with life as it comes. If you wish to discuss the meaning of life, you must ask Ali to debate with you. He will be happy to talk of these things for hours. I am a man of action and I do what I have to do.'

'That is why you became a mercenary,' Anne said, for he had revealed more than he knew. 'You were cheated of what was yours and had nothing. The only thing you knew how to do was fight.'

'Perhaps…' His expression was harsh, because he fought the memories that might have softened him, made him vulnerable. 'I shall not prevent you making my house a home if it is your pleasure, but do not forget that you will leave here as soon as you remember who you are and whence you came.'

Stefan turned and walked from the room. She probed too deeply, disturbing him with memories he could not fight, touching places inside his mind that had been forgotten these many years. She was beautiful, and the more he saw her, the more he understood that her beauty was not just of face and figure. She was a lady such as his mother had been, gentle, compassionate, spirited and loving. Women like that were not intended to be taken lightly and discarded, as he would a mistress. They worked their way into a man's heart, stealing his soul and making him soft and destroying him. Stefan had known only whores and women who cheated or betrayed. A gentle, loving woman was a new experience, something he must avoid at all costs lest she made him weak!

The sooner they discovered who Anne really was and returned her to her family, the better!

Anne wore a thin wool cloak over her gown as they rode. When the horse was brought out she had been terrified, imagining that she was meant to ride it alone. It was a great, black, highly bred Arab and Anne had known that she would never be able to control it. However, she had soon realised that she was meant to ride pillion behind Lord de Montfort.

'I was not sure if you could ride,' Stefan said and gave her his hand to help her on to the saddle, mounting immediately in front of her. 'Besides, I think it best if you ride with me for the moment. You have not long risen from your sick bed and I would not have you grow faint and fall. You may hold on to me if you wish.'

Anne held on to his belt, but did not put her arms about his waist. Three armed men accompanied them; two she thought must be French and a third was English. The Lord de Montfort seemed to have surrounded himself with odd characters, for each of the men had some mark or disfigurement. One had lost two fingers of his left hand, another had a split in his nose and the third could not speak properly, but made signs with his hands that the others appeared to understand.

'Eric lost his tongue when he was captured by the Caliph's guards,' Stefan told her. 'He would not betray the whereabouts of his comrades and so they took his tongue. Had it not been for Ali's devotion, he would surely have died.'

. Anne said nothing. It sent icy waves down her spine when he spoke of such unspeakable acts, but she saw the way his men looked at him and knew that whatever else Stefan de Montfort might have done, he inspired devotion in his followers. Surely that meant he was not as cruel or unfeeling as he would have her believe?

The town was one of the old medieval-walled type and the centre was teeming with people who had come in from miles around to visit the fair. The marketplace was crammed with stalls selling all kinds of merchandise, and the air smelled of spices and meat cooking slowly on a spit. Anne felt a surge of excitement, feeling that she had been to fairs like this before. Something about the noise and the bustle seemed so familiar that she could see figures moving in her mind, faces of people she ought to know. The feeling was a good one, but tinged with sadness because she could not remember the people she had gone with to the fair.

Stefan gave her his hand, helping her to dismount. Eric took the reins of the horses and two of Stefan's men followed close behind as they walked into the square.

It crossed Anne's mind that they were being guarded. She wondered why that was necessary. No one was taking much notice of them. Everyone was too busy looking at the merchants' wares and enjoying themselves in the sunshine. She saw children chasing each other, shouting and throwing sticks as they competed to see who could throw the furthest. One small lad took her attention. He had such a beautiful face and there was something about him that tugged at her heartstrings.

Why did she feel as if she wanted to pick him up and hug him? Who did he remind her of?

Stefan led the way to where the silk merchants had their wares laid out on wooden stands. Anne followed just behind, feeling a flicker of excitement. She saw the beautiful material and her eye fell on a dark green silk that had a shimmer to it and seemed to catch the light.

'That is lovely,' she said, fingering the cloth at the edges. 'And good quality I think, but it will be expensive.'

Stefan spoke to the merchant in rapid French. He nodded and the man beamed at Anne, obviously pleased with whatever had been said.

'Choose another cloth,' Stefan said. 'You will need more than one gown, Anne. I think this dark blue would suit you…or the paler green?'

'Are you sure?' she asked uncertainly. 'I have the gowns that were found at the chateau.'

'You are too beautiful to wear black,' Stefan said. 'We shall take these three. What else do you need?' He looked down at her feet. 'Shoes, of course. Those slippers are Sulina's and not suitable for outdoor wear. And you will need lace or braid to trim the gowns. Choose what you wish for while you have the chance, and do not count the cost. I am in the mood to indulge you—take advantage of it.'

Anne realised that he would not be pleased if she protested at the cost of all these things. She chose lace and beads, a gold braid that would look striking on the blue gown and two pairs of shoes. She did not dare to think of the cost, but she saw no money change hands. The merchants seemed to know the Lord de Montfort and were eager to please him.

'Everything you have chosen will be sent to the chateau,' Stefan told her when she had finished looking at the merchants' wares. 'Come, we shall eat and drink at the inn before we return. It may be months before we visit Cherbourg again.'

Anne felt that might be a good thing, for if he were always this extravagant it would cost him a fortune. She knew he had ordered other items from the merchants, and supposed the cloth was for himself or others of his household. Obviously, he was taking the opportunity to stock up on supplies they needed. She knew that a list of more mundane things they required had already been sent to merchants in the town and would be delivered in due time.

The inn was busy, but the landlord recognised Lord de Montfort and showed them into his best parlour where only one other lady and gentleman were seated eating their meal. They seemed to have finished for they stood up, the gentleman stopping to speak a few words with Stefan before they left. The woman sent a fleeting smile at Anne, but did not speak.

'Did you know those people?' Anne asked as they took their seats at a table near the window.

'The Chevalier Charles Renard and his sister are our nearest neighbours at the chateau. I have been asked to dine at their home before now, but I declined for I did not wish for visitors. However, I asked if he would call one morning and bring Maria with him. You might like a little company of your own kind, Anne. It will be lonely for you otherwise.'

'That was thoughtful of you,' Anne said. 'Did you tell them who I was?'

'I told him that you were a kinswoman come to live

with me for a while. If the truth were known, there would be gossip. I would not have your reputation sullied, lady. If your memory returns, you will not thank me if it is generally thought that you are my mistress. And now that you have been seen there will be gossip. I am known, but I do not often shop at the fair, nor do I generally have female company—at least not a lady of your class.'

'You are considerate for my good name, sir,' Anne replied. She glanced out of the window. Her eye fell on a young man with dark auburn hair. He was talking earnestly to one of the grooms, who was shaking his head. As the Chevalier and his sister emerged from the inn into the yard, the young man approached them and began to ask questions. They also shook their heads. The young man looked disappointed. He glanced towards the inn, seeming undecided, and then turned away, walking towards a group of men and women and beginning to question them.

'What would you like to eat?' Stefan asked and she turned from the window. 'The woman says there is soup, roast pork and cabbage with plums or a pigeon pie…'

'Oh, I should like some soup and bread, please,' Anne said. 'I am not truly hungry.' It was odd, but her stomach was full of butterflies and she was aware of a feeling of sadness. She glanced back through the window, but the young man who had obviously been searching for something had gone. She could see that he was riding away. She did not know why that should upset her.

'Is something wrong?' Stefan asked.

'No…at least I do not know,' Anne replied. 'I was watching someone from the window. There was something familiar…I felt that I should know him…'

'You felt that you should know him, but you could not remember his name?'

'It was his manner that attracted my attention,' Anne confessed. 'He seemed so urgent, so…distressed.' She sighed. 'If I knew him I would surely have recognised him at once and I did not.'

'What did he look like? Did you catch more than a glance?'

'He had dark auburn hair and was a tall, strong-looking man. He spoke to the Chevalier and his sister for a moment as well as others. I turned away and he had gone.'

'I shall make inquiries,' Stefan promised. 'If he was looking for someone—' He stopped, shook his head. 'It would be wrong of me to raise your hopes, Anne. It is unlikely that he was looking for you, but I shall send someone to discover who the young man was and what he sought.'

'I do not think he could have been looking for me,' Anne said. 'And yet I did think he seemed familiar.' She looked out of the window once more, her expression so wistful that Stefan was aware of a feeling of jealous anger in the pit of his stomach.

Who was this young man that had brought such a look to her face? Had she been lying to him all along? Did she know her name and where she came from—and had she recognised the man? He could not help the suspicions taking root in his mind, even though common sense told him they were ridiculous. He had plucked her from the sea half-dead, but his previous experience with women had taught him that too often they would lie and scheme to get what they wanted. The lady Madeline had wanted him dead, though he did not know what he had done to arouse her hatred. Anne seemed innocent and as lovely inside as she was beautiful, but was she lying to him? He could see no reason why she should, and the feeling of anger cooled as she turned and smiled at him. Surely she was as innocent as she seemed? And yet he might be a fool to trust her.

Stefan did not give her an answering smile. His thoughts were confused, because he did not understand why he had felt such jealousy. If Anne had a lover somewhere, she would return to him when her memory came back. Now that he was calmer, he knew that he owed it to her to try to find the young man she had seen from the window of the inn. He had always intended that she should go back to her family and friends—so why did he have this ache inside when he thought about what the man might mean to her?

She was young and beautiful, a lady of good family. It was likely that she would be betrothed to someone—a young man who would love her enough to go on searching for her weeks after she was lost?

Anne seemed content to live at his chateau. She had begun to turn it from a rambling, neglected house into a home. He had begun to enjoy the thought of seeing her at his table, the pleasure of talking to her and seeing her smile. The place would seem empty when she left, but once she remembered the people she loved she would want to go. He would tell her to go back to her family, because he could not love her.

It was best that she left as soon as possible. Something about the man she had seen outside the inn had seemed familiar to her. If by some sheer chance the man was looking for her, he would know things that would bring back the home and life she had lost. Anyone who had her welfare at heart must want that for her…and he did feel something for her. Stefan studied her profile as her eyes were drawn back to the window. Something was haunting her. She sensed that she ought to have known the man, was regretting a chance lost. Smothering the urge to sweep her up and take her back to the chateau, away from all contact with anyone that might claim her, Stefan forced himself to remain calm and dispassionate. She was not for him. He could not give her the life she deserved.

'If it is possible, we shall discover his name and my men will make a search for him. We shall find him, and if he looks for you we shall bring him to you, Anne.'

She turned back to him, shaking her head. 'I do not think I truly knew him, for I would have remembered. It must just have been that he seemed so urgent.' Anne smiled. 'We shall forget it. I have had a day I shall remember, sir. I thank you for spending so much money on my new clothes. I do not think I have ever been so indulged before.'

'You deserve much more,' Stefan said, his voice hoarse with emotion. He was seeing her dressed in the emerald green gown, her hair adorned with a cap of gold and precious stones. He could see her as she smiled up at him, her lips parted for his kiss…and later as they lay side by side in the great bed she presently slept in alone.

He wanted her. Stefan admitted the truth to himself. His body burned for her and it was the reason for his restlessness of late. He acquitted her of being false, because there was too much honesty in her eyes. Life had led him to mistrust others, but she reminded him of the one woman who had shown him love—his mother.

He had forgotten that women such as the late Lady de Montfort existed. He had accepted that women wanted him only for the pleasure he could give them or the gold he paid them. Love was something he had dismissed as being a myth, but now he was remembering that sometimes love could be true and sincere.

If no one claimed her he could take her for his own—as his mistress or his bride. Stefan acknowledged that he would not want to lose her once she was his, so perhaps marriage was the only way. Yet he was not worthy of her. He knew it and a part of him rejected the idea of marriage and children. He had vowed to be revenged for his father's death and his brother's murder. How could he set that aside in favour of taking a bride?

The answer was that he could not—nor could he take a bride with fresh blood on his hands. To murder his enemy and then go to her bed would be an abomination in the sight of God and man. Anne was too far beyond him and he was a fool to let the shine of her eyes or the softness of her lips make him weak, even though his body clamoured for her.

If he needed a woman that badly he should send for a whore and take what he wanted coldly and without emotion. Love ensnared a man, binding him with invisible chains. He could not allow himself to be enticed into that honeyed trap. Love had no place in his life!

'Your husband will buy everything your heart desires,' he said harshly. 'Here is our food. Eat what you want, Anne. We shall leave for home as soon as you have taken your fill.'

'But what of you?' Anne asked. 'I thought you were hungry?'

'I have something to do,' Stefan replied. He took a thick chop from the dish and bit into it. He turned away from her. 'I shall be only a few minutes. There is someone I must see…'

Anne stared after him as he left the table. He was such a strange man sometimes, his moods changing like the wind. All the morning he had been kind, indulging her like a loving father…or lover…but now he was angry again.

What had she done to make him angry? Anne had no idea. She did not know where he was going or why, but she knew that she felt a sense of loss every time he withdrew from her.

Stefan helped her to mount the huge black horse. Anne was not as frightened as before, because she knew now that he was an expert horseman, and she held on to his belt as they set out at a good pace. She suspected that Lord de Montfort was anxious to return to the chateau, though she was not certain why he was in such a hurry. His manner had changed so abruptly at the inn and he had hardly spoken to her since he returned after she had finished her meal.

She suspected that he was angry with her. Was it because she could not remember who she was? Did he grow tired of having to look after her? He had been so kind about the matter of providing the material for her gowns, but now he was like a silent stranger. She found his silence hurtful, as if he were deliberately shutting her out.

They had been riding for some time when Anne first suspected that someone was following them. She had heard noises once or twice, like the clinking of a harness and a horse snorting, and she saw from the look on the faces of their men about her that they too had heard something. Suddenly, she caught sight of several men riding hard down the road ahead of them; looking back, she saw others coming up swiftly from the rear.

'We are being followed,' she cried and Stefan turned his head to glance at her face.

'I know. I have been aware for some time. Put your arms about me, Anne. I must ride faster to avoid them. You see the woods to your right? We shall go through them. Hold on tight, otherwise you might fall.'

Anne obeyed, holding on tightly as he suddenly wheeled his horse to the right. His men followed instantly and she knew that they had expected something like this might happen. She heard shouting from the riders behind them, and then a cracking sound. It was loud and she tightened her hold about Stefan's waist. Could that sound have been arquebus fire? Had someone shot at them from one of those terrible weapons that were the Devil's invention?

There was no time to be afraid, no chance to do anything but press her face against Stefan's back as they plunged through the trees at a speed that astonished Anne. The huge horse seemed almost to fly as both she and Stefan ducked their heads to avoid low-hanging branches. She knew that this wood was on one boundary of the estate and when they reached the other side they would be nearly home. She was not sure if Stefan's men-at-arms were following, but she heard some yelling and screaming behind her and thought that perhaps they were fighting, covering their master's escape.

On and on they went through woods so thick it would be impossible to find the way unless one knew the trails.

All sounds of pursuit had ceased. Only the silence of the woods remained and the occasional call of a bird from deep within the forest. After what seemed a long time, Stefan slowed his pace, then stopped, looked back and listened.

'We should be safe enough now. Eric and the others will have led them astray. Some of the ground is marshy here and, if they wandered into the bogs, they will not get far.' He slid from his horse's back and lifted her down, gazing at her face. 'Are you all right? I am sorry if you suffered some hurt.' He touched her face where a branch had caught it. 'You are scratched, but there is no blood. Forgive me. I would not have had that happen to you.'

'Who were they?' she asked. 'Did they want to rob us? What kind of men would lie in wait and try to trap you like that? They must have known you would come this way.'

'I did not think he would dare follow me here,' Stefan said and frowned. 'There is a man who hates me, Anne. He would do anything to destroy me, but I did not believe he would come here. An attempt was made on my life when I was in England, and there have been others—but here near my home…' His expression was harsh, angry. 'He has declared war and I must respond to the challenge.'

'Why does this man hate you so much?'

'Because what he has belongs to me by right,' Stefan said. 'He knows that I shall not rest until I have my revenge for what he took from me and my family.'

Anne shivered as she saw the ice in his eyes. He was so cold, so angry. She did not know this man and she was not sure that she liked him.

'Come, I must get you back to the house and raise the alarm,' Stefan said. 'Eric and the others may be hurt. We must go in search of them. They protected my back so that I could get you away.'

Anne looked up at him as he gave her his hand. 'You would have fought them had I not been there, would you not?'

'To the death,' Stefan said. 'I have sworn that either he or I shall lie beneath the earth before this year is out.'

Sickness swirled inside her as she looked into his eyes. They were dark with hatred. There was no softness or love in this man. She had believed that he was a man she could trust...even love, but he had become a stranger.

Anne did not put her arms about him as they rode the last few leagues to the chateau. She hardly looked at him as he lifted her down, turning her face from him as she ran ahead of him to the chateau. What kind of a man was he that his enemies pursued him to the gates of his home? What kind of a man had vowed to kill another or die in the attempt?

Stefan de Montfort had warned her that he was a mercenary, and that he had killed men in battle. He had told her that sometimes innocents had died too in the aftermath of war. She had tried to put those pictures from her mind, because a part of her was drawn to him and when he kissed her she had wanted to stay in his arms—but what had happened today had brought the horror of death too close.

Stefan rallied more of his men and returned to the woods. Anne spent some time alone in her chamber. She paced the floor, feeling restless until sounds from the courtyard told her that the men were returning. Running to the window, she looked out and saw that at least twelve men were dismounting. A body was slung across one of the horses and when it was lifted down she saw that one of the men who had accompanied them to Cherbourg that day had been killed. Several others had been wounded.

Anne could not see their master. Her heart caught because she feared the worst. She hurried from her chamber, running down the wide stone steps to the hall below. Stefan was not with his men! Surely they would have brought him back had he been killed or injured?

She found Ali in the hall. The physician was going from one injured man to the next, examining their wounds. He turned and beckoned to her as she hovered uncertainly.

'Does the sight of blood offend you, lady?'

'No, sir,' Anne replied. 'I shall be glad to help you if I can.'

'I have sent Sulina for water, salves and linen. The linen must be torn into strips and the wounds of these three men bound with salves and clean linen. I shall attend to the more seriously wounded, but if you can tend these men it will ease them sooner. The slight sword wounds are easiest dealt with, but a bolt from a crossbow can be deadly, and some of the men may have burns from gunpowder, though such weapons are seldom accurate enough to kill.'

'Yes, of course,' she said. 'I think I can do that, for it would not be the first time I have bound cuts and bruises.' Anne was too concerned about the men who had been hurt to notice the way the physician looked at her.

Sulina and another serving girl brought pewter bowls and cans of water, also soft white linen and salves. Anne poured water into a bowl and began to wash away the blood from the head of one man who had been slightly hurt in the battle. The cut was not deep and she applied salve and a bandage, working deftly and as gently as she could.

'You should not take harm now,' she told him. 'I am sorry if I hurt you.'

'You did not, lady.'

Anne passed on to the next, who had a cut hand, and the third, who had suffered a slash across the face. She asked each of them if they had seen Lord de Montfort but all of them shook their heads, seeming surprised that he was not with them.

She had finished her work when she heard a cheer and turned her head to see Stefan walk in. He was carrying a man in his arms and seemed near exhausted as others hurried forward to help him lay his burden down on a blanket. Anne saw it was the man Eric and she knew at once that he must have become detached from the others as they sought to lead the enemy astray. He had been shot in the chest by a bolt from a crossbow, the tip of which was still protruding from his chest.

Ali finished bandaging the man he had been helping and went to look at Eric. He made a thorough examination before glancing up at Stefan.

'He is alive,' he said. 'But I shall have to cut that iron tip out and he will bleed a great deal. We shall need the opium juice, otherwise he will not bear the pain.'

'Do whatever you must,' Stefan said. 'Where do you want him?'

'You must place him on the board there. Clear everything else away and scrub it first. And I shall want boiling water for my instruments. I can remove the tip, but he may not recover from the shock, my lord.'

'Do your best,' Stefan said grimly. 'He deserves his chance. He has served me well and I could not leave him to die alone in the forest.' Stefan glanced round, frowning as he saw Anne. She had blood on her hands and her cheek. 'You should not be here. Such sights are not for a gentle lady.'

'I am not afraid of a little blood,' Anne replied with a proud lift of her head. 'I shall help Ali if he wishes it.'

'Eric will fight us,' Stefan said, his mouth thinned, eyes stony. 'Go to your chamber. If we need you to help when he is recovering, you will be asked.'

Anne's cheeks were on fire. How could he be so harsh to her when she had merely tried to help? Was he blaming her because his men were injured? She knew Eric and the others had covered their escape and she felt guilty because one man had died and another looked close to death. Walking away, her head high, Anne hid her feelings of distress. For a time that morning she had believed Stefan might care for her, but his manner since had made it quite clear that she was nothing but an extra burden he could well do without.

She held the tears back until she was alone in her chamber. Sinking down on the edge of the bed, she wept then, feeling terribly alone. Lord de Montfort had rescued her from the sea, but she was nothing to him.

He would be glad when she remembered who she was so that he could send her home.

She wished so much that she could supply a name for him. If she still had a family, she would rather be with them than live here in a house where she was not wanted. She did not know what to think of a man who could be kind one moment and an avenging devil the next. If only she knew who she was so that she might leave this place and never be forced to see him again…

Stefan knew that he must apologise. Ali had said nothing until they were alone, but then he had spoken out in defence of the young woman who had come instantly to offer her help.

'I do not know what ails you, my lord,' Ali told him. 'Why did you speak so unkindly to the lady when she had done so much to help me? I have seen her work and she makes a good physician's assistant. Sulina will hold a bowl for me if forced to, but she cannot bring herself to touch a bloodied limb. The lady Anne deserves your thanks, not your curses.'

'I did not curse her!'

'You sent her away without thanks, and your looks were harsh. What has she done that so displeases you?'

Stefan had not answered him—he knew that Anne had done nothing to deserve the way he had behaved to her since their return from Cherbourg. It was he who was at fault. Anne was not to blame if he had lustful thoughts of her! Stefan knew that he was fighting a battle with himself, and that his harshness to Anne was a result of his fear that the saner half of him was losing the war. He wanted her more with each hour that passed, and yet he knew that to take her as his mistress would wrong her. Anne was a lady, even though she did not know her name. If he wanted to lie with her, he should wed her in all honour.

The thoughts chased themselves through his mind like a puppy after its tail. How could he ask a gentle, lovely woman like Anne to marry him when his life might be forfeit at any moment? They had beaten off one attack, but they had not caught all Cowper's men and he himself was not amongst the dead or the prisoners.

Ali was even now tending the wounded amongst Cowper's men who had surrendered rather than die, and a detachment of Stefan's men were directing the burial of the enemy who had died. A priest would say prayers for them over the woodland graves.

It was night now and Stefan was conscious of a need to speak to Anne. He was not sure if she would be sleeping and he paused outside her door before knocking softly. No answer came. Lifting the latch, he discovered that her door had not been locked and, after a moment's hesitation, opened it and went inside. One small candle was set on a table at some distance from the bed. The light was dim, but Stefan could just make out her face as she lay in the great bed. Her pale gold hair was spread about her on the pillows, one arm flung out, and another tucked beneath her face as she slept.

She made a little whimpering sound, rolling from her side to her back. Clearly, she was dreaming and her dreams disturbed her. When she cried out, Stefan bent over her. His hand was reaching towards her when she called a name.

'Harry…Harry…' she cried. 'Help me…'

Stefan stared down at her, withdrawing his hand.

Who was Harry? Was he her lover or just a friend? Had he been on the ship when she was washed into the sea? Surely if he cared for her he would have gone in after her even if he drowned in the attempt to rescue her!

And yet Stefan had discovered that the agitated man Anne had seen from the window of the inn had indeed been searching for a young woman who might have been pulled from the sea half-alive. In his heart Stefan knew that Anne must be the woman the stranger sought. He owed it to her to make further inquiries concerning this man. If Anne had family, she must be restored to them.

He knew well enough that if she came from a good family it was unlikely that his suit would be welcomed, even if he were to ask her to be his wife. He would be a fool to allow himself dreams that could never be fulfilled. Far better to keep his distance. He had wanted to apologise, because he knew that she had not deserved his harshness, but perhaps it was better this way. If he told her he was grateful, she would smile at him and he was not sure that he could resist her. He turned away, leaving the room and closing the door softly.

Anne gave a little start as the door clicked to, opening her eyes and looking about her. She felt that someone had been in her room, but no one was here. She knew that she had been dreaming of the night that she was lost at sea. She had felt the swell of the sea and seen the huge waves coming at her, and then she was lifted from her feet and swept into the sea. After that there was nothing but darkness in her mind.

Anne could not even be sure that what she had seen in her dream was true. She thought that there had been a man in her dream and that she had called out to him, but now that she was awake she could not remember him. Who was he—and what did he mean to her? Could it have been the agitated stranger she had seen from the window of the inn? Had he been asking people about her?

Anne wished that she had made some sign to him. If he had been looking for her, surely he would have known her? She longed to regain her memory so that she could remember the people who had loved her—surely someone must have loved her?

Perhaps the Chevalier Charles Renard and his sister would know something of him. If he had been looking for her, Anne might be able to send a message to the stranger...though if he were looking for her he would not be a stranger. Was he her brother or her lover?

Instinctively, Anne knew that she did not have a lover. She would not have these painful tortured feelings for Stefan de Montfort if that were so. Perhaps the stranger was her brother...

The thought made Anne tingle at the base of her spine. Did she have a brother? Something told her that she did and perhaps a sister too. All the things she felt about keeping a good house must mean that she had a loving family. Someone had taught her about being the chatelaine of a large house, because she instinctively knew what needed doing here—and that person must have been her mother.

'Why can I not remember?' she asked herself.

Anne threw back the covers and got out of bed. The night was warm and sticky and she thought with longing of the bathing pool in a secluded part of the gardens. The custom had been brought from the east, Anne knew, because Sulina had told her so when she showed surprise the first time she saw it.

'It is not for washing,' the Arab girl told her, 'but for refreshing yourself when it is hot. There is another small pool within the house that the master uses to bathe. He likes the ways of the east and it is common there to bathe for pleasure.'

The idea seemed strange to Anne. She was certain it was not her way, though she liked to use a hip bath in her chamber sometimes. She washed all over herself every day, though she did not believe it was the custom in her own country. Many people did not bathe or wash as often as they might, but Anne had noticed that Stefan always had a clean fresh smell about him.

Slipping on a silken wrap, Anne put on flat slippers and went downstairs. She would walk in the cool of the night air; if no one was about, she might take a swift dip in the outdoor pool.

Anne felt much better when she was outside. Her restlessness fell away. Some sweet perfume floated to her on the air and she tried to place the night-blooming flower that was the source of the scent. Walking through the maze of rose bushes that guarded the pool from anyone who might chance to disturb the privacy of the bather, Anne was thoughtful. She was beginning to enjoy living here and it would be a wrench when the time came to leave, though she knew she must as soon as her memory returned. Her family—her mother would be worried about her. She had a feeling that her mother was in great distress because she feared Anne lost.

When she came suddenly upon the pool, Anne was not immediately aware that someone was in the water. It was not until he stood up and began to ascend the graduated steps that led from the shallow pool that she saw him properly.

Stefan de Montfort was a handsome man when dressed, but in the moonlight his body had the pale gold perfection of a statue made from some polished stone. He stood for a moment at the edge of the pool unmoving, completely unaware that he was being watched.

Anne could not take her eyes from him, even though she knew she must leave. It was wrong of her to stare so, but her heart was thumping wildly against her ribs and she was aware of a hungry longing deep inside her. As he bent down to retrieve a long robe made of some striped material, wrapping it about his nakedness, she suddenly found that she was able to move. Turning, she hurried back the way she had come. She had no right to be here in Stefan de Montfort's private place! If he knew she had seen him, he would be angry!

Going straight back to her own chambers, Anne found that once again she was being torn in two. A part of her longed to be home with her family, wherever they were, but the other part of her wanted to stay here with the master of this chateau for the rest of her life.

Chapter Four

Sulina came to her the next morning as she was dressing. She brought a message from Ali asking if she would help him to tend the wounded, who were housed together in the great hall. Several of the men had developed a fever, and lay moaning on their pallets when Anne went down a little later to join the physician.

'I need to change all the dressings and to administer a healing draught, but there are so many of them,' Ali told her. 'Could you give each man a measure of this mixture if I show you exactly how much is needed?'

'Yes, of course,' Anne told him. 'You know that I am more than willing to help—if Lord de Montfort does not object.'

'He spoke too harshly to you last evening, lady,' Ali said, because he could sense her hurt. 'I remonstrated with him and I am sure that he will apologise to you when next he sees you.'

'I need no apology,' Anne replied. 'I dare say he was distressed by what happened yesterday, as we all were.'

'He has seen worse,' Ali said, 'but his own wound may be troubling him again.'

'Lord de Montfort was wounded?'

'Superficially yesterday,' Ali told her. 'However, he received a severe wound some weeks ago. It has not healed as well as it ought and could have broken open again in the fighting yesterday.'

'I did not know he had been wounded before,' Anne said and looked concerned. 'He showed no sign of it.'

'Would you expect him to? To complain of pain would show weakness. He would never let his feelings show. A man, who has seen the things and suffered as Lord de Montfort has, learns to hide his pain.'

'No, I suppose he would not.'

Anne was thoughtful as she tended the wounded, working carefully and methodically as Ali directed her. The men all welcomed her with a smile and she talked to them, as she would a brother, as she offered each a cup with the carefully measured potion. She was unaware that Lord de Montfort had come into the hall and was watching her until she straightened up and saw him standing there, his eyes intent on her.

'You are compassionate, Anne,' he said as she came to him. 'The men are grateful to you.'

She met his gaze with a quiet pride. 'I do not forget that they were injured helping to save your life and perhaps mine.'

'You would certainly have been killed,' Stefan told her, his expression grave. 'You could not have been allowed to live to tell the tale of an unprovoked attack.'

'No, I do not suppose I could,' Anne replied and looked at him with troubled eyes. 'Is there no one who would support you, sir? Can you not have this enemy taken before the courts?'

'I asked an audience of King Henry of England,' Stefan said and frowned. 'I was refused a hearing. Lord Cowper has powerful friends at court. I might be heard by Louis of France, but Cowper would have returned to England before anything could be done.'

'That is unfair,' Anne said, feeling angry. 'I am sure that my father would support you if he knew—' She broke off, her eyes widening. 'I believe my father hath influence with the King...'

'What have you remembered, Anne?'

'I remember a man being angry once when I was a child. I cannot see his face, but I know my mother was upset and she said that he should use his influence with the King.' She placed the palms of her hands to her cheeks. 'Sometimes I feel the past is very close. I can almost see it and I dream...' She shook her head, gazing up at him with real distress. 'Why can I not remember who I am? I remember things my mother taught me, but not my name or hers.'

'I believe everything will come back to you soon,' Stefan told her and his tone was gentle, for he had sensed her grief. 'You must be patient, Anne, and perhaps soon we shall discover something that will help you.'

'What do you mean?'

'I learned yesterday that the man you saw from the inn was seeking a woman who might have been rescued from the sea. It seems highly likely that it is you he is looking for and I have set one of my men to searching for him. Once he is found, he will come here and then perhaps you will remember.'

'Perhaps...' Anne frowned. 'Last night I dreamed

of someone. I think his name may have been Harry. I think he may be my brother for I called to him to save me when I was swept into the sea. Yes, I think he may be my brother…' She stared at him in wonder. 'I am almost certain of it, but I still do not remember my name or my home.'

'Is that what happened to you—were you swept overboard in the storm?'

'In my dream I was swept overboard by a huge wave, but it was just a dream. I cannot tell if it was true.'

'No, for our dreams are often distortions of the life we live,' Stefan agreed. He looked serious. 'If I was harsh with you yesterday I ask you to forgive me, Anne. I was angry, but you were not the cause and I should not have spoken as I did.'

'You were distressed at the injury to Eric,' Anne said. 'He is being nursed separately from the others, for he was the most seriously hurt, but Ali told me he is as well as could be expected.'

'Yes, he lives,' Stefan said grimly. 'No thanks to the devils who tried to murder me!'

'You must lay your complaints before the King again,' Anne said. 'I would testify for you. You were attacked for no reason and the man responsible should surely be arrested and imprisoned.'

'You would not be heard. Do you think they would listen to a woman? They would think you my mistress and deny you a hearing.'

'But that is so unfair!' Anne cried.

'Life is oft unfair. Have you finished here?' Stefan asked, as if he wished to dismiss the subject. 'The things we ordered yesterday were delivered this morning and I have ordered them taken to your room. However, if you have time I would walk with you in the garden.'

'I thank you for your generosity towards me,' Anne said. 'And I should like to walk with you, sir. Was there something you wished to ask me?'

'You recall that I met some neighbours at the inn yesterday?' Stefan asked as they left the house and went into the walled garden. The sun was warm and the scent of the flowers wafted towards them, carried by the light breeze. Anne nodded, slightly puzzled. 'Since I purchased this house I have remained much in seclusion from choice. However, you spoke to Sulina of guests and I have thought that perhaps it is time I became acquainted with others who live near me. It is many years since I had anywhere that I could truthfully call a home, but what I meant to say was—would it trouble you to arrange a dinner for perhaps ten guests?'

'You would like me to plan this entertainment for you?' Anne was surprised and then pleased. 'It would not trouble me at all. I should enjoy the task, sir.' It would be a way of repaying him for all his kindness to her. She would be a part of his life, of use to him, instead of just someone he had pulled from the sea.

'I should want to provide everything that you think necessary for a dinner fit for a gentleman and his friends. I fear I have grown lax these past years and my tastes tend towards eastern dishes. You would need to instruct my cooks what to prepare and the servants on how the food should be served.' He raised his eyebrows. 'I think it would be a hard task—do I ask too much?'

'No, of course you do not,' Anne said. 'I had planned to begin waxing the furniture today, but Ali needed help. When were you thinking of holding this dinner?'

'Shall we say in ten days?' Stefan bent to pick a dark red rose. She noticed that he was a little stiff, as if his side pained him. 'Would that give you time to prepare?' He held the rose to his nostrils, inhaling the perfume, and then handed it to Anne. 'This is one of my favourites.'

Anne took the rose and smelled it. 'That is gorgeous,' she said. She would keep it and treasure it, because it had come from his hand. 'I think ten days is perfect—most of the men will be well again by then. Do I have your permission to set the servants their work in the house?'

'Yes, of course. If you need more help, I can send to the village. I have not bothered, but I think perhaps a house like this needs many servants to keep it as it should be.'

'You need a…housekeeper or a steward to order the servants,' Anne said. She had almost said a wife, but stopped herself just in time. 'But I shall be happy to fill that position while I stay here.' She hesitated, then, 'Should you not ask Ali to look at your side, my lord?'

'Ali has others more in need of his services for now,' Stefan said. 'I was not cut; it is merely bruising that a salve will cure.'

'But you cannot rub salve into your own side,' Anne said. 'Would you allow me to do it for you?'

His eyes seemed to blaze at her for a moment and she trembled inwardly. Had she made him angry again?

'Forgive me. It is not my place…' She was immediately uncertain again, fearful of making him angry.

'There is nothing to forgive.' Stefan's mouth relaxed into a smile. 'I do not think that it would be sensible for you to tend me, lady. I find you too…disturbing. I am a rough soldier and used to taking what I want of the women I meet—women who are not as you are, Anne. Such intimacy might be more than I could bear, and I might take advantage of your sweet innocence.'

The look in his eyes made Anne's heart race wildly. What was he saying to her? As he gazed down at her she felt a sensation of melting, of such sweet longing that she wanted him to take her in his arms and kiss her. She had never felt anything like this in her life and it thrilled and yet frightened her. She hardly knew this man and yet she was almost ready to surrender herself to him.

'Stefan…my lord…' The spell was broken as she saw Hassan approaching them. He inclined his head to her, his ugly features softened by a smile.

'We have visitors, my lord. The Chevalier Renard and his sister have this minute arrived. Sulina took them to the parlour the lady Anne has been using, because she says it is the only one that has been properly cleaned— and the hall is being used to nurse the wounded.'

'I shall come at once,' Stefan told him. He held out his hand to Anne. 'You must come too. Do not forget, Anne, I have told them you are my kinswoman.'

'I will remember that.'

'I believe that for the moment that may be best,' Stefan said. He looked thoughtful. 'Shall we meet our guests and ask their advice about whom we should invite to our feast?'

Mademoiselle Maria Renard was a pretty young woman, vivacious and good humoured. Anne liked her immediately. She said at once that she had plagued her

brother to bring her that morning because she had heard
that Lord de Montfort had a guest staying.

'I caught a glimpse of you at the inn and was curious,'
Maria admitted to Anne softly when the gentlemen had
removed themselves to another part of the chamber. 'We
are all curious about Lord de Montfort's household, for
the rumours abound. We have heard tales of his bravery,
and his courage, but no one really knows much about
him. I could not come here while he lived alone with just
his servants, but as soon as I understood from Charles
that he had a lady staying here I was determined to visit.
I am so glad I did, for we shall be friends, I think.'

'You are very kind,' Anne said, warmed by her
engaging manner. 'And your visit is well timed for my...
cousin and I were just talking of giving a dinner for
his neighbours. Lord de Montfort believes it is time he
became acquainted with his neighbours and he means
to ask your brother whom he ought to invite.'

'Well, you must invite us, because I should just die
if you did not,' Maria said and threw a laughing glance
across the room at Stefan. 'But you must invite the
Chevalier Lamont, his wife and their two sons, of course,
for they live a few leagues to the east of our manor. And
there is Madame Dupré and her son Armand—she has
land to the west. I do not care for her, for she is very
proud and talks of nothing but how different things were
when she was young. Your other important neighbour is
the Comte Henri De Vere. He lives in great state and I
am not sure he would accept, but he should be invited.
He was widowed two years ago and they say he looks
for a wife, but I do not know if it is true, though I dare
say it may be, for he has no heir.'

'There are not many ladies amongst the guests,'

Anne said with a little frown. 'Are there no more we could ask?'

'Well…there is Madame Leclerc,' Maria said, but looked doubtful. 'She does not often accept invitations. She was once the mistress of Comte De Vere. I am not sure, but I think they quarreled.'

'I see…' Anne was thoughtful. 'Well, I shall consult with Lord de Montfort and see what he has to say.'

'How long do you stay here?' Maria asked. 'We must meet as often as we can. Do you ride?'

'Yes, but I am not sure that there is anything suitable for me to ride in the stables.'

'Have you a palfrey that Anne may ride?' Maria asked of Stefan as he glanced their way. 'If not, my brother will provide a horse for her so that she may ride with me.'

'Would you like to ride?' Stefan asked, looking at Anne directly.

'Yes, I think I should.'

'Then I shall make sure we have something suitable.'

'I cannot ride tomorrow, for I have a prior engagement,' Maria said. 'But on the following day you must come to us, eat your dinner with us. Charles will see you safely home, will you not, brother?'

Her brother gave her an indulgent look. 'If it is your pleasure, you know I shall. Mademoiselle de Montfort is welcome to visit us whenever she pleases.'

Anne almost protested that she was not Mademoiselle de Montfort, but changed her mind. She had no blood claim on Lord de Montfort; if her new friend knew the truth, she might not wish to continue the friendship. It was highly irregular for a young, unmarried woman to reside in the house of a single gentleman, especially when they were unrelated. Maria would think the worst and she would certainly not ask her to visit, nor would she think it proper to visit here.

It was a little uncomfortable to deceive her new friend, but Anne pushed the guilt from her mind. Her circumstances were awkward, but there was little she could do about it so she allowed the misconception to stand unchecked. Until she remembered her name— or someone came to claim her—she could do nothing else.

'You will forgive the intrusion,' Harry said as he was admitted to the Comte De Vere's elegant salon a day or so after his visit to Cherbourg. 'I have been making inquiries in the area concerning my sister, Anne Melford. She was lost at sea some weeks ago. I was told that a gentleman plucked a young woman from the sea— perhaps a lord or a nobleman who might live in this region of Normandy. Unfortunately, the sailor did not recall the gentleman's name.'

'And you are?' The Comte looked at him, one eyebrow raised. He glanced down at the letter that had been handed to him. 'Ah, yes, Sir Harry Melford, a courtier of some note, I see. Comte St Orleans is a friend of mine. His letter asks me to give you all the assistance I can, sir. I fear that I am unable to help you at this moment. I have heard nothing of such an occurrence. However, should I hear something I would certainly send word. Where are you staying?'

'I am travelling from town to town,' Harry replied and sighed. 'When I first heard that a young woman had been rescued, I thought it would be easy to find the man who had taken her, but it has proved difficult. No one seems to have heard anything. It is strange—one would have thought something like that would occasion some talk.'

'Unless it has been kept quiet for some particular reason,' the Comte said. 'Your family have not received a ransom note? It might be that some unscrupulous person is keeping her for nefarious purposes of his own, of course. Is she a pretty girl?'

'Anne is very attractive. I suppose she might be called beautiful, for she has golden hair and greenish-blue eyes.' He looked thoughtful. 'I do not know if a ransom has been asked for her, because I have not been home. I sent out agents, as did the Comte St Orleans, and it was through his good offices that I was given a lead. He has taken Mademoiselle St Orleans to my home in England, for we are to marry. I stayed here to continue the search.'

'I am sorry I could not have been more helpful,' the Comte told him. 'What will you do if you find no trace of her?'

'I intend to move on further north tomorrow,' Harry said, 'and then I shall return to England.'

'If you return this way, call and see me again,' the Comte said. 'I shall make certain inquiries in the district. As it happens, I am invited to dine with Lord de Montfort in a few days. I shall ask my neighbours if they have heard anything. If I should discover anything, I will send a letter to your home, unless I see you first.'

Harry smiled and offered his hand. 'I thank you for your hospitality, sir, and your kindness. If you hear even the smallest detail, do not hesitate to contact me. I must soon return to my duties at court, but I know my father would make the journey here if I could not. He will, I am certain, offer a reward for any information leading to the whereabouts of a girl who could be my sister. She is precious to her family and will be much missed.'

'It may be best not to mention a reward, for there are unscrupulous rogues about,' the Comte said. 'However, I would hope that whoever has your sister will ask for a ransom for her. Of course, if she did not long survive her ordeal, it may be that she has since died and the man who rescued her does not know who she was...' He shrugged his shoulders—it was not his concern. He would make inquiries, but would not trouble himself to do more, unless it suited him.

'Yes, that is a possibility,' Harry said. 'It grieves me that she may be buried in an unmarked grave. My parents will know that she is lost by now and I cannot think how this hurts them.'

His face reflected his sorrow. He bore the guilt of Anne's loss and the thought of his mother's pain lay heavy on his mind.

'It grieves me to be the bearer of such news,' Comte St Orleans said as he sat closeted with Lord Melford. 'We were delayed on our journey, because the ship was held in port. The weather was stormy and I would not risk the crossing until it settled.'

'Very wise,' Rob said, a nerve flicking at his temple. The news of Anne's loss had shocked him, and he knew that Melissa was in her bedchamber weeping. She would emerge soon and there would be few signs of her grief, but the worst nightmare for any mother was to lose a child. 'I wonder that Harry did not write to us sooner, for I might have gone out there to help in the search.'

'I believe that he wished to find her himself if it were possible,' Comte St Orleans said. 'He blames himself for her loss, but I can tell you that he was knocked unconscious to stop him jumping into the sea to search for her.'

'Had he done so, we should have been grieving for a son as well as a daughter,' Rob said. 'We are glad to have you with us, sir—and to welcome your daughter to our family. Harry told me what a beautiful girl Claire was and now I see it for myself. I just wish that things were happier so that we might even now be preparing for the joyous occasion of their wedding.'

'It will be a happy occasion, but I have hopes that Anne may be found. I was able to give Harry some news and he is searching for her.'

'I shall consult with my wife,' Rob said. 'If Lady Melford agrees, I shall travel to Normandy and see if I can help Harry search for her. I would not have him blame himself for this, and I know he must soon return to his duties at court.'

'If you wish it, I would come with you,' the Comte offered. 'Claire would be happy to stay here and offer what comfort she can to Lady Melford until we return.'

'I shall not refuse your offer,' Rob said. 'The more of us that search the better, for Anne might be anywhere.'

'I had wondered if you might have received a ransom demand,' the Comte said. 'I did not mention it to Harry, but it was one of the reasons I decided to bring Claire on ahead. Whoever has Anne has either kept her for some purpose of his own or he is ignorant of her identity.'

'Unless she has since died,' Rob said and his expression was bleak. 'After being in the water for some hours, as she must have been, it is likely that she did not recover her senses before she died.'

'In which case she may have been buried in an unmarked grave.'

'I would pay just to know where she is,' Rob said and groaned. 'Had she died at home of a fever it would have broken our hearts, but not to know if she is alive and safe or dead is a cruel thing. I do not know how her mother will bear it.'

'Harry has been devastated,' Comte St. Orleans said. 'I gave him a letter to a gentleman I know slightly—the Comte De Vere. Henri has some influence in the district and may use it to discover any news of her. I think our best course would be to call on him first and see if he has heard anything of your daughter...'

Anne entered the house fresh from her morning ride with Maria. Immediately the scent of lavender greeted her and she smiled, for she could see that the servants had been working hard. Furniture that had been dull and neglected had been polished until the surfaces shone enough to reflect your face. The tapestries had been taken out into the yards and beaten until the dust flew and then re-hung, and the floors had been scrubbed clean. There was now an air of activity about the house, giving it a lived-in feeling, which had turned an empty, neglected house into a home.

Anne had found herself growing more content as the days passed. Stefan seemed to smile more and there was a different atmosphere in the house. Everywhere she went, the servants and men-at-arms greeted Anne with pleased looks and the deference they would normally show to the lady of the manor. Anne supposed it was because she had helped to nurse some of them when they were ill, though it was her duty to help them—at least, it would be her duty if this were truly her home.

It was odd, but she had had no more disturbing dreams of late. Since the talk with Stefan in the garden and her new friendship with Charles and Maria Renard, she had felt much calmer. She believed it possible now to contemplate a life here. She sometimes felt sad when she thought about the mother who had taught her all the skills she had used to turn Stefan's house into a home, but the ache inside her had eased a little. She could remember a house and she believed she had had more than one brother or sister, though perhaps she had not been truly close to all of them—but she had loved her mother. She missed her mother and wished she could remember her. However, she had begun to enjoy her life here at the Chateau de Montifiori.

Anne thought that she could happily live here if... Stefan cared for her enough to take her as his wife. She knew that he had a score to settle with his enemy, and sometimes when she watched him train with his men, she feared for his future. There was no doubt in her mind that he intended to find and punish his enemy. She could not forget the wild ride through the forest when their lives had been at risk. Stefan had not told her anything more about that day, and she was not certain whether he believed there was a risk of a further attack.

Stefan was courteous to her, even gentle at times, and the look in his eyes told Anne that he felt something for her. She could not be certain whether it was love or merely the lust any man might feel for an attractive young woman living in his house. She knew that she was attractive, for she had seen herself in a small mirror provided for her use. The sunshine suited her and her skin had begun to glow with health, because of the long rides with Maria and her brother Charles, and also the time she spent in the walled garden tending her herbs.

Anne had discovered that she knew a lot about herbs. She knew what they were and their uses in cooking and in medicines. Ali had shown her some new ones that he had brought with him from his homeland, and he had praised her for her knowledge.

'Someone has taught you well, lady,' he said. 'You could be of great help to me while you stay here.'

'I should love to help you tend the herbs and in the preparation of cures,' Anne told him wistfully. 'I wish that I might—' She had stopped suddenly, for her wish had been that she might stay at the chateau for the rest of her life, but she was not certain it was possible.

Ali had smiled in that knowing way of his, but said little. He was not the only one to notice the changes in the house and its master. Stefan de Montfort laughed more and shouted less, though there were times when his mood changed abruptly and he became harsh, angry without reason. Those who knew him best understood the tussle he was having with himself.

He was smiling as he greeted Anne on her return that morning. She had blossomed in these past days and he could hardly recognise the woman he had pulled from the sea more dead than alive. Sometimes he felt that he might have seen her before the day he pulled her from the sea, but it was an elusive memory and would not come to him. Perhaps he did not wish it, because he

might then know who she was and would be honour
bound to return her to her home.

'You enjoyed your ride, Anne?'

'Yes, as always,' she said. 'But it was lovely to come
home and see how good the house looks now. Do you
not think so?'

'I hardly know it,' Stefan admitted 'I have not seen
many of the things you have used to transform it. Where
did you find them?'

'So much had been stored away,' Anne said. 'I was
not sure whether the chests we unpacked were things
you brought here or the last owner had packed away.'

'I believe much of the brass and pewter was brought
from the east, though I had never seen it all, but I collected things as I travelled and had the chests stored.
Some of the furniture must have been here.'

'Yes, it is French, I think,' Anne said. 'It is strange
how well the different styles contrast and yet blend
together.'

'That is your magic touch,' Stefan told her. 'I
should probably never have bothered to have the chests
unpacked. Even had I done so, I should not have known
what to do with the contents.'

'It is a woman's place to make a house a home,' Anne
said and laughed. 'Are you ready to greet your friends
tonight, my lord?'

'Yes, of course. It is strange, but I find myself looking
forward to it,' Stefan said. 'I had forgotten what it felt
like to be a gentleman, Anne.' Something in his eyes at
that moment made her feel light headed. The longing
to be in his arms, to feel his lips on hers was so strong
that she almost swayed towards him, but he stepped back
and she felt the barrier come down once more, shutting

her out. He frowned. 'I must tell you that my enquiries
have come to naught. The man you saw did ask for his
sister—and you may be her, Anne—but no one seems
to know his name or where he may be found. He must
have moved on. I am sorry that I cannot give you better
news.'

'I am grateful that you have taken so much trouble on
my behalf,' Anne said. 'I should like to remember my
family, but sometimes I think…' She shook her head.
'Of course I must not expect it. You have been more
than generous, but I do not belong here.'

'Do you not?' Stefan asked, and the tone of his voice
made her eyes fly to his face. 'There are times when I
think this is just where you belong, Anne. If you were
to leave—' He broke off as Hassan came up to them,
his attention caught by the man's manner. 'You have
news?'

'Cowper was seen at Cherbourg,' Hassan said.
'He was heard making arrangements for a ship to
England.'

Stefan's expression was grim. 'Has he given up, do
you imagine, or is he simply slinking back to his lair to
lick his wounds?'

'Or is it a trap? Does he want us to believe he has gone
so that we relax our guard and call off the search?'

'Exactly,' Stefan said. 'Perhaps we should put it to
the test?'

'What are you suggesting, my lord?' Hassan frowned.

Stefan looked at Anne and his eyes held the coldness
she dreaded once more. 'Excuse me, Anne. Hassan and
I must talk. I shall look forward to your company this
evening.'

Anne nodded. She went on past him, walking up the

wide stone stairway to the gallery above. Glancing down at the men in the Great Hall she saw that Hassan was shaking his head as if disagreeing with something Stefan was saying to him. She was thoughtful as she went into her chamber. Stefan had seemed as if he had something important to say to her before Hassan's arrival, but the news about Lord Cowper had interrupted him. She knew that he could not afford to neglect such news, because of the attack that had been made on them the day they went to the fair. Until Lord Cowper left the country—or was dead—they could not feel safe whenever they left the manor.

'I want him dead,' Cowper said, scowling over his wine cup. 'I do not understand how he managed to escape that day. There were ten of you and only four of them and a woman. You should have taken him easily.'

'In the woods they scattered and we could not follow the trails—and the land was boggy. Our horses refused to go on. Had we been on foot, we should have been sucked into it.'

'Damn you for lily-livered cowards,' Cowper snarled. 'I should hang the lot of you.'

'He is too well protected,' Fritz said. 'But there was a woman with him. She rode with him and I think he fled to protect her. She may be his weak spot…a chink in his armour at last.'

Cowper stared at him, a gleam of malice in his narrow-set eyes. 'She must be guarded day and night. We could never get into the house to snatch her.'

'She has friends,' Fritz said, smiling inwardly as he saw he had his master's attention. 'She rides out with them sometimes—just a man, two grooms and the two women. If there were enough of us, we could snatch them.'

'We only want de Montfort's woman,' Cowper warned. 'The others should not be harmed if it can be avoided. Thus far we have not attracted the notice of the French court or the nobility, but if one of their number were harmed it might go ill with us. We are not on English soil here.'

'I have heard a rumour that she is not who she pretends to be,' Fritz told him. 'Her friends call her Mademoiselle de Montfort, but in a tavern I heard that she was found in the wreckage of a ship more alive than dead and that his physician nursed her back to health.'

'If that is true, she must be his mistress,' Cowper said, a glint of excitement in his eyes. 'So much the better. If she means something to him, he will come after her.' He glared at Fritz. 'Bring her to me alive. We shall take her to England with us. If he wants her back he will come for her—and then we shall have him.'

'What is in it for me?' Fritz asked, the gleam of avarice in his eyes. 'I have served you well, my lord. I want more than life as a servant. I would be my own master.'

'You want freedom and gold, I suppose?' Cowper smiled nastily. He would teach the fool a lesson, but not until he had the girl safe. 'Get de Montfort's woman for me; once I have what I want, you shall have your just reward.'

Fritz inclined his head and left the tavern. He had not missed the gleam in Cowper's eyes and knew that his master was not to be trusted. He also knew that several of the other men in Cowper's pay were dissatisfied with their lot. His plan was a good one. He was certain that Lord de Montfort would pay well to recover the woman, and he would pay even more for information that might lead to Cowper's downfall. The late Lord de Montfort had never signed his manor away. The signatures were false, and Fritz had the proof—Cowper had practised Lord de Montfort's hand many times, carelessly discarding the parchment afterwards. He, Fritz, had seen the moment when the proud old man realised that he had been duped, and the wicked murder that had taken place that night. He had a letter in the late Lord de Montfort's own hand, written to his son begging him to return and help him.

Fritz had kept these things secret, waiting for his chance to use them. Cowper was a ruthless, brutal man, and while his cousin Sir Hugh lived it had been impossible to destroy him. Sir Hugh was a clever, devious man, but Fritz had lost all respect for his master. Cowper did not deserve all he had acquired through murder and deception. It would give Fritz pleasure to see him pulled down. He had had enough of watching his sister being treated almost as a slave. If Fritz had enough money he could take her and his family away, somewhere they would all be free of Cowper's brutality.

But there must be some profit in it for him. He needed to think about this carefully—he must not be implicated in the kidnap of Lord de Montfort's woman.

Anne was wearing the dark emerald silk gown the seamstress had helped her to fashion and sew. She had done much of the needlework herself, including the embroidery about the squared neckline and on the cuffs of the hanging sleeves. The full skirt was cut so that it flowed to a little train at the back, and Anne had a sash of gold, which matched her cap. She wore slippers of black leather embroidered with gold, and Stefan had sent her a gold chain to wear about her neck that night.

She looked what she was, a young gentlewoman, a lady of quality, and the chatelaine of a large manor. All she lacked was the ring on her finger that would proclaim her the wife of the lord of that manor.

Going downstairs to meet Stefan, she felt a flutter of nerves in her stomach. So far she had managed to keep up the pretence that she was Stefan's cousin—but supposing one of the guests knew the truth? If she were exposed as an impostor, everyone would believe the worst and think her Lord de Montfort's mistress. Her reputation would be gone and it would shame her.

She almost wished that she had told Maria Renard the truth at the start, but had she done so Maria would have withdrawn her offer of friendship. No, she must continue the masquerade, at least until she remembered who she really was.

What if she never remembered? Would Stefan declare his feelings? Would he ask her to become his mistress— or his wife?

There were moments when Anne felt that she would willingly be either. He could be harsh and his anger was terrible at times. However, the longer she stayed in his house, the more she felt herself drawn to him, and wished he would speak to her of love.

Stefan was in the hall as she entered. He turned to look at her as she entered, his gaze intent as it swept over her. Anne's heart fluttered as she saw the richness of his dress that night. She was used to seeing him dressed simply, but that night he wore the robes of a nobleman, embroidered with gold thread and jewels. He looked handsome, proud, even arrogant, and she knew that she was happy to be his lady for the evening, his hostess, standing by his side to meet the guests he had invited.

He called himself a mercenary, and perhaps he was, but she was proud to be the mercenary's lady.

Stefan watched the way Anne greeted his guests. If he had ever doubted that she was a lady, he could not do so now. Her manner was almost regal and he felt pride in seeing her dressed the way she should be dressed. He knew a fierce desire to make her his own. If his plan worked and Cowper was fooled into making a move against him, the feud might at long last be over. He might then be able to think of a future that included all the things he had denied himself.

He was not sure that he was worthy of the beautiful young woman who had wormed her way beneath the shield he had for so long kept in place, but it seemed increasingly unlikely that she would remember her identity. He could not abandon her to her fate. Perhaps it might be the best solution to wed her.

'Your cousin is a beautiful woman,' a voice said at his side and Stefan turned his head to look at the Comte De Vere. 'She is English, of course, as you are.'

'Yes, Anne is English,' Stefan agreed. 'Her French improves daily. She is intelligent and knows she must learn the language if she is to live here.'

'It is your intention to keep her here, then? Has she no family of her own?'

'Anne recently lost her family,' Stefan said. He realised that he had given more information than he had meant to concerning Anne. 'She came to stay here, for she had nowhere else to go. We may wed if the idea agrees with us both.'

'Ah, I see,' Comte De Vere said. Something about de Montfort's cousin intrigued him. He felt there was some mystery about the girl, though he was not sure why he did not quite believe his neighbour's story. However, he found the young woman charming and was loath to think badly of her. He knew that some whispers had started, which inferred that de Montfort had a mistress, but he thought the girl innocent. She was fresh and wholesome and beautiful, and he felt a strong attraction to her. 'Well, I wish you happiness of her, de Montfort.'

Stefan cursed beneath his breath. De Vere's tone told him that he thought Anne could be Stefan's mistress. His brow furrowed as the Comte moved away to greet Charles and Maria Renard. Had it been a mistake to invite his neighbours to the chateau? Or would the stories have begun to circulate anyway once it became known that a young woman was living at the manor?

Stefan's gaze narrowed as De Vere approached Anne, engaging her in conversation. He did not know his neighbour well, and yet there was something about him that Stefan found odd, a certain look in the eyes, as if he were calculating the odds. Hassan had told him about frequent visitors to the Comte's chateau and he wondered why a Frenchman should have so many Spanish friends.

Anne's laughter rang out, drawing Stefan's attention. It was obvious that she was enjoying herself and found her neighbours good company. She looked very beautiful, completely at home and happy. Their eyes met and she smiled at him in a way that made his throat catch and set up a burning desire to hold her in his arms.

As the evening wore on, Stefan increasingly realised that he had been neglectful. For Anne's sake he must either make more effort to find her family or he must wed her. It would be wrong to let her stay here and drift into the position of being his mistress simply because she had nowhere else to go. The musicians had begun to play and the guests called for the dancing to begin. Stefan walked to where Anne was standing with her friend, Maria, and made his bow. He held his hand out to her.

'Come, Anne, as my hostess, you should lead the dancing with me.'

Anne took his hand. Her heart leaped as she allowed him to lead her into the centre of the floor. For a moment she worried that she would not know how, but then as Stefan bowed to her and lifted her hand with his, she found that her body understood. Dancing was natural to her, and she followed him instinctively, knowing that this was a pleasure she had always enjoyed. And yet there was something special about this dance with this man, something she knew instinctively she had never felt before this evening.

When their dance was over, Stefan took her back to where Maria and the Chevalier Renard were standing. He bowed to Maria and led her on to the floor, and the Chevalier asked Anne to partner him.

Anne enjoyed her dance with him, but it was not quite the same, and she could not help her gaze straying to Stefan and the young woman who was clearly enjoying her dance with the master of the chateau.

Smothering her slight pangs of jealousy, she danced with other guests. Stefan danced with all the ladies, but he did not ask any of them more than once.

Anne woke early the next morning. The night had been warm and she felt sticky, her body damp with sweat. Pulling on a loose wrapping gown, she went down the stairs, through the house and out into the garden. It was so early, the sun hardly risen, and she was sure that no one would be about. The servants had worked hard for days to get the house ready for guests, and would take their time about beginning the new day. If she was quick, she might have time to bathe in the pool.

No one was about as she made her way through the garden. Slipping off her robe, Anne walked down the steps to the shallow water and dipped down below the surface. The water felt so cool against her skin. She had kept her night chemise on, but in a spirit of recklessness she pulled it off and began splashing about in the pool. Anne could not swim—she had never been taught—and she thought that perhaps swimming in the river would have been a forbidden pleasure for young women. However, the pool was shallow and she was able to walk on the bottom and splash in the water to her heart's content.

It was only as she turned to leave that she became aware that someone was there. She instinctively covered her breasts with her arms as Stefan bent down to pick up her wrapping gown and hold it out for her.

'Come out, Anne. I wish to talk with you.'

'Put the gown down and turn your back.'

'Do you not think it a little late for that?' he asked, a gleam of what she thought was amusement in his eyes.

'I did not come here to spy on you, but the night was hot and I thought to cool myself—as you clearly did too.'

'I am not coming out until you turn your back.'

Stefan laughed, laying the wrapping gown on a stone bench by the pool and turning his back. Anne rushed up the steps and slipped it on, tying the sash at the front.

'Very well, you may turn now,' she said. The gown immediately became wet and clung to her breasts and wherever else it touched, making her aware that it revealed more than it hid. 'I thought it was your habit to bathe here at night and that everyone would sleep late after the feasting.'

'Most are still sleeping,' Stefan said, letting his eyes travel over her as he turned. Her hair was wet as it hung down her back, for she had immersed herself completely in the water as she played. 'I come here whenever I am not able to rest. The water helps me to relax.'

'Are you disturbed about something?' Anne asked, her eyes wide and innocent as she gazed at him. 'Were you not pleased last evening? I think our guests enjoyed the feast.'

'I am sure they did, but they are all wondering about you, Anne. I am not sure that some of them believe you are my cousin. The speculation will multiply unless we do something about it now…'

'What do you mean?' She caught her breath, her heart beating wildly. 'Are you going to send me away?'

'Would you prefer to leave? I could send you to the nuns. If I gave you a dowry, they would take you in.'

'No! No, please do not send me away,' Anne said desperately. 'Have I done something to make you angry?'

'No,' he said, his voice soft and caressing. 'Nothing but keep me restless in my bed each night. You haunt my thoughts, Anne…' He moved towards her, reaching out to catch her and draw her close. His eyes seemed to burn with a dark flame and then he bent his head and kissed her. It was not the gentle kiss he had given her before, but a hungry, passionate kiss that seemed to draw her soul. She felt the heat and the hardness of his arousal pressing against her body; the thin material of her wrapping gown was no protection as his hands found and cupped her buttocks, clasping her to him as the kiss went on endlessly. When he let her go at last, she felt her senses swim and gasped. 'I cannot go on this way. I have tried to ignore my feelings, because you deserve more than I can give, Anne. I am not a gentle or a good man and I am not sure I know how to love—but I want you in my arms, in my bed.'

'What are you asking me?' Anne said, her lips parting softly on a sigh of relief. He was not angry with her. He did not mean to send her away from him. 'If it is to be your mistress—'

Stefan put his fingers to her lips. 'I shall not so insult you,' he said. 'I do not know your name or where you came from, but I do know that you are a lady. I cannot offer less than marriage, and it must be soon, otherwise your reputation will be lost. I had thought to wait, because I had not planned to wed. You must know that in the past I have found women to be deceitful and unworthy of trust, but I think you honest, Anne. I am not worthy to be your husband, but I shall do my best to make you happy—if you will wed me?'

'Oh…yes,' Anne breathed. She would have agreed to anything rather than be sent away to a nunnery where she would never see him again. Thoughts of home and family were far away. She knew that she would regret her lost identity sometimes, but her feelings were too strong to be denied. 'Yes, I shall marry you…but when shall it be?'

'If I pleased only myself, I would summon the priest and have him wed us today,' Stefan told her. His fingers trailed her cheek, down her throat to the open V of her wrapping gown. He went further, his hand moving beneath her gown, caressing her breast, feeling the nipple harden beneath his touch. 'I want you now, this instant, but you shall be my wife before I take what I desire. We shall invite the guests we entertained last night, and the banns shall be called in the village church so that all shall know it is my intention to wed you. Even those that have wondered if you were my mistress will not be able to slander your name—and our first child will not be born too soon and give them the satisfaction of thinking they were right.'

'But how shall we marry when I do not know my own name?'

'I have given you my own,' Stefan said. 'You are Anne de Montfort and you shall be Lady de Montfort as soon as I can arrange it—if you truly wish it?'

'Oh, yes,' she said, happiness spreading through her. Perhaps he did not love her as she loved him, but he cared for her, he wanted her. At that moment all that mattered to Anne was that he would keep her with him for always. She would be his wife, live in his home and bear his children. She could ask for nothing more— except to know the name of her family. Even if she knew it, knew where to find them, Anne was certain she would never want to leave this man. 'Yes, please, Stefan.'

He smiled oddly. 'I am hoping that the feud between

Lord Cowper and myself can be settled soon, Anne. If he will agree to return to England and give up this fight, I shall try to forget that he and his cousin murdered my brother and father.'

'You will give it up?' Anne asked, looking at him uncertainly. 'But you swore that either he or you would lie in the grave before the year was out.'

'Could I come to you with blood on my hands?' Stefan asked. 'I have killed in battle and innocents have sometimes died, but not by my hand. I did my best to save those I could. I do not count myself innocent of their deaths, but I am not a murderer. If I kill Cowper in revenge, I shall have his blood on my soul—and I could not come to you, Anne. I could not soil you with the knowledge that I had done murder. So I shall meet with him and give him the chance to make a truce. He may keep the lands he stole from me, for I have all I could want here.'

'Oh, Stefan,' Anne cried and pressed herself against him. 'I love you so…' The fire rushed to her cheeks, but she would not let herself feel shame. Her confession was instinctive and could not be denied. 'You may not love me yet, but I pray that you will one day, for I love you.' She was so innocent, so sweet that it tore at his heart, yet he did not say the words he knew she longed to hear. He wanted her, desired her so fiercely that his body burned for hers, but love made men weak. He did not want to love her in the way she wished.

Stefan bent his head and kissed her once more. 'Go in and dress before the household rouses. If you were seen with me here, some would think the worst. I have been careless of your reputation, Anne, and I must be more circumspect in future. We shall be wed as soon as I can arrange it.'

Anne impulsively kissed him once more and then left his arms, running towards the house. When she reached the door she turned and waved to him before disappearing inside.

Stefan stood staring after her. He had lain all night torn between wedding her and sending her away so that she should not lose her good name. Seeing her in the pool had broken his resolution. He could not let her go therefore he must take her to wife—and that meant he must try to make peace with Lord Cowper if he could.

It would not be easy, for his hatred was still fierce. Yet he must kill the man or make peace with him, and for Anne's sake he would forgo his revenge. He began to walk back to the house. He would summon the priest and make the arrangements for his wedding.

Watching from the shrubbery, Fritz pondered over what he had seen. He had not dared to get close enough to hear what they were saying, though he had found a breach in the thick thorn hedge that formed a part of the boundary where the wall had been allowed to fall into neglect. Normally, a guard patrolled the walls, but for some reason this morning he was missing from his post.

Fritz was certain now that Lord de Montfort would pay anything for the return of his mistress, for his mistress she must be from what he had seen of their kisses. She must have come to bathe at the pool, but he had not been in time to see her, only the embrace they shared. Now that he had discovered how to enter the grounds of the chateau, it would be an easy matter for a few of his hand-picked comrades to come at night and snatch her when everyone was sleeping.

He had thought to seize her when she was out riding with her friends, but his new plan was even better. He would lie in wait in the early morning and when she came to bathe he would capture her. He smiled as he crept back the way he had come. There might be a guard the next time, but one man was easily disposed of and there would be at least six of them. He had tested them out and they were all willing to betray Cowper in the hope of getting their hands on Stefan de Montfort's gold.

Once he had the gold he could return to England, take his sister and parents and go far away. They would go somewhere that Cowper would never find them. He knew that the lord was his master and perhaps his father, but he hated him with a fierce passion. If he thought he had the chance he would kill him, but Cowper was too well protected. Revenge for all the slights Fritz had suffered could be won in quite another way…

Chapter Five

'The banns will be called this Sunday for the second time,' Stefan said as they walked together in the gardens some days later. 'It will not be long to our wedding day, Anne. Are you still content that it should be so?'

'Yes, of course,' she said, gazing up at him, her eyes reflecting her inner beauty. 'I shall be happy to be your wife and live here with you, Stefan.'

'And you will not regret all that you have lost?'

'I should like to know who my family are and to let them know I am well,' Anne told him, and there was a wistful look in her eyes. 'But even if I knew where they were to be found, I should still wish to be your wife.'

'Then I am content,' Stefan told her. He reached out and touched her cheek, smiling in the way that set her heart racing. 'But if ever you should remember and wish to change things, I would set you free from your promise, Anne.'

'No, no, I wish to be your wife, your lady,' Anne told him.

'You know that many think of me as a mercenary?'

'I know what you have been and what you have done,' Anne said. 'It makes no difference to the way I feel.'

'I have had a message from Lord Cowper,' Stefan told her. 'He will come to the meeting tomorrow and we shall talk. I hope that the quarrel between us may be settled, for I wish to have peace at last.'

'I pray it may be so,' Anne said and smiled. He bent his head and kissed her softly.

'Go in now, Anne,' Stefan said. 'I have things I must do and I dare say you have work enough.'

'Yes, I have,' Anne agreed. 'I shall see you this evening, my lord.'

'St Orleans, I was told you were in England,' the Comte De Vere said as the gentlemen were shown into his sumptuous salon that evening. Two whole weeks had passed since the evening he had spent as a guest of Lord de Montfort and something was hovering at the back of his mind. 'I understand Claire is to be married?'

'That is true and she is indeed with Lady Melford. Lord Melford and I have made the journey here to discover what we can about the disappearance of his daughter.'

'Ah, yes,' De Vere said. 'Mistress Anne Melford. Sir Harry was here a few days ago. I do not wish to raise your hopes only to see them dashed again, but I was on the point of writing to you, Melford. I could not help Sir Harry then, but something has happened since then…'

'You have news of my daughter?'

'I am not certain,' De Vere told him. 'I have seen a

lady I think might be her. I was not sure enough to say anything at the time, but it was in my mind to send a message. Now that you are here, the matter may soon be resolved.' De Vere smiled inwardly. If the girl was Melford's daughter, he might be angry enough to do what Cowper and his idiots had so far failed to achieve. De Vere would then lay claim to the chateau and lands that de Montfort had bought from King Louis of France, and which he had long coveted.

'Where is this lady?' Rob asked. 'And where would I find her? Her mother is beside herself with worry and I have promised to do whatever I can to find her. I did not think there was much hope, but now—' He stopped as De Vere shook his head. 'Please tell me as much as you can, sir. I shall not hold you responsible if it comes to naught.'

'She is calling herself Anne de Montfort. I met her two weeks ago at the Chateau de Montifiori, where she is the guest of the man she says is her cousin... I am not sure why I feel there is some mystery about her, and I am not sure what she is to de Montfort—but there was a slight resemblance to the man who came inquiring for his sister. She does not have the same colouring as Sir Harry, but there is something about the eyes and mouth.'

'Anne...my God! What has this man done to her?' Rob said and his expression was murderous. 'When I heard that she might have been rescued I praised the Lord for His mercy, but if she has been forced into a life of shame as de Montfort's mistress—' He broke off, for he could not contemplate something that horrified him so much.

'I am not sure that she is his mistress. There are

whispers of it, but she seems an innocent to me. I believe she may have some feeling for Lord de Montfort, but I do not know if he returns it or even if she is the lady you seek.' De Vere smiled inwardly as he saw the anger in Melford's face. He had said enough to ignite the fires, but he would not interfere further. Until de Montfort was dead he must live in peace with his neighbour, unless he wished to storm the chateau and take it by force, which might bring King Louis' wrath down on his head.

'Where does he live—this Lord de Montfort?' The pulse throbbed at Rob's temple. 'If he shamed my daughter, he will answer to me.'

'He is some ten leagues or more from here,' De Vere answered. 'But there is no point in going there at this hour. The house will be locked and the guards will not take kindly to anyone who approaches under cover of darkness. Stefan de Montfort has lived as a mercenary for some years. There was some tale of his being attacked on his return from Cherbourg some weeks back. I understand that there was some bloody fighting. It would be wiser to go in the morning. I will accompany you there and we shall conduct this in a gentlemanly way.'

'If he has seduced my daughter—' Rob began angrily, but the Comte St Orleans touched his arm.

'I know this is painful for you, Melford, but you must think of Anne,' St Orleans said. 'If she has indeed become his mistress, it might be better if a marriage could be arranged discreetly.'

'I would see him dead first!'

'As any father would,' De Vere agreed smoothly. 'But her affections may be engaged. Besides, we do not know that any force was applied—or even if the rumours are true. It may be that she has been merely an honoured guest in his home. I have heard stories about him, and I know he has acquired some odd servants, but I know little of the man. Had I seen any sign of distress in her I should have spoken out, but she seemed content… and she may be Anne de Montfort for all I know. Had Sir Harry not visited me, it would not have crossed my mind to doubt her.' Some of those odd servants had escaped the Spanish Inquisition, which had not pleased De Vere's masters. Stefan de Montfort was no friend of Spain. The Inquisition would no doubt reward him if they learned that Stefan de Montfort had been dealt with satisfactorily.

'Anne would never live there as de Montfort's cousin or his mistress unless he forced her,' Rob said. 'She is a spirited girl and her temper is sometimes hasty—but she would not shame her mother.'

'Then perhaps it is not her and I have wronged them both,' De Vere said, his usual urbane self. No one could have known from his manner that he detested everything English and had sworn to help his Spanish masters win superiority over that arrogant nation. 'We may go there on the morrow and speak with her ourselves, for she is a charming lady, and if I am wrong no harm will have been done. Please, stay as my guests tonight and tomorrow this business is easily settled.'

'Give yourself time to think,' St Orleans urged Rob. 'If by some wondrous chance your daughter still lives, the rest must be as nothing. She will be restored to you and I dare say something may be arranged to protect her from spiteful tongues.'

'Her mother would welcome her back whatever the

case,' Rob admitted. 'If her affections are engaged and he will wed her, it might be best that she is married.'

'He will wed her if she has been his mistress,' De Vere said and smiled inwardly. 'The three of us will see to it…' He knew that Stefan de Montfort would never bow to dictation, and a quarrel might bring about the very result he desired.

Anne could not sleep. Her room seemed stuffy and airless and she thought longingly of the pool in the garden. There was a moon and it would be easy to find her way there. She knew the path well enough, and she would love to cool herself in the water. She knew that Stefan had set the date for their wedding and it was less than a week until their wedding day. Until then he was determined that he would not seek her bed, though they had kissed and touched intimately when they walked in the gardens.

She could hardly wait for the day she became his wife. Her mind had settled to it that she would not now remember her past. The flashes of memory had ceased to come and she thought it must be because she was happy and at peace in this house. She was always busy—she enjoyed helping Ali with the cures he made, and there was usually some small task needing her attention. Her life was much as it must always have been, helping to run a large house, except that she would soon be wed. The thought excited her and she knew that she might as well get up, for she would never settle.

Slipping a thin wrapping gown over her night chemise, she slid on a pair of soft leather slippers and went down through the house and into the gardens. The moon was very bright and she hummed a lullaby to herself as she walked. She knew exactly what she wanted to do and went directly to the pool. Sometimes Stefan came to bathe at night. If he chanced to come, perhaps they might bathe together…

Lost in her dreams of the happiness that was soon to be hers, Anne had no idea of what was about to happen. She did not see the men hiding in the shrubbery or hear them as they crept towards her. When something struck her on the head everything went black and she fell like a stone.

'Damn you!' Fritz snarled at the man who had hit her. 'I told you we needed her alive and well. He will not pay one gold piece if she is dead.' Stefan de Montfort would seek a terrible revenge on the man who murdered his mistress!

'It was only a light tap,' the man said. 'I didn't want her to scream and bring the guards down on us. If they caught us here, we should be trapped. For God's sake hurry up. We need to get out of this place before someone sees us.'

Fritz hoisted the girl over his shoulder. As he did so, one of her slippers fell off. None of the men saw it as they began to creep away into the darkness. Fritz's plan had seemed a good one when they talked of it over their ale at the tavern, but Stefan de Montfort was known to have the devil of a temper. If he discovered them before they spirited the girl away, none of them would live to see the dawn!

'I'll be glad when this is over,' one of them grumbled. 'You planned this, Fritz. If anything happens to the girl, you are to blame.'

'Nothing will happen to her, unless Marc struck her

too hard,' Fritz said. 'If she doesn't come to her senses, we'll dump her in the forest and disappear.'

Stefan rose at first light as was his habit. He walked down to the bathing pool because the night had been hot and he liked to refresh himself in the cool water. He knew that Anne enjoyed it too and he smiled as he thought of the pleasure it would give him to teach her how to swim once she was his wife. The pool was not deep, but there was a river with a sandy bed on his manor and they might swim there together if she mastered the art. She seemed to embrace new things easily—she had already begun to speak French more often than she had and would soon be fluent. Once they were wed he would make it his business to teach her. The thought brought a smile to his face, because he would enjoy teaching his wife many things...

Stefan saw the leather slipper lying on the grass near the edge of the pool. He bent to pick it up, instinctively knowing it belonged to Anne. He was sure it was part of a pair they had bought when they visited the fair at Cherbourg. He frowned as he wondered how it came there. It was possible that Anne had come to the pool to bathe, but why would she leave one of her shoes behind?

Glancing about him, he saw that the grass had been trampled by feet heavier and larger than Anne's. A bush had been damaged, some of its leaves hanging, as if someone had brushed past it carrying something. An icy chill went down his spine and he clenched his fingers about the delicate slipper. It was not possible! No one could enter these grounds without being seen by his guards...unless they had been negligent. No, it could not be. The footmarks must belong to the gardener or one of his men-at-arms…but none of them would come here. This part of the garden was private. Only the gardeners and a few others were allowed here. Besides, he was certain that none of his men would harm Anne. They all knew that he was intending to marry her.

Turning, Stefan strode back to the house. His heart was thumping wildly as he faced the fact that his enemy might have somehow found a way into his gardens and stolen the woman he had promised to wed. If that were so, he would kill whoever had taken her! Yet perhaps Anne had merely dropped her slipper and not bothered to stop for it. He prayed that it was so; if she had been taken, he did not know how he would bear her loss.

He entered the house at a run, halting in surprise as he saw that three men were standing in the Great Hall. One he knew at once as his neighbour. The others were strangers to him. Hassan was with them and something in his face warned Stefan of trouble. He went towards them, barely controlling his impatience.

'I do not know what brings you here so early, De Vere, but it is not convenient. I must speak with Anne before I can see you.'

'Anne has been sent for at Lord Melford's insistence,' Hassan told him. 'However, she is not in her room…' He saw the slipper that Stefan had crushed in his hand. 'What has happened?'

'I found this by the pool,' Stefan said and his expression was icy. How dare these people come to his home at this hour and demand to see Anne! The rage boiled inside him, but something about Hassan's manner made him hold his tongue. 'There were signs of what may have been a struggle. If Anne is not in her room, it is possible that she may have been taken—'

'No!' one of the strangers cried angrily. 'I demand to know what you have done with my daughter!'

'Your daughter?' Stefan's startled gaze flew to his face. Now he understood Hassan's message, and, looking at the man's face intently, he saw that there was a certain resemblance. 'What makes you think she is your daughter?'

'This gentleman is Lord Robert Melford,' Comte De Vere said in a reasonable tone, for it suited him to play the diplomat. 'He is looking for his daughter. She was travelling to France some weeks ago with her brother when a freak wave washed her over the side of the ship. Having seen her brother a few days ago, and noted a faint likeness, I thought that the lady calling herself your cousin might possibly be Anne Melford.'

'Damn you!' Stefan cried. Instinct made him distrust his neighbour, though he had no real reason for it. 'Whether she is Anne Melford or my cousin hardly matters for the moment. If she is not in the house, it is likely that she has been stolen.'

'Why would someone do that?' Rob asked, his eyes as hard as iron. Clearly he did not believe Stefan! 'What reason could there be for Anne to be abducted?'

'If Cowper took her, he did it to gain revenge on me,' Stefan ground out. His temper hung by a thread and it took all his control not to lash out at the newcomers. They were wasting his time when he needed to look for Anne! 'He hates me and would see me dead. I had hoped to make peace with him, but if he has taken her I shall see him dead!'

'Why should he gain his revenge by taking my daughter? What is she to you?'

'Anne was to marry me as soon as the banns were called.'

'Never! I shall not allow it,' Rob said furiously. Lord de Montfort was a stranger to him and his first thought was for his daughter's safety. 'If you cannot protect her in your own home, you are not fit to be her husband.'

'I thought us all well protected,' Stefan replied coldly. 'Believe me, you cannot be angrier than I am that this has happened. I do not know if Anne is your daughter or not, sir. It is possible that she may be, of course. However, she was more dead than alive when I snatched her from the sea and brought her here. My physician brought her through the fever and made her well again, but she could not remember her name or where she came from. At times she thought she remembered a house and recently she told me that she thought her father might have some influence with King Henry of England, but though she knew many things, she did not remember her family. And she chose the name Anne for herself from some I suggested.'

'My God!' Rob stared at him. A part of his frustration at this situation was that he had been on thorns to discover if the girl was Anne and just when he had hoped to find her she had gone. 'It must be her. Thank God she is alive!'

'She was alive last night,' Stefan said, his expression grim. 'But I do not know if she still lives…'

'This man—where can he be found?' St Orleans asked. 'What did you say his name was, sir?'

'Cowper. He is an English lord and a devil,' Stefan said. 'Years ago, he and his cousin murdered my brother and blamed me for it. After I left England under a cloud, Cowper gained influence over my father and forced him to sign away his birthright and mine when he became old and feeble of mind.'

'Can you prove that?' Rob asked, eyes narrowed, suspicious.

'I have a witness that my father was treated ill, but actual proof—no,' Stefan answered. 'At this moment it hath no importance. I mention it only because it explains why the man wishes me dead and why he may have stolen my promised bride.'

'Anne may have given you her promise,' Rob said, his temper controlled but still simmering. 'If it is what she truly wants, I shall not deny her—but if you have brought pressure to bear, she shall not be forced to it.'

'Anne has not been ill treated in any way,' Stefan said haughtily. 'There were rumours, however, and I sought to protect her reputation by asking her to be my wife. Anne accepted me and I believe it was her true wish. She could not have continued to live here unless it was as my wife, and she had nowhere else to go. If she is your daughter, the case is altered. You should take her home with you and I will come for her when my business with Lord Cowper is ended. If Anne still wishes to be my wife, I shall honour my promise to her.'

'Spoken like an honest man,' Rob said, his frown clearing, because, despite some of the rumours he had heard, he discovered that he liked this man. 'We shall let Anne decide her future.'

'First we have to find her,' the Comte De Vere reminded them. 'Have you any idea where he might have taken her?'

'I have had one of my men keep an eye on him,' Stefan replied. 'He was staying at the King's Arms in Cherbourg, though I understood it was his intention to take a ship for England soon, for he had been making inquiries. His men made an attack on me some days ago, but were beaten off and several of them were killed. We had hoped that Cowper might have given up the fight. Yesterday, I sent word to him that I was ready to talk. We were to meet at the Abbey of St Michael, which is some twenty leagues on the road to Cherbourg, later today. If Cowper has stolen Anne, he may have hoped to fool me into going to the meeting with him while he slips away to England.'

'He will not try to ransom her?' Comte St Orleans said. 'You believe his motive is to gain revenge rather than for money?'

'If it were money, I would pay his ransom willingly,' Stefan said and Rob muttered agreement. 'Yet I fear he may try to strike a blow at me.' His eyes met Rob's. 'I thought she was safe here. Forgive me for not protecting her. This will be thoroughly investigated; if I find negligence, the men involved will be punished.'

'There must be a breach in the boundary somewhere,' Hassan said. 'I shall have the grounds searched, my lord—unless you have other work for me?'

'Detail a party of men to search for any clues. I shall take six of our best men and ride to Cherbourg to discover if they have taken Anne there.' He glanced at the three men who had come in search of Anne. 'Do you wish to ride with me?'

'What of your meeting with Lord Cowper?' Hassan asked.

'I suggest that you might wish to keep the appointment. If he comes to the meeting, Cowper knows my terms. I shall renounce all my claims to my late father's estate if he agrees to a peace between us. However, if anything has happened to Anne and I discover that he is responsible, I shall kill him.'

'If I have not done so first,' Rob growled.

'I shall detail the men,' Hassan said and bowed his head to Rob. 'I pray that your daughter will be found alive, sir.'

'Thank you,' Rob said stiffly. 'I shall accompany you to Cherbourg, Lord de Montfort. If they are about to board a ship, we shall need a strong force to stop them.'

'I think I shall take my men and help to make a search of the area,' the Comte De Vere said. 'St Orleans, I suggest you accompany Hassan to the meeting with Lord Cowper. If an agreement is reached, there will be need of an impartial witness.'

'I am not exactly impartial, for our two families are to be joined by the marriage of my daughter and Melford's son, but I shall be glad to witness the contract if one is drawn up.'

'Then we are agreed,' Stefan said. 'If Cowper defaults, you must return here, Hassan, and we shall return this evening if we have no luck at Cherbourg. If Anne has been taken to England I shall go after her, but we must search the area thoroughly first. Tell the men that no hut is to be left unsearched nor any bush or ditch lest her body has been discarded. I need to know whether she is alive or dead.' His eyes were bleak, as cold as the North Sea.

'Your men will search your own estate,' Comte De Vere said, a flicker of dislike in his eyes, for things had not gone quite as he'd hoped, 'and mine shall make a search of the surrounding area. They must have taken

Anne somewhere and they will have been seen. We shall find them between us.'

'Has she stirred yet?' Fritz entered the wooden hut where they had laid the woman on a pile of sacking. He looked down at her face, frowning as he saw how still and pale she was. 'Damn you, Marc! You have killed her. She is no use to us dead.' He bent down, placing a hand to Anne's forehead. 'She is not cold yet, but I fear she will die.' He rounded on Marc in a fury. 'You fool! Lord de Montfort would have paid a fortune in gold for her return, but if she dies he will hunt us down. He can be a ruthless devil and will have no mercy for the men who took his woman.'

'I didn't hit her that hard,' Marc replied in a surly tone. 'It was your idea to snatch her, not mine, and I'm not staying around to be killed by that devil.'

'Where do you think you are going?' Fritz grabbed his arm as he made to leave the hut. 'We're in this together! I want you to take the message to de Montfort. Tell him we have the girl and we'll return her for five thousand gold pieces.'

Marc shook off his hand angrily. 'You go and deliver the message yourself,' he said. 'I'll stay here and guard her.'

'You'll cut and run the minute I leave,' Fritz muttered, frustrated as he saw his dreams of riches melting into the mist. 'The others have run off with their tails between their legs. We have to stick together or we're dead.'

'You're dead,' Marc muttered in a surly tone. 'You should have left it to Cowper. You cheated on him; if de Montfort doesn't kill you, Cowper will! You're a fool and I'm getting out of here now.'

'Damn you!' Fritz said and threw a punch at him. Marc drew a knife from beneath his jerkin and thrust it into Fritz's side. 'Fool…we could have been rich.' Fritz staggered and then fell to his knees, his eyes wide with horror. 'You've killed me…'

Marc withdrew the knife and walked towards the door. As Fritz fell flat on his face, Marc kicked at his body, then left without a backwards glance. If he returned to his master with the story of what had happened here, Cowper might reward him for the information. He would gain something from this if he could.

'That English pig left for his ship at first light this morning.' The innkeeper spat on the floor of the taproom, which was covered in rushes and none too clean. The stink of stale ale and body odour permeated the air, bringing a look of distaste to the men's faces.

'Did they have a young woman with them?' Stefan asked. 'Did you hear them speak of a woman at all?'

'The wenches would have naught to do with them, for they said they stank, dirty pigs,' the innkeeper growled.

'I meant a young gentlewoman, perhaps injured or in an unconscious state—a girl who did not look as if she belonged with them?'

The innkeeper shook his head. 'A man arrived late last night. Whatever he said made the lord angry and there was some shouting. They mentioned a man named de Montfort…' His eyes narrowed as he looked at Stefan. 'It was of you they spoke.'

'Did you hear what was said?'

'They said that once you knew you would seek vengeance.'

'My God!' Stefan looked at Rob, his expression bleak. 'Cowper must have ordered them to take her, but something went wrong—unless they took her straight to the ship!'

'I'll send two of my men to make enquiries. We'll discover the name of his ship and whether anything was seen of a woman,' Rob said and went outside to dispatch the men.

'I thank you for your help,' Stefan said and took a pouch of gold from his jerkin. He gave the innkeeper five gold pieces. 'Is there anything more you can tell me?'

'The man who brought the news was called Marc. He mentioned someone called Fritz. He said that Fritz had betrayed his master and had been dealt with.'

'Which means he is dead,' Stefan said grimly. 'Thank you. If you see any of these men again, please send word to the Chateau de Montifiori and you shall be rewarded.'

The landlord bit one of the gold coins and grinned. 'I'll do that, my lord,' he promised.

Stefan went outside. Three of Lord Melford's men had already set off towards the harbour to make inquiries. He turned as Stefan came up to him.

'One of us should return to England and see what can be discovered there.'

'I have a score to settle with Cowper,' Stefan said grimly. 'I know what a coward he is. He will run to his manor and hide there, thinking himself safer inside its walls, but he forgets that it was once my home. He shall answer to me, I promise you that—but first we must return to my home and discover if anything has been heard of Anne. Hassan will know that Cowper has not turned up and he will have joined the search for her.'

'What happened to the poor devil?' Rob asked, remembering the horrendous disfigurement of Hassan's face.

'He was sold into slavery as a young lad and was unfortunate enough to be bought by Sir Hugh Grantham when he was travelling in the east. Sir Hugh had his slave master beat him many times for disobedience. However, they could not break his spirit and he tried to run away. For that sin he was tortured and sold. Fortunately, I saw him being beaten by the slave master in a market place. I bought him and set him free.'

Rob's gaze narrowed as he looked at him, for he remembered hearing recently of Sir Hugh's murder, and that of a young woman. However, he said nothing, because for the moment only Anne's safety mattered. He would join forces with the devil if by that means he could find his daughter safe and well!

'We must go back and help them,' Rob said. 'If my men bring news of her, I shall follow and report her abduction to the King. Cowper will give her up to Henry or end in the Tower—and if he has killed her, his life is forfeit.'

The two men nodded, in perfect agreement. 'If I discover that she is dead, I shall kill him myself,' Stefan said. 'But if she lives, we shall seek justice from the King.'

The two men mounted their horses and set off for Stefan's home, but it was a sombre journey, for neither held much hope of Anne being found alive after the news of Cowper's hurried return to England.

* * *

Anne's eyes flickered open. She was immediately aware that her head ached and she moaned softly, looking about her as she tried to discover what had happened to her. Where was she? Not in her own bed at Melford… Melford… Her name was Anne Melford and… Suddenly, her head was filled with such frightening pictures that she screamed.

Where was she? What had happened to her? Anne's thoughts were whirling round and round like the wheels of a capsized hay cart, so many confusing thoughts in her head that she was terrified. Her hand moved out, discovering that she was lying on a dirt floor with nothing but a pile of sacking under her. To one side of her there was a crack in the wall and moonlight filtered through it. She struggled to her feet, dazed and confused. She was Anne Melford…she knew that her name was important, but at this moment she could not think why she needed to know that fact.

As she stood for a moment, her head going round and round and the sickness rushing up to her throat, she could not make sense of the whirling pictures in her head: a huge wave rushing at a ship, darkness, a man's face…and then more darkness. She stumbled towards the crack of light, her hands exploring the rough texture of wood. Was she in some kind of a hut? Following her instinct without knowing what she was searching for, Anne moved round the walls, feeling each piece, unable to see much because there was hardly any light, and finally finding metal. Her fingers ran over its smooth curves as she found it was a latch. She lifted the latch, which gave easily, opened the door and felt the rush of cool air on her face.

Stepping outside, she discovered the moon was

high, though sheltered behind a cloud, making the night darker than it might have been, but as her eyes accustomed themselves to the light she could see a little. She was in a clearing. The hut must belong to a woodcutter, perhaps the charcoal burner. Beyond the clearing were dense woods on all sides, dark, eerie and frightening. Which way should she go? Her mind was dazed, struggling to cope with all the pictures that kept crowding in on her. There was a place she wanted to be, and a man…but she could not make her thoughts keep still long enough to remember the things she needed to know. They went round and round so fast that she felt dizzy. At the back of her mind she heard a voice telling her that there was marshy land somewhere in the wood, and she resisted the urge to run blindly. She must follow a trail because it would lead somewhere rather than wander off and get lost.

Something told her that people would be looking for her, but for the moment she felt too ill to think who those people were or why they would be searching for her. As she hesitated, the moon came up overhead and she saw what was clearly a well-used trail ahead of her. It looked as if a cart had come that way recently, for the undergrowth was flattened. She began to walk and then to run as she heard an owl hooting deep in the wood, her gown catching on a bush. She tore it away, leaving a scrap of fine material clinging to its thorns. Her mind was still confused, but her instincts told her that if she followed the trail she would find a man who was important to her and safety.

'Any news?' Hassan said as Stefan entered the hall, closely followed by Rob and a few of the men. 'Cowper was not at the meeting. I am certain he never intended to come. He sent word that he would be there in order to cover his tracks.'

'She has not been found, then?' Rob asked, a nerve flicking at his right temple as Hassan shook his head. 'Cowper has run back to England. I had hoped that Anne might have been found. If she is not found by morning, I think one of us should follow him and see if any news can be heard of her in England, though the landlord at the inn in Cherbourg had heard nothing of her.'

'Cowper is afraid of what I will do to him,' Stefan snarled. 'And he is right to be afraid after what he has done. Tell me, where have you searched so far? If Cowper did not have her, she could be somewhere in the woods. I want the search to continue throughout the night.' It was a desperate hope because his instincts told him that something bad had happened to Anne—what else would have sent Cowper scurrying for home? His mind conjured up pictures of rape and murder and a red mist formed before his eyes. He had to dig his nails into the palms of his hands to stop the rage boiling over. If Cowper had not run, he would have torn him limb from limb!

'I have detailed the woods to be searched bit by bit,' Hassan told him. 'There were some signs of men and horses in the woods near the chateau, but they split up and went different ways. I am not certain why they should do that.'

'I think they most likely fell out amongst themselves,' Stefan said, but he did not voice the worst of his thoughts. The man called Marc had carried the news to Cowper that had set him running for cover—and if Cowper was afraid for his life, that must mean that

Anne was dead. He had a sick burning at the pit of his stomach, because he ought to have protected her from the evil men who sought to revenge themselves on him. He had not dreamed that someone would breach their security and snatch her and he was torn by grief and regret. If anything had happened to her, he would never cease to blame himself!

'If Anne is not found by morning, I shall take some of the men and find a ship bound for England,' he said, because he knew he could not stand the agony of seeing her lifeless body brought back to the chateau. 'You will stay here and continue the search, Hassan. Lord Melford should stay in case Anne is found. If she is hurt, she will need her father.' Rob nodded his head in agreement. 'Besides, Cowper did this because of me. It is for me to find and punish him for what he has done.'

'You need me to watch your back,' Hassan said, his dark eyes anxious. 'Lord Melford will do all that is necessary here.'

'No, you must stay,' Stefan said. 'If you love me, do as I ask, Hassan. Anne means more to me than my life. Ali made her well once. She may need his skills again. Stay here and see that everything is done as it ought to be, but I pray that we shall find her this night...' He turned as he heard the sound of excited voices, a look of expectation and hope in his eyes. 'There is news...' One of his men came rushing into the Hall, clearly bringing news of import, and Stefan started towards him. 'Have you found her?'

'No, my lord, but we found a man stabbed and near to death in the woodcutter's hut. We think he may have been one of them—'

'What makes you think it?' Rob asked bluntly. 'Did he say anything?'

'He has not spoken, sir. But there was a scrap of cloth caught on a bush nearby and it matches a piece we found near where the lady Anne was snatched. We think that she must have run away into the woods after the man was wounded…or was carried that way.'

'Have you set men to searching the trail?' Stefan asked fiercely. 'What of the man you found—have you brought him here?'

'Ali told us to take him to the men's quarters. He is with him now, but he said it might be too late to save him for he has lost much blood.'

'I shall speak with Ali,' Rob said and looked at Hassan. 'Send more men to look in the area of the wood-cutter's hut. If she was there, she may be nearby. One of those trails leads to the village. Send some of the men there—though De Vere may have gone that way, unless he has given up and gone home.'

'He would not have done that,' the Comte St Orleans said. 'I will ride there and discover if he has heard any-thing. Stay here, Melford. If I have news, I shall send word or come myself.'

'I shall join in the search,' Rob said. 'I cannot rest until my daughter is found.'

Anne saw a light moving ahead of her. She knew that someone was carrying a lantern and she instinc-tively turned towards it. Her head was aching again and her mind was still confused, though she had begun to remember. She had been washed overboard the ship carrying her and Harry to France, and then someone had rescued her… She could see his face in her mind and she knew she wanted to reach him, to be with him, because she loved him.

'Stefan…' His name was on her lips. She remembered that he had rescued her, cared for her, but she felt so ill that she could not think clearly. Her head was going round and round. She seemed to have been stumbling through the woods for hours and hours, but she was nowhere near finding her way through them, even though she could see that the trail had been used recently, for the undergrowth was flattened by horses and wheels. 'Where are you? Please help me…'

The light was just ahead of her now, and the trees were thinning. Anne could hear voices. She tried to call out, but no sound came. Her throat was too dry and her mind too confused to form the words she wanted to say. All she could do was to stumble on towards the light, but she felt so ill. She was going to faint. As she did so a faint cry issued from her lips and then she fell, clutching at a bush as she did so, causing it to crack and the leaves to rustle.

'What was that?' Comte De Vere listened, but the cry was not repeated. He called to one of his men who was carrying a lantern. 'Over here—to the right, Etienne. I am sure I heard something. Bring more lights. It may have been a fox, but it sounded like a woman's cry.'

Several men hastened to do as he bid them. They had been searching all day, save for half an hour when food and ale had been distributed. Most of them were beginning to think fondly of their beds, but their lord would not give up the search. It had seemed hopeless, but as they began to search the trail they had already been over earlier, one of them saw something lying on the ground and gave a shout that brought the others running.

'Here! I think I've found her. Yes! It is a woman! God be praised. It must be her.'

Comte De Vere dismounted quickly and went to join the others crowding about the woman on the ground. He knelt down, feeling for a pulse, then looked up, the light of triumph in his eyes.

'It is her. There will be a gold coin for each of you when we return. Lift her into the cart, Jean—help him, Carl and Philip. We are closer to my home than de Montifiori so we'll take her there. One of you must ride ahead of us and have a room prepared. We shall need a physician—and de Montfort must be told. And Melford too. We do not yet know if she is his daughter, but he will want to see her as soon as she is well enough to receive visitors.'

Comte De Vere smiled inwardly as he watched the men lift Anne into the cart they had commandeered from a neighbouring farmer. It was fortune that had led him to find her—or perhaps the will of God. De Vere was a devout Catholic, and he believed in fate. It was one of the reasons he had decided to take Anne to his home rather than back to de Montifiori. If she was Lord Melford's daughter, it might be that once she recovered her memory she might not wish to keep her promise to wed Stefan de Montfort. At his home she would be given the freedom to recover in peace and decide her own future without any pressure being brought to bear.

Besides, his plan might have failed to cause a breach between Lord Melford and de Montfort, but he could still hold the whip hand if he had Anne. She was beautiful and he needed a wife. It would give him pleasure to snatch her from under de Montfort's nose. First the woman, and then his house and lands...

* * *

Stefan looked at the man Ali had been tending. Half of him wanted to finish off what had been done to the devil who had taken Anne, but the part that still retained a modicum of compassion held back his anger. He could not be certain what part this rogue had played in the abduction.

'Will he live?' he asked harshly.

'He may if Allah wills it,' Ali replied. 'He has bled a great deal, but had vital organs been damaged he would not have lived this long. With careful nursing he should live—is it your wish that I continue to tend him?'

'Do what you can for him,' Stefan replied. 'It may be that he can tell us what happened to Anne—and why.'

'You want me to save his life so that you can hang him?'

'Perhaps,' Stefan growled. 'If he harmed her, he does not deserve to live. But I shall give him a fair trial—do you ask more of me?' He glared at his friend. If this man had harmed Anne, he deserved to die and he would!

'I know she means a great deal to you,' Ali replied. 'As long as I have your word that he will have a fair trial, I shall do my best to save him.'

'Did he have anything with him?'

'Just his clothes and a pouch. I have not looked inside.'

Stefan glanced at the man's clothes and the leather pouch. He made a move towards it and then stopped as he heard heavy footsteps. Going out into the hallway, he saw one of his men coming at a run towards him.

'You have news? She has been found?'

'She has been found, my lord. At the far side of the

wood close to Comte De Vere's land. He sent word that he is taking her there.'

'Why not here?' Stefan demanded and then shook his head. The soldier could not answer for the Comte. 'Thank you—has Lord Melford been told?'

'He was about to leave with a fresh search party when the news came, my lord. He asked that someone take him there immediately—and he rode out even as I came to find you.'

'She is alive?' Stefan breathed more easily as the man nodded. 'Melford wishes to know if she is his daughter. In his place, I should do the same.'

'He did not wait for you, my lord,' Ali said. He had come to the door and heard what the soldier had to say. 'If she is Anne Melford, he is her guardian, and will have the charge of her welfare. You cannot deny him in law. Do you wish me to come to Comte De Vere's house with you?'

'You have work here at the moment,' Stefan said. 'I shall speak to De Vere and Melford. If you are needed, I shall offer your services, but we do not know yet—' He stopped, his expression harsh. 'I shall ride to De Vere's home and see how she is. If they need you, I shall send word—but until then stay with your patient. We may need him alive, because I want the truth of what happened here.'

Chapter Six

'May I see the girl?' Rob asked as he was shown into the Comte's presence. His expression was one of extreme concern. 'Is she well? What has happened to her? How did you find her?'

'It was sheer chance that we were the ones who found her,' the Comte said. 'We were at the edge of the woods, our search almost done for the day. Indeed, we had already searched that part of the woods, but I was reluctant to give up and we had begun to search the common ground at the edge of the woods when I heard something. The sound was faint, but I thought it a woman's cry and I was right. She must have been wandering the trails for a while and she fainted when she became exhausted…'

'Is she much hurt?' Rob asked anxiously.

'When my physician looked at her he found blood in her hair. He says that she must have been struck on the head. The blow was not a heavy one, for the wound is not deep. However, she may have been unconscious for a while. I do not know how she escaped from her captors, but I think she must have given them the slip somehow and then become lost in the woods.'

'A badly wounded man was found in a woodcutter's hut,' Rob told him. 'He was brought to de Montifiori more dead than alive, but if he recovers we may discover the truth. May I see her…please? Is she awake?'

'Not at the moment,' the Comte said. 'She recovered her senses when my physician examined her, but nothing she said made sense—except that she asked for de Montfort, apparently.'

'I must see her to make sure it is Anne,' Rob said. 'If she is not…then I must go on with my search, but if it is Anne—' He stopped abruptly, too emotional to continue.

'Yes, I understand,' De Vere said. 'I shall take you up. She has been given something to help her to sleep. My physician said it was what she needed to rest her mind. I thought it best to abide by what he said—but I shall take you to her room and you may see her for yourself.'

Rob was on thorns as he followed the Comte up a wide staircase. The house was in a much grander style than de Montfort's and he knew that his host was a wealthy man. He had not taken much notice the previous evening, but now he was more aware of the opulence of the furnishings. However, his mind was busy with thoughts of his daughter. If it was Anne, he would have good news to carry home to his wife and family, though he could not be sure that Anne would wish to accompany him. If she had called for de Montfort, there must be some feeling between them. He had witnessed Stefan de Montfort's anger at her loss and it echoed his own, but he was not certain of the cause. If Anne loved de Montfort and he loved her, there could be no real objection to a marriage between them—if both wished for it to continue.

If Anne wished to come home once he told her who she was, the circumstances would be altered. The choice must be hers, which was why he had wanted to speak to her first. To Rob it seemed that Lord de Montfort was a harsh man, though that was not cause to forbid the marriage by itself. Rob would have preferred to know more about him before he sanctioned the marriage, but he knew he could not deny Anne if she loved him— but would she once she knew she had a choice? If she was his daughter… The thought tailed away because he could not yet be certain.

Pausing outside the room, Rob felt the tension inside himself. He was building so much on the chance that it had been his daughter that Stefan de Montfort had plucked from the sea. He followed the Comte into the dimly lit room. A serving woman had been bending over the bed. She glanced at her master and curtsied.

'She seems to have a fever, sir,' she said. 'She cries and tosses restlessly. Perhaps the physician should be called?'

Rob moved towards the bed. His heart caught and he felt a rush of emotion as the sob left his lips. 'Thank God!' he cried, tears stinging his eyes. 'She lives…Anne is alive…' He turned to the Comte, his face working with the strength of his emotion. 'Yes, she is my daughter. I have thought it might be so for something similar happened to my wife once when she suffered a trauma. For a time she lost her memory, though eventually it was restored to her.'

'God be praised!' Comte De Vere came towards him and they shook hands. 'Should I send for the physician, sir? She is your daughter and I bow to your judgement.'

'I think I shall send to de Montifiori,' Rob said. 'The physician there helped her before and he may have some idea of her condition now—if that does not offend you?'

'I bow to your judgement,' De Vere repeated, though he might have wished otherwise. He had hoped that his own physician might tend her so that she would have something to thank him for rather than de Montfort's man, but he was too much the diplomat to go against her father. He would be no use to his Spanish masters if his true feelings were known, and much of his wealth had come from them. 'I shall go downstairs now and arrange it. Please stay with her, Melford. If she wakes, she may know you…'

'I should like to sit with her for a while,' Rob said. 'If de Montfort comes, tell him the glad news. My daughter is found and I shall do everything to make her happy.'

'Yes, of course,' De Vere said. He left Rob standing by the bed and went out. As he descended to the Great Hall he was in time to see that Stefan de Montfort had just arrived. He smiled, at his most charming, most convincing. 'Ah, the very man…'

'How is she?' Stefan asked, his voice harsh with anguish. 'Will she live? What happened to her?'

'She received a blow to the back of the head, but she must have escaped from her captors somehow and wandered into the wood. She was unconscious when we found her, though she later came to herself and cried out in pain. My physician gave her something to help her rest,' the Comte said, though he did not mention the fact that Anne had called for de Montfort. 'Her father is with her now and he asked me to tell you that she is indeed his lost daughter. He is determined to do all that is necessary for her happiness. He has asked if your physician will come to her—she may have a fever.'

'I should like to see her,' Stefan said. 'She should be at de Montifiori where she can be properly cared for.'

'Your physician may stay here,' De Vere told him smoothly. 'I think it would be unwise to move her for the moment. Besides, her father is her guardian now. You must speak to Melford if you wish to take her with you. I am not certain he would agree.'

Stefan hesitated. He sensed that Comte De Vere was against it, and he knew that Anne's father would probably prefer to stay here. She was Melford's daughter and he had no right to force the issue, even though she would have been his wife in a few days. Had that happened, he would have fought his way to her room and taken her by force if necessary, but she was not his wife. He was not sure that she would wish to be once she knew who she was and where she belonged.

He had asked Anne to marry him because she could not continue to live at his home without the protection of his name, but a part of him had always known that he was not worthy of her—he could never be worthy of a lovely innocent woman like Anne Melford.

'You will tell Melford that I came to inquire how she was?'

'Yes, of course. Certainly—and you will ask Ali to visit her as soon as is possible?'

'He will come at once,' Stefan said. 'Please tell Lord Melford that I go to England to finish the business we spoke of. Anne is safe in his care and I shall visit her at her home when…I can…'

'I shall give Lord Melford your message,' De Vere promised. 'Is there a message for the lady Anne?'

'None for the moment, except that I shall visit her when I am able.'

De Vere inclined his head. 'It shall be exactly as you ask,' he said. 'You go to find and punish the man who did this, I presume?' He would send word to Cowper, warning him that de Montfort was on his way. Cowper was a fool, but still useful as a spy at the English court, and much of what he disclosed when in his cups had found its way to Spain. De Vere's Spanish masters were not happy with the way Prince Arthur's wife had been treated since his death. Katherine of Aragon was a Spanish princess, and some thought both she and her dowry should be returned to Spain—unless Prince Henry were to wed her.

'Cowper does not deserve to live,' Stefan said, a nerve flicking in his cheek. 'If he wished to be revenged on me, he should have come to me like a man in single combat. To kidnap an innocent girl and—' He broke off as the bile rose in his throat. 'I shall not rest until justice is served!'

'Then I wish you well,' Comte De Vere said, his manner seemingly open and concerned. 'If Lord Cowper was behind this dastardly attempt to steal the lady Anne, I should like to see him punished.'

'He knew that I would kill him once I had discovered what he had done,' Stefan said. 'I do not know what went wrong with their plans. Perhaps they thought she was dead and abandoned her. We may discover the truth if the man we have at the chateau recovers consciousness.'

'We must hope that he does,' De Vere said, though privately he thought it better if the man died without speaking. 'If there is anything I may do for you?'

'Nothing—except take good care of her,' Stefan said. 'She will be safer here. At least you have no enemies!'

'You cannot blame yourself for what happened, de Montfort,' the Comte said, though there was a gleam of satisfaction in his eyes.

Stefan inclined his head, but did not answer. He turned and left the room without another word, leaving De Vere to stare after him. He smiled as he thought of the young woman lying upstairs. Anne Melford had been in a difficult position at de Montifiori. She might have agreed to a marriage because she thought she had no other option. If Anne loved de Montfort there would be no changing her and she would wait for him to visit her at her father's home, and if she did not…she would be grateful to De Vere.

De Vere was pleased as he contemplated a future with the lovely young woman who had attracted his attention from the first. He would find it amusing to take her from his neighbour, and to flaunt her as his wife under de Montfort's nose. It would give him almost as much pleasure as he would have when the Chateau de Montifiori finally belonged to him.

'Do you want me to come with you?' Hassan asked as Stefan prepared for his journey to England. 'I know you wished me to stay here to protect Anne, but she is with De Vere and her father now. I can do nothing.'

'Yet still I would ask you to stay here,' Stefan told him. 'If Ali is with her, he cannot watch over the injured man, and you know something of healing yourself. I would have the truth of what happened that night and what part Cowper played.'

'I shall obey you, of course,' Hassan said. 'But as soon as I have news I shall follow. I do not like the idea of your being in England without me to cover your back.' He smiled as Stefan raised his brows. 'I know that you have others to watch out for you, but we have been as brothers these many years.'

'Yes, we have,' Stefan said. He was tempted to change his mind and yet something told him that Hassan should remain here for a while. 'I trust no one as I trust you, Hassan. I feel you are needed here for the moment, though I cannot say why.'

'Your instincts have always served you well,' Hassan said. 'I shall do as you ask, but if I feel I am needed by your side or if I have news I shall come.'

'Yes, that is fair,' Stefan said. 'You are closer to me than the brother I lost, Hassan. Your instincts are good; if they tell you to come, then no doubt I shall be in need of your help.'

The two men embraced briefly. Stefan nodded his head, turned away and went down to the Great Hall. He knew that Ali was already on his way to De Vere's house and he prayed that Anne would soon be well again. However, he had done his best to thrust all thought of her from his mind. He would not forget her, but he would give her a chance to forget him, because she deserved better. Besides, he had vowed to seek revenge on Cowper for the ill he had done, both to Anne and others. It would not be easy, for Cowper knew that his life was forfeit. He would do all he could to have Stefan murdered before he was killed himself.

'Stefan…' Anne muttered, her eyelids fluttering. 'Stefan…please help me…'

'Rest now, my little one,' a voice said and a cool hand touched her forehead. 'She feels cooler—has the fever gone?'

'It is on the wane,' another voice said close by. 'I think she is nearly over it, my lord. The mixture I made will help her grow stronger once she is herself again. Do you wish me to stay until she is completely recovered?'

'You have another patient, I believe?'

'Yes, but he is being cared for,' Ali said. 'However, I believe that your daughter is almost better. I know you have been concerned for her, but believe me, she was not as ill this time as before. We nearly lost her then, but she is in no danger now. I cannot tell whether she will be herself again, because a blow to the head sometimes causes problems, but in every other way she should soon be well.'

'What kind of problems?' Rob asked, looking at his daughter anxiously. She seemed to have settled again, and there was no sweat on her brow.

'As you know, she could not remember her name,' Ali said. 'It may be the same case. I cannot promise you that she will be as you remember her. A blow to the head is not predictable, though I do not think it was hard enough to have damaged her brain.'

'If she lives, her mother will make her well again,' Rob said. 'I shall take her home and with love and care she will come back to us.'

'Then I shall leave you,' Ali told him with a smile.

'Anne is in good hands. I know she has a good home, for it was evident in all that she was and did. She is as wise as she is beautiful and we shall miss her at the chateau. As I have told you, Lord de Montfort has gone to England. I have a feeling that I am needed at the chateau, though I cannot tell you why.'

'Then you should go,' Rob said. 'I cannot thank you enough for saving my daughter's life—if not this time, then last time. If ever I can be of help, you have only to ask.'

'All I ask is that you should be fair to Anne—and to Stefan de Montfort. I know that some think ill of him, but he is a good man in his heart, and I believe their destiny lies together.'

'We shall see what Anne wants,' Rob said. 'But I give you my word that she shall choose whether she wants to marry de Montfort or another.'

'Then I know what she will do,' Ali said and smiled. 'She may not know it yet, but they are bound together— it is written that when you save a life, that life is yours and you must care for that person all your life.'

Rob frowned as the Arab physician bowed his head and left the chamber. He did not deny that something was owed both to him and to Stefan de Montfort, who had pulled her from the water. Anne undoubtedly owed her life to them, but it did not mean that she was destined to be de Montfort's wife. If she chose to change her mind, he would see that she was free to return home and live as she pleased amongst her family.

Hassan bent over the sick man, bathing his forehead. He was muttering feverishly, tossing on the sweat-soaked pillows, his hands working on the covers.

'Hit her too hard,' Fritz muttered. 'You fool…if she's dead he will kill us…'

'You do not know how truly you speak,' Hassan said. He poured some of the mixture Ali had left into a cup, adding water and a little honey to sweeten the bitter taste. Putting an arm beneath his shoulders, he lifted his patient and held the cup to his mouth, letting some of the liquid slide down his throat. 'Swallow! It will do you good, though I am not sure it will prolong your life once Stefan knows it was you.'

Fritz opened his eyes and stared at him. 'He'll pay a fortune in gold if I tell him what I know,' he said clearly. 'Cheated…he was cheated and I have the proof…'

Hassan's eyes narrowed as he lowered the man to the pillows. 'What do you know of this?' he demanded. 'Cowper cheated Stefan, but there was no proof.'

'Signature forged…' Fritz muttered. 'Never meant to hurt the woman…stupid fool…Marc killed her…'

'If you can prove that Cowper stole Stefan's birthright, he might spare you. Tell me where to find the proof.'

Fritz's eyes had closed. He was moaning again, the moment of lucidity passed. Hassan considered pouring water over him, but dismissed it as unlikely to bring him round. If he were telling the truth, he was worth saving, because his testimony could be exactly what Stefan needed to recover his birthright.

Hassan's eyes fell on the pile of clothes lying nearby. He crossed the room in quick strides and made a search. Finding the leather pouch attached to the man's belt, he opened it and found some papers folded and folded again. Opening them, he saw the signature scrawled over and over again, understanding at once what it showed.

Someone had copied Lord William de Montfort's hand until they had a fair copy—had it then been used to sign away everything the lord owned? Everything that Stefan ought to have had by right.

In itself it was not clear proof of anything except that someone had tried to forge a signature, but it did not prove Lord Cowper was guilty. Only the man lying there in that bed might be able to do that with a sworn testimony.

Hassan tucked the papers away inside his jerkin. The wounded man was lying quietly now. Ali's mixture would help him to sleep as it cooled the fever. Hassan returned the pouch to the pile of clothes. He would keep the papers and give them to Stefan, though they were only proof that his suspicions had been correct. Someone had forged those papers, but it would still have to be proved. However, if Fritz recovered, he might be persuaded to sign a sworn statement. He would do so if he valued his life. Once he had that too, Hassan could go to England, because he had a premonition that before too long had passed Stefan would need him.

Hassan left the room. As he walked across the court-yard to the main house, he saw Ali dismount from a horse and go into the house. He hurried to catch up with him. The physician would want news of his patient, and Hassan was anxious to discover if the lady Anne had recovered her senses.

Anne's eyes fluttered and opened. She moaned because the light hurt her eyes. She put her arm across her eyes because the sunlight was full on her face. Someone went to the window and drew the curtains, shading the room.

'Does that feel better?'

Anne was comforted by the familiar voice. 'Thank you,' she said. She opened her eyes again and saw the man looking down at her. He smiled and she made a little whimpering sound. 'I am so thirsty, Father. Is Mother here? Tell her I have such a headache…'

'Anne dearest,' her father's voice said, and his voice shook. He sat down on the edge of the bed and reached for her hand, much affected by her recovery. 'We did not know what to expect when you woke. You know me? You know who I am?'

'Yes, of course,' she said and wrinkled her brow, because she hurt too much to think about the things that hovered at the back of her mind. 'Have I been ill?'

'Yes, my dearest daughter, you have been ill,' Rob said, his throat caught with emotion. 'Your mother is not here, Anne, but as soon as you are well enough to travel I shall take you home to her—if you would like that?'

'Yes, please,' Anne said and sighed. 'I am so thirsty…'

'I shall ask the servant to bring you a drink, something that will ease your head,' Rob said. He bent down to kiss her forehead. 'Is there anything you want to tell me or ask me?'

Anne shook her head. She knew there was someone she wanted to see, but just for the moment she was too tired to think who it was.

It was a while before Anne woke again, and this time there was an elderly woman bending over her. She smiled and offered her a cup, slipping an arm about her shoulders to help her drink.

'This is a tisane I made for you, mistress,' she said. 'Your father said your head pained you. This will ease the pain for you. Drink it all and you will soon feel better.'

Anne tasted the honey and swallowed eagerly. The honey eased her throat as she finished the drink, and she could feel drowsiness washing over her.

'Is Stefan here?' she asked. 'I do want to see him… please tell him I love him…'

'Yes, mistress, you rest now and he will come,' the woman said and smiled at her. It was not her place to answer. Besides, the girl was drifting off to sleep again. Sleep was what she needed now. The fever had gone and now she was just tired.

Anne opened her eyes as someone drew the curtains back. She saw a servant, a young girl. The girl turned and looked at her, smiling as she saw she was awake.

'Madame Bacall told us you were better,' she said and came towards the bed. 'I have brought you some breakfast, mademoiselle. And then I shall bring water and help you to wash, if you wish.'

'Yes, please,' Anne said. She felt sticky and uncomfortable, as if she had been sweating a lot. She eased herself up against the pillows, looking round the room in a puzzled way. 'Can you tell me where I am, please? This is not my room at the Chateau de Montifiori.'

'You are at the house of the Comte De Vere.'

'Why am I here?' Anne asked. 'I do not remember. I was ill. I thought my father was here…' She frowned as her thoughts cleared. 'I am Anne Melford and my father was here.'

'Yes, Mistress Melford. Lord Melford has sat with

you day and night since they brought you here. He went out riding this morning only because he knew you were better. I believe there was someone he wished to see.'

'But why am I here? I was at the chateau and then...' Anne's eyes widened. 'Someone hit me when I was going to the pool... What happened? Where is Stefan? Does he know I am here?' She threw off the bedcovers and swung her legs over the side of the bed, but as her feet touched the floor her head swam and she sat back on the bed hurriedly. 'Oh, my head...I feel dizzy...'

'You should not try to get up too soon,' the girl said. 'Madame Bacall said you were better, but would need to rest for another day or so.'

'I want to speak to my father as soon as he returns to the house,' Anne told her. 'Where is Lord de Montfort? I must see him.'

'I believe Lord de Montfort came to the house once, but he went away,' the girl said. 'I shall leave your tray, mistress—and I will tell Madame Bacall that you wish to see her.'

The girl hurried away. Mistress Melford seemed most upset and she did not wish to be the one to tell her that people were saying that Lord de Montfort had gone to England. It was bound to distress her further since she had been promised to marry him. Jeanne had heard rumours that the banns had been called in church, but since then the marriage had been cancelled. If Lord de Montfort cared for his promised bride, he would surely not have left her while she lay ill.

Was that not always the way of men? They took what they wanted from a woman and then left her while they went off about their business.

* * *

Anne ate a little of the fresh bread and honey that had been brought to her, and she drank a mouthful of the sweet wine, but she pushed it away impatiently as the older woman entered her chamber.

'I wish to see Lord de Montfort,' she said. 'Is he here?'

'No, Mistress Melford. He is not here. Your father went out riding, but he will be back very soon. I shall ask him to come up to you.'

'Will you have a message sent to Lord de Montfort, please? Does he know I am better? I know he thinks it is not proper to visit me in my bedchamber, but I need to see him…I must see him…'

Madame Bacall hesitated, then, 'Lord de Montfort is not at home, mistress. You must not distress yourself. The Chevalier Renard and his sister have visited and send their good wishes, and my master has had fresh flowers picked for your room every day. Your father has sat with you for hours…'

'But we are to be married,' Anne said and her throat caught with tears. 'I want to see him. Please send word that I want to see him…'

'I will speak to your father,' Madame Bacall said. 'If you have finished your breakfast, I shall send Jeanne up with some water. She will help you wash. Then your father will come up and talk to you.'

Anne lay back against the pillows, tears trickling down her cheeks. Where was Stefan? Surely he would come to her soon? He had asked her to be his wife. He must know that she had been ill—that she needed him.

Closing her eyes, she rested until Jeanne came to help

her wash. The perfumed water made her feel better and fresher, and the housekeeper's tisane had made her headache less severe. She was resting with her eyes closed when the door opened.

'Anne…' She heard her father's voice and opened her eyes, smiling at him as he came towards her anxiously. 'They told me you were awake and much better. Is that so, my dearest?'

'Yes, I am better, Father,' Anne said. 'Tell me, how did you know where to find me? I could not remember my name—but I saw Harry once in Cherbourg, though I could not recall his name or what he was to me. He had been asking questions and Lord de Montfort thought he might have been asking about me. He sent men out to try to trace Harry, but he had moved on.'

'Lord de Montfort told me how ill you were,' Rob said, choosing his words carefully. 'I was angry that you had been stolen from his house when you were under his protection, but it seems there was a breach in the thorn hedge that forms a part of the boundary. I believe the hedge is being cleared and a high wall built so that it cannot happen again.'

'It was not Stefan's fault,' Anne said. 'I went out to the pool in the early morning, because the night had been so hot. I did not think anyone would be there, but they must have been waiting, for they grabbed me from behind and someone hit me on the back of the head. When I came to my senses, I was in a hut. It was so dark that I could hardly see, but I felt my way round the walls and the door was not locked.'

'We think that you were left for dead,' Rob said, reaching for her hand. He held it in his own. 'Perhaps when you were unconscious for a long time they feared you would not recover—and we think they fell out over it. They may have been afraid of the consequences if you should be badly hurt.'

'So they abandoned me to die,' Anne said and shuddered. 'What terrible men they must be—but does Lord de Montfort know I have been ill? The housekeeper said that he had gone to England, but surely he would not leave while I was ill?' She looked hurt and bewildered and her father stroked the back of her hand to comfort her. 'We were to be married soon...'

'The wedding has been cancelled,' Rob told her gently. 'Lord de Montfort left you because he knew I was here to care for and protect you. He believes that a man called Lord Cowper arranged your kidnap and he has gone to England to seek a reckoning with him. We are all very angry about what happened to you.'

'Oh...' Anne frowned. She seemed to remember Stefan telling her about his enemy. 'It was Lord Cowper who robbed Stefan of his birthright and ill treated his father.'

'That is what he claims,' Rob agreed. 'I know they are old enemies.' He wondered if he should tell Anne that Lord Cowper's cousin had been murdered some months previously, and that it was possible the culprit could have been Stefan de Montfort. However, there was no proof of that and he decided to say nothing for the moment, lest it was just an unfounded rumour.

Anne looked at him uncertainly. 'Do you not like Lord de Montfort, Father?'

'I hardly know him,' Rob admitted. 'It is what you feel that matters here, Anne. I know you agreed to wed him, but you did not know who you were and you were beholden to him. You may wish to change your mind now that your family is restored to you.'

'I...love him,' Anne said and frowned. 'He saved my life, Father, and I was happy at the chateau, but—' She broke off and plucked at the bedcovers with restless fingers.

'What troubles you, daughter?'

'I feel love for him,' Anne said, the words coming slowly and with difficulty. 'Yet I am not certain that he loves me. He may have asked me to marry him because he felt sympathy for my plight.'

'Surely he spoke of love?'

'Not in so many words,' Anne said. 'He spoke of desire...' Her cheeks heated—it was not a subject she would normally have discussed with her father. 'I think men often feel desire for a pretty woman. I was living in his house and he told me that people had begun to gossip about my position. It was for that reason that I pretended to be his cousin, but it did not stop the speculation. Stefan said that either I must go to a nunnery or... he would marry me...' She faltered, her eyes moist with the tears that hovered. 'I love him, but I should not wish to marry him unless I was sure he truly loved me.'

Rob hesitated. Stefan de Montfort had been demented with fear for her safety, which in his opinion was not the behaviour of a man who had offered marriage as a matter of honour. Yet he had relinquished Anne into her father's care without a struggle, and he had taken himself off to England in pursuit of his enemy. He had said that if Anne still wished for the marriage he would honour his promise, but he had not spoken of undying love.

'The choice shall be yours, Anne,' Rob told her. 'We

shall return to Melford as soon as you are well enough to travel. I have sent word to your mother that you are safe and she will be anxious to see you as soon as possible. Once you are at home, you will be able to think more clearly. If you wish to marry, I shall send word to Lord de Montfort and I am certain he will honour his promise. He is a gentleman and could not break his word to you.'

'No, Father,' Anne said swiftly. 'Please do not ask him to come. If he loves me, he will seek me out. I shall not hold him to his promise unless he truly wishes to wed me.'

'You were always proud, Anne,' Rob said and smiled oddly. 'I believe you get that from me, daughter. You have my pride and you have my temper. Sometimes pride is best forgotten. I almost lost my chance of happiness with your mother through pride.'

'I could not be happy in a marriage without love,' Anne told him. 'I would prefer to live at home with you and my mother.'

'You will think differently when you are truly well again,' Rob said with a smile. 'However, Lord de Montfort is not the only man who may wish to wed you, Anne. The Chevalier Renard has called twice to ask after you, and Comte De Vere has been very concerned for your well-being.'

'I hardly know either of them,' Anne said and sighed. Neither of the gentlemen concerned made her heart race the way Stefan did when he looked at her.

'I am not suggesting that you should marry either of them,' Rob told her. 'I am saying that there will be others. Give yourself time to think about the future and decide what you wish to do, my love. As soon as Harry returns, and I have hopes that will be soon, we shall have his wedding to celebrate. We shall have many guests and you may meet someone you like. Besides, I promised you a trip to the court, and, if you wish it, we shall go in a few months—but first you must get truly well.'

'You are very kind to me, Father,' Anne said. She thought that she had not properly appreciated her father's love for her in the past. 'It was good of you to come looking for me.'

'You are my daughter,' Rob said. 'I may not always show how dear you are to me, but when you were lost it almost broke our hearts. Only the hope that you might be found gave us the strength to carry on.'

Anne clung to his hand. She was glad of his love and support, but it did not prevent her heart aching. She knew that she would never love anyone else as she loved Stefan de Montfort, and if he did not come to find her it would break her heart.

Chapter Seven

'Who are you, and what do you want?' Stefan asked as the woman was shown in to the inn parlour. He was staying some five leagues from his father's estate, but she had found him. She had come asking for him that morning, but, looking at her, he did not know her. 'And who told you where to find me?'

'Edmund, your late father's steward. You sent him word that you were here, my lord. Many of us have heard it and long for the day you rid us of a cruel master.'

Stefan's gaze narrowed. Could he trust her? 'You are one of my father's tenants—but I do not know you.'

'My name does not matter, for you would not know me, my lord,' the woman said. 'I am someone who wishes you well, and I bring you a gift. I have here your father's ring with his seal and his chain of office that Lord Cowper stole from him.'

Stefan looked at the things she placed on the table before him. 'How did you come by these things?'

'I stole them that from that pig Cowper as he lay in

a drunken stupor,' the woman told him with a look of disgust. 'He forced himself on me when I was a child of fourteen and I have been his whore ever since—but now he grows careless and I stole these while he slept.'

'If he discovers the theft, he will punish you.'

'I mean to take my parents and flee,' the woman said. 'If I had money I would go far away where he would not find me.'

'So that is why you came to me,' Stefan said and nodded. 'Tell me some more about Cowper's habits and I shall give you the money you need. I thank you for these things, for they were my father's and it is good to have them.'

'They were stolen from your father as he lay dying, and should always have been yours, but Cowper stole much that was yours.'

'I know it, but I have no proof. Do you have proof?'

'No,' the woman said. 'I saw things, but it would be only my word against his.'

Without proof of his enemy's guilt, Stefan knew that his only chance was to challenge Lord Cowper to single combat. It was a lawful way of settling differences between the barons, and had superseded the time-honoured warring that had gone on between disputing noblemen. Before Henry Tudor came to the English throne, the barons had been unruly, fighting against one another, laying siege to an enemy's castle and taking what they wanted by force. King Henry had done his best to stamp the practice out, replacing the use of force to settle petty quarrels with his own law. However, Stefan had been refused an audience only a few months earlier and doubted he would fare any better now. Indeed, after the fight with Sir Hugh Grantham, which had resulted in his death, he had even less chance of being heard. If he attempted it, he might find himself being thrown in the Tower.

Stefan needed proof and he needed someone of influence to stand by him. Neither was easy to find, for he had few friends in England, and those that would speak for him were of the common folk and had no influence. He could, of course, enter the house that he had been born in secretly and murder Cowper in his bedchamber, but then he would have blood on his hands and be no better than his enemy.

If he wanted to go to his promised bride with his honour intact, he must challenge Cowper to meet him in combat. The fight must take place before witnesses and be seen to be fair. He would issue his challenge through the court, but he knew that Cowper was a coward and would avoid meeting him if he could. Cowper would have no scruples about sending assassins to do his dirty work for him. Stefan would need someone to stand with him, as his second, and the only man he wanted by his side was his friend.

Stefan did his best not to think of Anne, though she filled his dreams, causing him to toss restlessly on his bed. It was best not to sleep, for when conscious his iron will denied her, but when he slept she haunted him and he saw her lovely face, her eyes accusing him of deserting her.

Damn it! He must not allow himself to think of her. Anne's father and friends were caring for her. To wish that he had seen her before he left Normandy was useless, and to long for something that might never be made him weak when he needed to be strong. So he struggled to keep his need at bay. First he must deal with Cowper. Only after that would he be free to seek Anne and ask her once again to be his wife.

Anne woke suddenly from her dream. It was still very clear to her and she knew that she had been walking in the gardens at de Montifiori with Stefan. He had put his arms about her, drawing her close to kiss her on the lips, and she had been so happy. Then something had happened to drag him from her arms and she had seen him disappearing into the mist. She had called to him, but she could not reach him. Something was between them, keeping them apart, and she did not know what it was.

Tears trickled down her cheeks, because she wanted to be with Stefan more than anything in the world. She loved him, needed him, and yet her pride would not let her beg him to come to her.

'Stefan, my love...' she whispered. 'I wish you would come to me. Please come to me...I need you so...'

She had a loving father and mother, a sister and brothers. She was no longer alone in the world, but she still loved Stefan and she still wanted to be his wife. She wished with all her heart that he would come back to her and forget the feud with Lord Cowper. She was certain that if her father went to the King, Lord Cowper would be called to account. There was no need for Stefan to fight him. No need to risk his life when he might be with her.

'Stefan, I love you...' she whispered. 'I love you so much...'

She longed for him to return to her, but she did not

know if she would ever see him again. Why had he left her here and gone to England? Surely if he loved her, he would have stayed to make sure that she was well? Tears trickled down her cheeks, for sometimes she felt so alone.

'I am happy to see you well again, Mistress Melford,' Comte De Vere said to Anne when she came downstairs the next morning. Her clothes had been sent for and she was wearing one of the gowns that she had made with the cloth Stefan had purchased for her. It suited her well, and she looked beautiful, almost regal. 'We were very worried for a time, but my physician tended you and you have made a good recovery.'

'I must thank you for bringing me here,' Anne said and smiled at him. 'My father says that you have been generous in letting us stay here while I recovered and I cannot thank you enough for all you and your people have done for me. I believe it was you that found me at the edge of the woods?'

'I was fortunate enough to be in the right place at the right time,' the Comte said. 'We had been searching for you for many hours and were about to return home when I heard something. We had already looked for you in that area of the woods, but I think you must have been wandering for some time.'

'I was very fortunate,' Anne replied. 'Had you not heard my cry, I might have lain there all night—and perhaps I should have died.'

'If that had happened, I should have been most distressed. You are too young and beautiful to leave this life just yet, Mistress Melford.'

Anne saw the warmth in his eyes and blushed. Her

father had told her of the Comte's great concern for her, but she had not truly thought about it until this moment. She did not wish for his attentions, but felt conscious of the debt she owed him.

'You are kind to say it, sir. Ali would say that it is as Allah wills, but we prefer to think of it as God's will. Either way, I have escaped death twice and must believe that I was meant to continue to live.'

'You speak of de Montfort's physician. It was he that saved you after you were rescued from the sea. He is an Arab and an infidel, a believer in the Muslim religion. I dare say he is a good physician. However, I think my own as capable or better.'

Anne merely smiled. She knew that many people would feel as the Comte did, because of what Ali was by birth and religion. However, she respected the man who had saved her life and had felt happy to be his pupil and learn of many herbs and cures that she had not previously known.

'I know only that I was grateful to him, sir.'

'And to de Montfort as well, I dare say? He saved you from the sea and gave you a home when you had none—but things are altered now. Your father will take you home soon.'

'Yes. He speaks of leaving in a few days.'

'I shall miss you when you go,' the Comte told her with a look that made Anne glance away, her cheeks warm. She wished he would not look at her that way. 'Perhaps I may come and visit you at home one day? I should wish to make certain that you are truly well and happy again.'

'Of course you would be welcome to visit us,' Anne replied, for what else could she say? He had found her when she lay close to death, brought her to his home and had his physician care for her. She was still his guest and would remain so until she returned to England. Anne sensed that more lay behind the Comte's words than he was prepared to say at that moment. She did not wish to give him false hope, but she could not be rude to him. 'I know my mother would wish to thank you in person for all your kindness to her family.'

'Then I may follow in a few weeks,' he said and smiled at her. 'In the meantime, if I hear from your brother I shall tell him that you have been found alive.'

'Poor Harry must be so distressed,' Anne said. 'It was not his fault that I was swept overboard, for he asked me to go below earlier and I wished to stay on deck. The storm was magnificent to see and I found the cabin stuffy and uncomfortable.'

'You are a very brave young woman,' Comte De Vere said and reached for her hand. He carried it to his lips and kissed it briefly. 'I have remarked it from the start, which is why I admire you greatly. I hope the thought of a sea voyage does not fill you with too much trepidation?'

'I am a little nervous,' Anne replied. 'However, the storm was very fierce and I do not believe that such huge waves are normal. Besides, I shall go below and stay there, even if it makes me feel unwell.'

'Yes, for your own sake and your father's peace of mind you must,' he replied. 'However, it is unlikely to happen again. I have crossed the Channel safely in winter and many times in the spring and summer. I cannot think you in any danger this time.'

'I believe you are right, sir,' Anne replied. 'Besides,

I must risk it, for there is no other way to reach my home.'

'Yes, that is true,' he said. 'You will be safe this time I am sure. I believe you may return to France one day, and I pray that next time, you will have a happier outcome.'

'Yes, perhaps,' Anne said. She was not sure what he meant by that statement, but if her prayers were answered she would return to France as the wife of Stefan de Montfort. If he did not come to claim her, she thought that she might remain in England for the rest of her life.

Stefan woke sweating and crying out a name. He had been dreaming of the day in the forest when he was a young man and he had discovered his brother's body lying there, his throat cut. Gervase had been cruelly murdered and Stefan had believed he knew the name of his brother's murderer. Stefan had recently quarrelled with one of their neighbours over his treatment of a servant. Stefan had fought with Sir Hugh, giving him the scar he carried to the end of his life. He had taken his revenge by murdering Stefan's brother, but even that was not enough. Sir Hugh was the kind of man that harboured a grudge.

He had not been certain at the time, but Sir Hugh had admitted the truth the day he died. He had been responsible for Gervase's death, but it was Cowper that had convinced Lord de Montfort that his elder son was a murderer. Because of his lies, Stefan had been banished from his home, cast out by his own father. He had harboured the bitterness for many years, his life hard though rewarding as he became known for his skill and cool head in battle.

He had been haunted by the need to kill his enemies, to have his revenge at any cost. Now he was torn between the need for revenge and his feelings for an innocent girl…his desire to wed her.

He could not have both. His father's shade seemed to cry out for vengeance and yet he longed for Anne and her sweetness.

Anne had told the Comte De Vere that she was not afraid of returning home on a ship, but she could not help feeling a shiver of apprehension as she went on board. It was, however, a larger vessel than the one she had travelled on the first time, and her cabin was larger, less stuffy. She went below immediately with the maid her father had engaged for her, deciding that she would stay there until they reached port, even if she did feel sick.

Her heart beat frantically as she heard the orders to cast off and then felt the movement as the ship's sails filled with wind. However, the sea was calm and, though there was a good stiff breeze, there was no sign of a storm. The crossing was uneventful and Anne was soon stepping on to dry land again.

'It was not so very bad, then?' her father said as he glanced at her face. She was smiling, looking happier than she had for a while. 'Are you glad to be back in England?'

'Yes, Father, I am,' Anne said. 'I want to see my mother again, and to meet Claire. It was unfortunate for her that my disappearance should delay her wedding. I hope that it will not be too long before Harry joins us at home and the wedding can go ahead.'

'Comte St Orleans went home to leave a message in case Harry should make his way back there. It may be that they will meet and make the journey to England together. Otherwise, he will return immediately.' Rob looked at his daughter thoughtfully. She seemed quieter than she had once been and he wondered what lay behind the new face Anne showed to the world. 'Are you thinking of Lord de Montfort?'

'Yes, I am. We have heard nothing since he left for England. I cannot help wondering where he is and whether he has achieved his aim of bringing his enemy to justice.'

'You wished to see me?' Hassan asked as he went into the Great Hall to meet the visitor asking for Lord de Montfort. 'I am not the master here, but in Lord de Montfort's absence I stand in his stead.' His gaze narrowed, for he had seen an older version of this man not long since. 'Have you come in search of Mistress Melford?'

'I received a message that Lord de Montfort might have news for me concerning the lady I searched for,' Harry said, hope dawning in his eyes. 'Have you found her—is she alive?'

'Anne is alive and returned to England with her father,' Hassan told him. 'Lord de Montfort went to England before them, and I was about to follow. In another hour you would not have found me.' He smiled at Harry. 'Come, the servants will bring you wine and food and we shall talk. There are many things you should know, for they will help to ease your mind…'

* * *

'Anne, my dearest!' Melissa swept forward, her silk skirts rustling as she gathered her daughter into her arms and embraced her. 'Thank God you are home and safe again. I have prayed every night and every morning since I learned that you were missing, and God has answered my prayers. At times I feared I should never see you again, but come and sit down, dearest. You must be exhausted from the journey.'

'I am a little tired, but not exhausted,' Anne told her. 'I am much recovered now, Mother. I have been very ill since I last saw you, but the last time was not as serious as the first. I think I almost died then and owe my life to two people—Lord de Montfort and his physician. Ali is of Arab descent and skilled in the arts of medicines. He was teaching me many things before I was kidnapped.'

Melissa looked into her eyes, a little surprised at what she found there. Her daughter had changed, grown up since she last saw her. 'You sound as if you were content at the Chateau de Montifiori. I had your father's letter, but he told me only the bare facts, Anne. I would learn all of it from you, my love.'

'I shall tell you everything, Mother,' Anne said. 'I could not remember your name when I was at the chateau, but I remembered your love and the things you had taught me. It was the belief that I had a mother and that she loved me, which helped me in the early days. And then I began to feel as if I belonged at the chateau.'

'And would have remained there happily had your memory not returned?' Melissa asked.

'Yes, I believe so,' Anne agreed. 'Father has told you that I was to be married to Lord de Montfort?'

Melissa nodded, her eyes intent on her daughter's face. 'He told me that the marriage had been cancelled… Was that your wish, my love?'

'No, Mother, for I was content to wed him. However, he left Normandy to come here to settle an old score with an enemy. If he loved me, would he not have waited to see how I fared?' There was a sad, wistful expression in her eyes.

'Perhaps,' her mother said. 'We shall discuss this later, Anne. I am forgetting my manners. You must come and meet Claire. She has been as anxious for your safety as any of us. She is a dear sweet girl and I am happy that she will be your brother's wife.'

'I have longed to meet her,' Anne said. 'Mother, it has worried me—will Harry be in trouble because he did not return to court at the time he should have? Will the King be angry with him?'

'Your father sent word of Harry's search for you before he left for France,' Melissa said. 'I believe the King will understand, though he may demand that Harry return as soon as he is in England. If he does, we may have to postpone the wedding for a time.'

'That would be so unfair on Claire,' Anne said and looked thoughtful for a moment. 'Perhaps we might all travel to London so that the wedding may be held there?'

'It would be a good solution to the problem,' her mother agreed. 'But should you wish to make the journey so soon after you returned home?'

'I would not mind,' Anne said. She glanced at the young woman waiting a little nervously in the Great Hall and went to greet her with a smile, her hands outstretched. 'You must be Claire. I beg you will forgive me for the delay to your happiness. I am sure that Harry must come home soon and we shall all be together for a while.'

'My dear sister,' Claire said and opened her arms. They embraced warmly, emotion overwhelming them both. 'No words of mine could ever express my joy when I heard that you were safe. Harry blamed himself dreadfully for what happened on the ship. He was sure that his parents would never forgive him for your loss.'

'They would have grieved for me, because we are a happy family,' Anne said and smiled. 'I did not know how fortunate I was in my family until it was lost. I am so pleased that Harry has found you, because I know you must be special. My brother has waited some years to marry. I believe Mother had begun to think he never would.'

'I am delighted that he had the good sense to wait until he found the right wife,' Melissa said and looked from one to the other in content. 'How good it is to have you both here. I think that we should invite Andrew and Catherine to stay. Your sister was much distressed when she heard of your disappearance, Anne. I know they were planning to visit the court, but delayed it until they heard news of you, my love.'

'I should like to see Catherine again. It is a while since we met. Perhaps we should all go to London together, Mother.'

'I shall write to them tomorrow,' Melissa said. 'Much depends on whether or not Harry is given leave to come home or commanded to attend the King.'

'How dare he issue me with a challenge like this?' Cowper demanded of the courier. 'I am innocent of all the charges he would lay against me—and shall lay some of my own. Lord de Montfort murdered my cousin Sir Hugh and the lady Madeline. Such crimes are punishable by death and must be answered before a higher court.'

'I am merely the messenger,' the courier said. 'The challenge has been issued according to the ancient law and must be answered. Lord de Montfort awaits your answer. If you will not meet him in single combat, he will lay a charge of murder and abduction against you before the King.'

'This is mere speculation,' Cowper cried and his hand shook as he read the paper through once more. 'I bought this estate in good faith and the late Lord William died by his own hand when his mind became confused. As for the charge of abduction, I know nothing of it.' He tore the paper in two and flung it in the face of the courier. 'I shall lay charges of murder before the King. Stefan de Montfort is an adventurer and a murderer and it is time he was brought to justice.'

'Is that the answer you would have me take back to Lord de Montfort?'

'You have the answer, now go before I have you flogged,' Cowper raged. 'I will not meet him in single combat. He has no proof of any wrongdoing on my part, and cannot prove it before the court.'

The courier bowed his head. 'I shall inform Lord de Montfort of your decision, my lord. I bid you good day.'

Cowper watched as the man left the chamber in which he sat. The remains of a meal lay scattered on the table before him, an empty wine sack discarded on the floor. The room had not been cleaned in days and the stench of rotting food emanated from rushes that were much in need of changing.

Cowper scowled. He had not dared to leave the house since he returned from France for fear that Stefan de Montfort was waiting for him. The servants went in dread of his rages, and several of them had run away. Those that remained hardly cared if they did their work, because he was drunk for the most part of the day and walked the house at night searching for assassins that might be hiding in the draughty passages.

'Curse him! Why did he not die in some foreign land as he was meant to?' Cowper lifted his wine cup and drained it to the dregs. Discovering that he had drunk all that had been brought, he yelled for a servant to bring more. Some minutes passed and no one came. Cowper threw his cup at the wall and cursed furiously. Where the hell were they all? They had begun to desert him in droves, like rats leaving a sinking ship. He stank of sweat and unwashed raiment, and they knew he was losing his grip on reality. He had ruled his household by fear and he knew they all hated him, the men he had brought with him and those he had forced to work for him after their old lord died. 'Damn the rogue! He shall not have it. I'll write to the King…'

He searched for a quill, writing vellum and ink. His brow knit in thought as he began his accusation. It was many years since Stefan de Montfort's brother had been murdered. His fool of a father had believed his own son capable of murder and sent him away, leaving himself vulnerable. He had soon regretted it, but under the influence of a man he believed his friend he had delayed sending for his heir until it was too late. Cowper had all he had coveted, and revenge for a love unrequited.

Stefan de Montfort's mother had rejected him in favour of an older, richer man, and Cowper had hated her, her sons and the man he believed had stolen her from him. Twisted and bitter, he had destroyed all that she had loved, but the jealousy had never left him.

A smile of malicious pleasure curved his mouth as he penned his poison, accusing Stefan of the murder of his own brother, the lady Madeline and Sir Hugh Grantham. Now the arrogant de Montfort must answer to the King. When he was dead, the debt would at last be paid.

'We have travelled thus far together,' Harry said when they reached the shores of England. 'I must return at once to London, for the King may be angry with me for deserting my post. I was given a month's leave and I have been gone more than twice that time…'

'You searched for your sister,' Hassan said. 'Surely the King will listen to your plea for clemency?'

'Henry is a fair man, but there is no doubt that I have abused my position of trust. I ought to have returned and asked permission to search for Anne, but I could not bring myself to give up the search once it was begun. I might have been searching still if Lord de Montfort had not sent out messengers to find me.'

'He thought Anne might be the person for whom you searched,' Hassan said. 'He wanted her to remember who she was, though had she not been snatched away from us she would even now be his wife.'

'She owes her life to him,' Harry said. 'Yet my father will not allow the marriage unless it is what she truly wants.' He offered his hand to Hassan, who took it and clasped it with his own. 'I am glad to have met you, sir. My family is in Lord de Montfort's debt. If there is ever anything I can do to be of service to you, you must send word. I am mostly at court unless the King has work for me elsewhere.'

'I shall give my lord your message,' Hassan said and smiled. 'You are very like your sister, though you have not quite the same colouring. Please send my good wishes to her when you see her again.'

'I do not know when that may be,' Harry told him. 'I shall send word to my family that I am in London, for I may not be able to go home for a while.' He frowned as he thought of his wedding. Would Claire have grown tired of waiting? Had her father taken her back to France? Many a lady would not have shown as much forbearance as she had, and he could only hope that she was content to wait until he could arrange their wedding.

'We must part,' Hassan said. 'My way lies in another direction, for I know where my lord will be. I know that he has Lord Cowper penned up like a caged animal. He will not let him escape this time.'

Anne stared out of the window. It was raining again, the sky grey and forbidding. She longed for the blue skies of Normandy, and the sunlit days she had spent there seemed an idyllic memory. A memory it seemed that must last her a lifetime.

Stefan had not come to her, though they had been home for some days. She had begun to despair that he ever would. She knew that he needed to settle the score with his enemy, but why had he not sent her word of some kind?

If he truly cared for her he would surely have come or at least written her a letter? Her heart ached and sometimes she thought it would break if Stefan did not come for her soon.

* * *

'I have a letter from Harry,' Rob said as he entered the small chamber where the three women were sitting at their sewing. 'He has gone straight to court, as I expected. He must wait on Henry's pleasure, for his extended leave of absence will not meet with favour in his Majesty's eyes. I doubt he will be punished for it, because I wrote begging the King's indulgence—but he will not be given further leave just yet.'

Melissa looked at her husband expectantly. They had discussed this eventuality and she knew his feelings on the matter.

'Shall you write to Harry and ask what he wishes to do—or shall we all travel to London together?'

'Claire's father is of the opinion that the marriage had better take place in London rather than be postponed yet again. He has business at home, but has delayed his return to be here for the wedding.'

'My poor father does not like to be so long from home,' Claire said. 'I am quite content to be married in London—if it is Harry's wish.'

'He might not ask it of you,' Rob said. 'I am sure it is what he would wish.' His dark gaze travelled to Anne, who had sat quietly at her embroidery, saying nothing. 'Do you feel like accompanying us to London, Anne? I have wondered if you felt quite well of late?'

'I am perfectly well,' Anne said as she looked up and met his concerned look. 'If I am quiet, it is because I have things on my mind. Forgive me, Father, if I have worried you, but I am not just as I was before I left home with my brother.'

'Your suffering has changed you,' Rob said. 'I am

sorry for it, Anne. I would like to see you happy again, as you used to be.'

'I am content to be here, Father.'

Anne bent her head over her work, smothering a sigh. They had been home for two weeks now and she had hoped that Stefan would come or at least send a message. It was possible he did not know that she was at home, of course, though she believed Hassan would have been in touch with him. The two were close, more like blood brothers than master and servant, and she knew that Stefan relied on his friend to keep him informed of what went on at the chateau.

She had no idea of whether Stefan was still in England or whether he had returned to his chateau. She had hoped that he would come to claim her, and she still clung to that hope, though it was not as bright as it had been once.

She stood up, excusing herself to the others. Going upstairs to her room, Anne fought the tears that threatened to fall. Did he even think of her? It was so long since she had seen him. She did not know how she could bear her life if she never saw Stefan again, but she was not sure he would ever come…

'So, she is truly well and at home with her father.' Stefan turned from his contemplation of a windswept scene to face his friend. 'It is good news that you bring, Hassan. I was sure that she would recover before I left her, but I have been torn with the desire to see her and the need to stay away until this business is finished.'

'And the papers I found?' Hassan asked. 'Are they of any help in your quest to have your birthright restored?'

Stefan had taken the papers, but as yet had hardly glanced at them. 'As you say, it is proof enough if I needed it that someone attempted to forge my father's signature, though it does not prove Cowper responsible.'

'What of the letter from your father?'

'Was there such a letter?' Stefan picked up the papers and looked again. He saw the wax seal and knew his father must have written the letter, though the hand was hardly legible. 'This was with the other papers in the man's pouch?' Hassan inclined his head and Stefan broke the seal. He read for some minutes and then made a moaning sound, screwing the paper into a ball as his hand clenched in distress. His eyes met Hassan's. 'My father begs me to forgive him for denying me all that ought by right to have been mine. He says that he knows Cowper lied to him and he no longer believes that I murdered my brother, for he has learned it was at Sir Hugh's murderous hand that my brother died.'

'This is the proof you needed,' Hassan said, a gleam of excitement in his eyes. 'No wonder Fritz believed that you would pay good money for these things.'

'If only Father had sent this letter a year or two earlier,' Stefan grated, his voice breaking with emotion. 'I could have been there—prevented the humiliation they heaped upon him as his mind weakened. That is worse than all the rest, Hassan. I do not care for the house or the land or the gold that Cowper stole. It is my father's pride, his dignity…'

'You have challenged Cowper to single combat. If he accepts you can kill him and remain within the law.'

'He has refused me,' Stefan said. 'I had decided that

I would go into the house and kill him there in his own filth like the rat he is.' He scowled at nothing in particular. 'They tell me he never washes, nor does he sleep. He wanders the house in fear of his life.'

'Is that not punishment enough?' Hassan asked, his dark eyes intent on Stefan's face. 'Go to London, my lord. Lay your case before the King again. You have proof now that Cowper lied all those years ago. If you kill him, you will never free yourself of the stain of his blood. What do you truly desire most—revenge for your father or a life with the woman you love?'

Stefan looked at him for a long time, and then inclined his head. He had battled with his conscience long enough, but now he knew that his father would wish to see him settled and happy above all else. 'You are right,' he said. 'I have fought for gold, but I am not a murderer. I shall go to London.'

Anne had envied her sister Catherine when their brother took her to court. She wished that she might go with her, but her parents had considered her too young at that time. She smiled now as she remembered fancying herself in love with Will Shearer. How young and foolish she had been, thinking only of her new gowns and the trinkets she would buy from the fair. She still took pride in her clothes, of course, though they did not mean as much now. However, she had made herself a new gown for the coming trip, because Claire had insisted on helping her.

'I have many pretty gowns,' Claire said when Anne asked if she did not wish to make something for herself. 'You lost the clothes you took with you to France and have only what you brought home with you.'

'I have enough,' Anne told her, but realised that Claire truly wanted to do something for her. 'But a new gown is always welcome.'

Anne was glad that Claire was to wed Harry. Her brother deserved the best and Claire had a sweet nature. The two girls had worked on Anne's new gown, becoming closer in the process, as Claire had confided her pleasure in her coming marriage.

'I love Sir Harry very much,' Claire told her. 'And yet I am a little anxious at the thought of becoming a wife, for I would not wish to fail him.'

'How could you fail Harry when he loves you so?' Anne asked with a smile. 'I know that you will make him a good wife and a wonderful chatelaine of his home.'

Claire thanked her shyly, a look of content in her eyes. 'In truth, I can hardly wait to see Harry again.'

Anne saw the dreamy expression in her face and knew she was thinking of her betrothed. Claire felt as Anne had when she had believed she was soon to be married to the man she loved. Anne's dreams had been shattered when she was stolen from Stefan's garden, and in the weeks since she had recovered her senses she had gradually come to think that he had asked her to marry him simply because she had nowhere else to go.

Now she was to visit the court in London. It was something she had longed for when she was still a child and impatient to be a woman. Yet, on the verge of achieving her childhood dream, Anne knew that the only thing she truly wanted was to be back at the chateau with Stefan. Her pride would not let her ask him to return to her, though if he did not she felt her life would be empty.

* * *

The journey to London was uneventful. Lord Melford's train was a large one—it was made up of his whole family, including the Earl and Countess of Gifford, their children and servants. The Comte St Orleans, his daughter and servants swelled their numbers. There were so many of them that only the most prestigious of inns could accommodate them, and several times they stayed with Rob's friends, who had large houses, but were pressed to find rooms for them all. Claire and Anne shared a room, but found this no hardship, for they had become great friends.

Rob had secured the largest available house he could find, but the Earl of Gifford had his own London house and so the family was divided by a few streets, though close enough to visit often. Lady Anne Shearer—for whom Anne had been named as a baby—had written to tell them that she would be visiting her house in London. She and Lady Melford were great friends and it was an opportunity for them to meet and entertain each other.

Although Claire had become her particular friend, Anne was happy to see her sister again. She was reminded of Catherine's determination to marry only the man she loved and no other and it heartened her. The general mood was one of pleasure and, by the time they reached London, Anne's spirits had lifted. Everyone was excited about visiting the court and the other pleasures of town, not least of which was the chance to visit shops they could only dream of most of the year.

'You must visit the silk merchants in Cheapside,' Catherine told Anne. 'You will love the fine materials you will find there, dearest. Andrew says I must take you to my seamstress and commission at least two new gowns for you to wear to court at his expense.'

'Your husband is generous,' Anne said, smothering a sigh as she thought of her visit to the silk merchants at Cherbourg. How excited she had been that day; it had been a wonderful day until the attack on them by Lord Cowper's men. She looked at her sister thoughtfully. 'Tell me, Catherine, are you as happy as you were the day you wed him?'

'I am much happier,' Catherine told her with a contented smile. 'I was not sure at the time that Andrew loved me, for the King ordered our marriage to settle the feud between our families.'

'Yes, I remember,' Anne said, looking at her curiously. 'How did you feel? You must have been torn in two, because you already loved Andrew and yet you were not sure of his feelings for you.'

'That is exactly how I felt,' Catherine replied and looked at her face. 'You were promised to wed Lord de Montfort—did you love him, Anne? I know there was a time when you thought you cared for Will Shearer.'

'I believed I loved Will Shearer,' Anne said. 'I was very young then, and I did not truly understand love.'

'You do now?' Catherine looked at her and nodded. 'Yes, I see that you do, dearest Anne. You have not heard from Lord de Montfort?' Anne shook her head and Catherine touched her hand. 'Do not despair. It may be that he has something he must do before he can come to you.'

'Yes, perhaps that is it,' Anne agreed. 'He has an enemy who has tried to kill him more than once and he must settle the score.'

'You speak of Lord Cowper?' Catherine frowned.

'Mother told me what you believed had happened. I spoke to Andrew about the matter and he promised to see what could be done.'

'What do you mean?' Anne's eyes widened as she looked at her sister, but Catherine shook her head.

'I cannot say more for the moment, but Andrew says there may be hope of Stefan's estate being restored to him if his cause is just. If he discovers anything that may help, he will seek an audience with the King.'

'Andrew would do that for a man he does not know?'

'I told him that I thought your happiness might depend on it,' Catherine said and smiled at her. 'My husband will do what he can, but I can promise nothing. If Lord William de Montfort truly sold his birthright, there is nothing anyone can do.'

'I do not think Stefan cares so much for the land and house,' Anne said, looking thoughtful. 'He intended to give up his claims in return for peace after that last attempt was made on his life in Normandy. For my sake, I believe. He wants justice, nothing more.'

'I see that you love him and believe in him,' Catherine said. 'Therefore I shall beg Andrew to intercede with the King on Lord de Montfort's behalf.'

'If he could be heard, perhaps he would think it justice enough,' Anne said, her face filled with a wistful longing she was not aware was there. 'He might then come to me…'

Anne had enjoyed her morning. She, Claire and Catherine had been to visit the silk merchants in Cheapside. They had each purchased several lengths of silk and the costly cloth would be delivered to the seamstress for making up into their court gowns. She was smiling, talking easily with her sister and her friend, and it was only as they stopped to admire a display of wares in the silversmith's window that she became aware someone was looking at her.

Glancing to her right, Anne saw the two men and her heart caught. Stefan de Montfort here in London! Hassan was with him, dressed as usual in the clothes that seemed so strange on an English street and yet suited the man, the bottom half of his face covered to hide the terrible scars. She hesitated, and then took a step towards them, such a look of appeal on her face that Hassan came to her at once, Stefan a step behind him. Clearly he was less pleased to see her than Hassan, and that hurt.

''Tis well met, my lady,' Hassan said and bowed to her. 'I am glad to see you well and happy. We were anxious for a time, but we heard that you were with your family.'

'Yes…' Anne's gaze flew to Stefan's face, looking for some sign that he was pleased to see her. His expression was sombre, though something in his eyes spoke to her despite his obvious reserve. 'My lord…you are well?'

'I am well,' he replied. 'I am glad to see you are much recovered, Mistress Melford. As Hassan has told you, you have been often in our thoughts.'

'In your thoughts?' Anne asked, and despite her determination not to let it show, her longing and regret were in her face. 'I have thought of you often. I had hoped you would come to visit me.'

'I had intended…they told you I would come.' A fire flamed in Stefan's eyes; the heat seemed to scorch her. She wished that they were alone, longed for him to put his arms about her and hold her close. 'You knew that I must settle with Cowper after what he did. You could never have been safe had I allowed his infamy to go unchecked. I challenged him to meet me in single combat…' His expression was so harsh then that Anne's heart caught. 'He refused to meet me and so I must lay my complaints before the King. I must hope that he will hear me this time. Otherwise…' He left the words unspoken, but Anne understood. He was telling her that if he could not find justice one way he would take it another—and until this business was settled he would not come to her. Her heart felt as if it would break. She loved him so!

'I pray that the King will listen,' Anne said. She considered telling him what Catherine had said to her, but decided it would be wrong to raise false hopes. Besides, her sister and Claire were looking curious and she knew they were waiting to be introduced. 'Lord de Montfort—may I present Mademoiselle Claire St Orleans, my brother's betrothed wife, and my sister, the Countess of Gifford…'

'Ladies—' Stefan made them a bow worthy of any courtier '—I am glad to make your acquaintance, and to see that Mistress Melford has such charming friends. I am sorry to leave you so soon, but I have an appointment.' He turned to Anne once more. 'Forgive me, I must go.'

'Of course…' She hesitated, then, gathering her courage, 'You will call on us, sir? I believe we have things to say to one another?'

Stefan's eyes dwelled on her face, making her heart beat wildly. 'Yes, I shall come,' he promised. 'I have waited because I was not sure…but you have my word that I shall come before I return to France.'

'Thank you,' Anne said and smiled suddenly. She had been so afraid that he did not truly care for her, but, despite his harsh looks and his neglect, something in his eyes told her that he felt this bond between them. He might deny it, as she had tried to do, but it was there. 'I shall wait for that day, my lord.' She looked at Hassan. 'It was good to see you again, sir.'

'So, that is Lord de Montfort,' Claire said, a hint of mischief in her voice as the two men walked away. 'Now I understand why you agreed to marry him. There is something exciting…dangerous about him. He would frighten me, but I think he may be just right for you, Anne.'

Anne laughed softly. The shadows had suddenly fallen away from her, her spirits lifting as if by magic. Whatever had kept Stefan from her side, it was not indifference.

'My lord's life has not been easy,' she said. 'He was cast out by his father as a young man and he has lived by the sword. Yes, there is something dangerous in loving such a man, but I would not have it any other way.'

'We should go home,' Catherine said. 'Mother will worry if we are too long, though she has Lady Anne Shearer to keep her company. I believe that Will is with her, and his wife. Lady Shearer has become reconciled to the marriage now that she has a grandson.'

'Oh…I shall be pleased to meet Will's wife,' Anne said, looking happy as they summoned the coach. She was thoughtful as they rattled over the cobblestones. Stefan had given her his word he would visit her before he returned to France. He would keep it and she must pray that he cared for her sufficiently to ask her once more to be his wife.

Busy with her own thoughts, she followed the others into the house, only half-listening to their chatter. It was not until she entered the parlour where her mother was seated with Lady Shearer that she realised that they had another guest. The Comte De Vere was standing by the fireplace, a cup of wine in his hand as he conversed with the ladies. He put down his wine cup and looked pleased as he saw Anne.

'Mistress Melford, how well you look,' he said and came towards her. 'I pray you, do not look so surprised—did I not say that I would visit you one day?'

'Yes, you did,' Anne said. She was conscious of a slight awkwardness, because the way he looked at her was too expectant, too satisfied, as if he thought she would welcome his attentions. 'It was good of you to come, sir. Have you business in London?'

'Yes, some business with a wine merchant,' the Comte said, lying with a practised ease. 'However, that is of secondary importance. My main reason for the journey was to see how you were. I have been concerned for you, Anne, as you must know.'

Anne smiled and thanked him, but her heart sank. She owed him a debt of gratitude and must be polite, though she wished that she could tell him his interest in her was unwelcome. All she truly wanted at this moment was to be alone with her thoughts. The meeting with Stefan had given her a new zest for life, and she could hardly wait until he kept his promise to visit her.

'I ask for an audience with his Majesty,' Stefan said. 'I have brought my complaints against Lord Cowper before the court once before, but was refused a hearing. This time I have new evidence. A letter in my father's own hand.'

'You will wait here, sir,' the courtier replied. 'The King is in council with his ministers and cannot be disturbed for the moment. When he is ready to see you, you will be sent for. If he does not send for you today, you must return every day and wait here until he has the time to grant you an audience.'

'How long before the King sends for me?' Stefan asked of Hassan as the courtier walked away. 'Last time I waited for hours each day for a week. In the end I was told that my request had been denied and the King would not see me.' His face darkened with anger and he struck the wall with his fist. 'Damn it! Why will Henry not give me a hearing?'

Hassan looked at him gravely. 'You have no choice but to wait here, my friend. I know it tries your patience sorely, but there is little else you can do for the moment.'

'I could go back to my father's house and kill his murderer!' Stefan muttered, his expression like thunder. 'I was a fool to come here. I should have known there was no justice in England for me!'

'You are impatient, my lord—' Hassan broke off as he heard heavy footsteps returning. 'I think someone comes.' The two men looked at each other as they heard the clink of armour. 'What…?'

The door was flung open and a palace guard entered. Behind them there were three more guards, all armed. Stefan's instinct told him that he had walked into a trap, but his pride would not let him run. He faced them, his eyes narrowed and angry.

'Have you come to take me to the King? I would be heard, as is my right under English law.'

'The King will hear you if he sees fit,' the guard said. 'I am here to arrest you for the murders of the lady Madeline and Sir Hugh Grantham.'

'That is a lie.' Hassan started forward, but Stefan caught his arm, shaking his head, but Hassan would not be denied. 'The lady lured Lord de Montfort to her house under pretext of needing help and Sir Hugh tried to murder him.'

'You were there?'

'Say nothing more,' Stefan ordered him. 'I am innocent of these foul charges and will answer to the King if I am given the opportunity.'

'My orders are to take you to the Tower, where you will be held in conditions according to your rank, sir. His Majesty will decide whether you are to be heard and when.'

'Here, take these,' Stefan said and thrust a leather pouch at Hassan. 'I need someone to stand for me, someone of rank and influence. It is a thankless task, my friend, but do what you can for me.'

'I shall find someone,' Hassan promised, his eyes meeting Stefan's. 'This is Cowper's doing, my friend. He must and shall be brought to justice.'

'Yes, somehow. If I fail, I know you will not,' Stefan said and smiled grimly. He turned towards his guards. 'I am ready to accompany you, sir.'

The officer inclined his head. 'I must do my duty, my lord. Please do not try to escape—if forced to it, I should have to kill you.'

'I shall not try to escape. I am innocent of the charges

and will clear my name when the King grants me a hearing.'

He turned to glance at Hassan one last time and then walked from the room with the guards.

Hassan stood for a moment, his forehead creased in thought. Stefan's message had been clear enough. If he should meet an unjust end, Hassan was to kill Cowper. In the meantime, however, he would do what he could to find someone who would stand for Lord de Montfort in the court. A man of his own class was needed, for the word of the late Lord de Montfort's steward would not be listened to, nor his own. Hassan had been willing to confess that it was he who had killed Sir Hugh after the lady was murdered by her uncle, but Stefan had forbidden it with a look, and Hassan knew why. He would certainly have been executed with barely a word said in his defence; at least, as a lord of the realm, Stefan was entitled to his hearing.

Chapter Eight

Anne dressed in her new gown of dark green silk. The neckline was squared and bordered with gold braid, the sleeves loose and hanging in long points; gold braid edged the sleeves, too, though the skirt was plain. She wore a peaked cap of matching green silk that framed her face, her hair hanging loosely beneath it and flowing down her back. It was to be her first visit to the court that evening, and her stomach fluttered with nerves.

Would Stefan be there? She knew that he was entitled by birth to take his place amongst the courtiers, but he had lived abroad for many years and might not wish to attend the gatherings. Her whole family was to attend that night, except for her younger brother who would remain at home with his nurse. The Shearer family would also be there, and Anne understood that both Comte St Orleans and Comte De Vere had been issued with invitations. Yet she knew that the evening would be empty for her if she did not see the man she longed for with all her heart.

'Harry arranged for Claire and her father to be presented this evening,' Lady Melford told her daughter. 'Comte De Vere is to attend as our guest.' Her eyes were inquiring as she looked at Anne. 'Comte De Vere seems to like you well, dearest. I think he means to make you an offer of marriage.'

'If he speaks to Father, please ask him not to allow the Comte to make the offer, Mother,' Anne said. 'The Comte is very kind and I am in his debt for what he did to help me, but...' She stopped and sighed.

'Your heart is given to Lord de Montfort, yes, I know, my love. Catherine told me that you met him briefly when you were out together this morning. I have noticed the difference in you since then. You seem more alive—more as you used to be.'

'I feel more as I used to,' Anne said, her eyes glowing. 'I love Stefan, Mother. I was afraid that he did not love me. I thought he might have asked me to wed him simply because at that time I had nowhere else to go.'

'Now you think it is not so? What did he say that gave you cause for hope?'

'He promised that he would call to see me before he left for France—but it was the look in his eyes, Mother. I believe he cares for me, even if he is holding back for some reason.' Anne's face was intense, her eyes wistful, revealing more than she knew.

Melissa nodded. 'Yes, I understand that, Anne. There was a time when your father and I had quarrelled. I had no cause to think he loved me for he was very angry, and yet there was something in his eyes that gave me hope even in the darkest days.' She smiled at her daughter. 'I am glad that you do not wish to marry Comte De Vere. You would not be his first wife and I am not sure he would make you a good husband, but you must be careful, my love. Do nothing to give him cause to believe you mean to accept him. If he should ask, you must say no in a way that does not cause offence.'

'I know that I must be careful,' Anne said. 'I have done and said nothing to encourage his attentions—except that I told him he would be welcome to call on us when he asked if he might.'

'Do you think that was wise?'

'He had been so generous to both Father and I—how could I refuse?'

'It was difficult,' Melissa agreed, but looked anxious. 'Well, be careful in future, dearest. It is very easy to give offence without meaning to and that can cause trouble.'

Anne nodded, but she was only half-listening to her mother's warning. Her thoughts were of the gathering that night and whether Lord de Montfort would be one of those summoned to attend.

Anne ate sparingly of the rich food brought to table. Her family were at the head of the board placed at right angles to the top table where the King and his most favoured courtiers were seated. Her brother Harry, the Earl of Gifford and Lord Melford were all amongst those so favoured that night, and Anne felt proud to see them there.

Catherine had warned her against eating too much of the spicy dishes offered her, because sometimes the food was not as fresh as they had at home. The palace was too large and the constant entertaining meant that sometimes standards lapsed, which was one of the reasons the court moved from one palace to another so that it could be properly cleaned. Anne had heard that another move was due to happen very soon. Many of the courtiers followed the King as he progressed from one royal palace to another, seldom finding time to visit their own estates.

Perhaps that was why some of the nobles took mistresses, Anne thought. Catherine had whispered to her that some of the courtiers were not to be trusted, warning her not to visit the courtyards with any of them. Anne listened to her sister's advice for Catherine had been to court many times since her marriage.

'If you are seen to be absent for too long, your reputation could be damaged,' Catherine advised her. 'Married ladies are not always frowned upon for taking lovers, for it is common enough at court, but it would not be tolerated in a single lady.'

'You do not have a lover?' Anne stared at her in shock and Catherine laughed, looking more beautiful than ever to her sister's eyes. Catherine had blossomed in her marriage.

'Andrew would kill him and me if I did,' Catherine assured her sister. 'No, dearest, I have never looked at another man, but it does happen. I was just warning you to be careful—and of whom you dance with, should there be dancing this evening. Wait until I bring you a partner. If I do, you may be certain that he is to be trusted.'

Anne had not bothered to tell her sister that she did not wish to dance with anyone, because she had not seen Lord de Montfort at the gathering. However, she was not asked since the entertainment that evening consisted of tumblers, minstrels and a miracle play, which she found diverting.

* * *

However, by the time the evening was done Anne was finding it hard not to yawn behind her fan. The Comte De Vere had sat beside her during the play, talking to her about the actors. Anne had found his commentary annoying, for she wished to listen to the play, but she had managed to conceal her feelings, though she was ready to go home before her father came to tell them it was time to leave.

Anne noticed something odd in his manner, especially in the look he gave her. She did not think she had done anything to displease him, but his manner was grave. It made her wonder if the Comte De Vere had approached him with regard to a marriage contract and she went cold inside. Surely her father would not agree to it without consulting her?

She walked ahead of her mother and Claire into the house. Her father called to her, asking her if she could spare him a few minutes.

'Yes, of course, Father,' Anne said, feeling surprised. He went into the back parlour and she joined him, closing the door as he bid her. Her heart was beating wildly and she wondered what had caused him to look at her that way. 'Have I done something wrong, Father?'

'No, Anne, of course not. I thought you behaved perfectly this evening. I am afraid I have some unhappy news for you.'

The expression on his face made her tremble. 'Something has happened…has Comte De Vere asked for your permission to address me?'

'I believe he intends it,' Rob replied. 'I fear this news is far worse—I have heard this evening that Lord de Montfort has been arrested for the murder of the lady

Madeline and Sir Hugh Grantham. I think you may remember that it was talked of shortly before you left for France? Two men were seen leaving the house at the time, but no warrant was issued for their arrest as no one knew who they were.'

'You cannot think that Stefan murdered them?' Anne's gaze flew to her father's face. 'It is not true! He is too honourable. I know he would not murder in cold blood. He would not!'

'I have found him honourable,' Rob agreed. 'However, the complaint has been laid and must be answered.'

'What does that mean?' Anne asked, an icy chill settling at the nape of her neck. 'Who laid the complaint?'

'Lord Cowper,' Rob said. 'Andrew is to discover more of it tomorrow and we shall see what can be done, though I fear de Montfort must remain in the Tower until his trial is set.'

Anne felt the tightness in her chest, and the tears burned behind her eyes. 'I must see him, Father. I must tell him that I do not believe this wicked tale.'

'I am not sure.' Her father looked at her doubtfully. 'The Tower is no place for a young girl.'

'I am not a child, Father, and I love Stefan. Had Lord Cowper not stolen me away, I should have been Lady de Montfort by now.'

'Yes, that is true—except that we have no proof that it was Lord Cowper.'

'Stefan knows,' Anne said and the desperation was in her face. 'He may not be able to prove it, but he knows. Lord Cowper arranged for me to be abducted, so that he could have his revenge on Stefan. He hates him because everything he has was stolen from Stefan—his home, his birthright. It is so unfair that Stefan has been arrested when he is innocent! Surely someone must listen to his side of the argument?'

'That much at least I can promise you. Henry is often morose since the death of Prince Arthur and the Queen. However, I still have some influence with Henry. I shall make certain that Lord de Montfort's trial is fair.'

'And you will arrange for me to visit Stefan in the Tower?'

Rob looked at her. Her mood of despondency had flown and she looked vital, alive in her determination to fight for the man she loved. He saw himself in her, even though she was a woman, and knew that she would not give up if he denied her.

'I shall try,' he promised. 'If it can be arranged, you shall at least speak to him, Anne.'

'He is innocent of these crimes, Father. I know he is innocent.' Her eyes blazed with passion. 'Lord Cowper should be made to prove his accusations.'

'Yes, that is fair,' her father agreed. 'I shall ask that he be summoned to the court to put his case. He has made claims and they must be proved.'

'They cannot be proved,' Anne said. 'Stefan did not murder that woman or Sir Hugh. I know he didn't!'

Unable to bear the distress any longer, Anne turned and fled from the room. The tears were very close, because she knew that the punishment for crimes of this nature would be harsh. Stefan would be executed, his name disgraced before his peers. She thought that the humbling of his pride would be even harder for him to bear than death, though for her his execution was too painful to contemplate. If Stefan died in such a terrible way, she would not want to live.

* * *

Ali bent over his patient. The man had recovered slowly, but of late he had seen signs of returning strength. He was not surprised when Fritz opened his eyes and stared at him.

'Where am I?' he asked.

'You are at the home of Lord de Montfort. Our men found you in the woodcutter's hut. You had been stabbed and they thought you near dead, but I have nursed you and you have recovered.'

'Did you save me so that de Montfort could hang me?'

'Perhaps,' Ali told him. 'All things are as Allah wills...but it might be that you could earn your freedom.'

'How could I do that?' Fritz asked, eyes narrowed and suspicious.

'What do you know that might be of service to the Lord de Montfort? Search your conscience, sir. I cannot tell you what you must do, but if you know something of worth, it might be your salvation.'

'I am too weak to remember,' Fritz said and lay back against the pillows. 'There was a letter and some papers...'

'The papers have been found, but someone who knew where they came from might earn my lord's thanks for revealing that to the right person.' Ali handed him a cup of water, letting him take a few sips. 'If you knew the truth of what happened at Lord de Montfort's estate, it could earn you more than freedom.'

'I am tired,' Fritz said and closed his eyes. 'Too tired to think...'

* * *

Anne slept very little that night. She tossed and turned restlessly, and when she did fall asleep at last, she woke crying Stefan's name, her cheeks wet with tears. In her dream she had been torn from his arms as they dragged him to the scaffold. She had witnessed his terrible death and the horror of it was still with her as she woke, making her cry out.

The dream had been so terrifying that she could not stay in bed. She got up and began to pace the room, weeping bitterly. It was so unfair that she should lose the man she loved just when she had found him again.

They had spent so little time together when you counted the hours, but she knew that from the first moment she had opened her eyes and seen his face she had loved him. Anne did not know why Stefan had such a hold on her heart, for he had done little to encourage her love. Yet the way he looked at her, his smile, his touch…and the kisses they had shared would never leave her memory.

If Stefan died, disgraced and branded a murderer, she would never marry. Indeed, she might end by taking her own life, though that would be a wicked sin. However, she could not bear the thought of life without him. She had thought that she would not take him if he asked her only to keep the promise he had made her, but now she knew that she would wed him whatever the case. Without him her life would be empty.

She loved him more than her life itself, and she would visit him at the Tower to tell him of her love. Perhaps if Stefan understood how much she loved him, he would fight even harder for his life.

* * *

Stefan lay on the hard bench that served as a bed, but did not sleep. There was little light in the room, though he had been provided with a table, chair, pen, ink and parchment so that he might prepare his defence. He had been given bread, cheese and a rough wine, also water that he could use to drink or wash. Late the previous night some of his clothes had been brought to him and an extra blanket.

Someone had paid the gaoler money for easement. He supposed it to be Hassan, for he had few friends in this country. He had fought as a mercenary under the flag of any prince or trader that would pay him, and had sometimes fought against his own countrymen. For that some would think him a traitor to his country and his King, though he had never taken up arms against them, merely defended those he served.

Stefan scowled in the darkness. The candle they had given him had burned low long ago. He knew well enough that men like Sir Hugh Grantham and Lord Cowper were respected, though they had raped and murdered any that stood in their way. However, Sir Hugh's crimes had often been done against the heathen infidel under the banner of Christ and were condoned for that reason. No one cared that he tortured and ill used the men and women he bought and sold as slaves.

Sir Hugh had been killed by Hassan and Stefan knew that his friend would testify to the truth if he allowed it. He might win his freedom at the cost of his friend's life, but Stefan would never allow Hassan to sacrifice himself in his stead. Stefan was innocent and he would demand his right to prove his innocence in the ancient tradition of single combat. He knew that Cowper would never meet him, but he had the right to appoint a champion if any one would stand for him.

Stefan would prefer to die by the sword rather than on the scaffold, though his skill was such that he could hold his own against most. However, he knew that the King was against the practice. He had brought new law to England and preferred to settle disputes in other ways.

Stefan rose from the cot and began to pace the floor of his cell. He had taken a risk coming to London, for he had known that Cowper would try to strike at him. He had not thought that it would be these false accusations, for there could be no proof. Only someone who had known of the plot to trap him could have known he was there, which must mean that Cowper and Sir Hugh had plotted these things together. He wished there was some proof of Cowper's perfidy, but he doubted it could be found. Even his father's letter was not clear proof of anything, other than a father's love for the son he had sent away in anger.

At least he had that, Stefan thought. Some of the bitterness had been cleansed from his mind, and he could remember a child's laughter and a man's kindness without anger. So much had been lost that could not be replaced, and yet he had a chance for happiness...

Stefan groaned inwardly as he remembered Anne's face. She had looked at him with love when they had met by chance in the street. He had known an urgent desire to sweep her up in his arms and carry her off with him. Had he taken her then, returned to France on the first ship, he might have avoided arrest. She might even now be his wife. Yet he could not have lived with the shadow of injustice hanging over him.

This business must be finished one way or the other. Only then could he be free to go to her.

'Are you sure you wish for this?' Rob asked. The dark shadow of the Tower loomed over them, its history forbidding and bloody, its very walls resonating with whispers of murder and torture within its shade. 'You may leave now and none will think the worse of you.'

'I am quite sure,' Anne replied. Her face was pale and she felt uneasy as they passed beneath an arch leading to some stone steps. 'I want so see Stefan. At least he will know that he has friends to help him.'

'I could have told him that,' Rob said but saw the determination in her. She would not be swayed, even though the sight of this place threw a chill into many a heart. 'He may not thank you for it, Anne. He is a proud man and will not want you to see him here.'

'I know he is proud, but he should know that I love him,' she said. 'Whatever happens in the future, he will have that to remember.'

The gaoler had come out to meet them. He beckoned them inside out of the chill breeze that blew across the Thames. Rob handed him a small leather purse and he weighed it in his hand, smiling at the clink of the gold coins inside.

'The young lady may go in,' he said. 'You will wait outside the cell for her, sir. Have you brought anything with you?'

'Only food and wine,' Anne said showing him her reed basket. 'You may look inside if you wish. I did not bring a weapon, for Stefan would not try to escape. My lord is innocent of the crime he has been charged with and will answer in court.'

'They are all innocent to their loved ones,' the gaoler muttered but quietened as he saw Rob's scowl. 'Well, you are not the first to bring him food. He has been well cared for. Ask him if you will, I have supplied all his needs.'

'Except for his freedom,' Anne said. 'But that is not yours to grant, I know.'

At the top of the stairs there was a wooden door studded with iron and fastened with bolts. At the top was a little grill so that it was possible to look inside and Anne could see a faint light showing through. She shivered as the damp chill of the ancient stones struck her and wished that she had thought to bring an extra blanket for Stefan. In a place like this it would always be cold.

For a moment a picture of Stefan in the gardens at the chateau came to her mind and she blinked as the tears stung. He had been so sure of himself, such a strong powerful man and the thought of him being shut up in this terrible place was almost too hard to bear. She pushed her weakness aside. Stefan would not want to see her weep. She waited as the gaoler unlocked the door and held it for her, allowing her to walk inside. Stefan was seated at a table, his head bent as he wrote industriously.

'Stefan…my lord…'

His head came up, his shoulders stiffening. He flipped his work over so that the blank side was face up and then turned to look at her, an expression of incredulity in his eyes as he rose to his feet. He stood by the table, making no attempt to come to her.

'Why have you come here? This place is not fit for you, Anne.'

'I wanted to see you.' She went forward, placing her basket on the table. Still he did not move. It was as if he were turned to stone, stunned by her presence in his cell, almost angry that she had come. She felt the pain lance through her, and tears stung her eyes. Pride aided her. She would not let her tears fall, even though her heart felt as if it were being torn from her body. 'I know you are innocent of the crimes they accuse you of, Stefan. My father…Harry, the Earl of Gifford…they are all trying to help you.'

There was no change in his frozen expression. 'Why should they do that, Anne? I hardly know your father and the others are strangers to me. Why should they help or believe in a man they do not know?'

'Because I ask it of them,' Anne said with a quiet dignity. Her love shone from her like an incandescent flame. 'You are my promised husband, Stefan. If I had not been stolen away, we should have been married.'

'Perhaps it was better that the marriage did not take place…' His gaze was flinty, distant, as if he were determined to keep her at a distance.

'No! How could you say that?' Anne asked and her lovely face reflected her hurt. 'You must know that I would wed you now—here in this place—if you wished it?'

'Perhaps you would, but I would not permit it,' Stefan said, though his expression relaxed a little. She had such fire, such passion! It was no wonder that she haunted his thoughts day and night. He longed to take her in his arms, to smell the intoxicating perfume that was hers alone, but held himself by his iron will. She should not be here! 'Do you think I would wish that fate on you, sweet Anne? If I die as a murderer, stripped of all honour—would you wish to carry my name?'

'Yes, for I shall never believe such tales,' she said. 'I know you are innocent. You would not murder a woman in cold blood.'

'No, though I am in part to blame,' Stefan said. He waited, watching for that shining belief to fade from her eyes, but it did not falter. 'The lady Madeline told me she was in dire need of help. I went with her, for she said that she had something to show me that I must see. When we were alone she threw herself at me and ripped her gown. She began to cry rape and accuse me of abusing her. The door opened so swiftly that I knew it must have been planned. I had no weapon, but I pushed the lady away from me. She staggered…and Sir Hugh thrust his sword into her. I am not sure whether it was an accident, though I believe he may have planned to murder her from the beginning and blame me. If we were both dead, there would have been no one to gainsay him. However, Hassan had been uneasy and he came looking for me. He threw me my sword and he killed Sir Hugh to stop him killing me. Some of Sir Hugh's men came in answer to his dying call and we fought our way out.'

'You need not have explained—I knew that you were not guilty of murder,' Anne said and moved towards him, her eyes shining with love. 'You must tell the court what truly happened.'

'Hassan would almost certainly lose his life in my stead,' Stefan said, 'and I might still be accused of complicity. I will not take the chance. I am innocent and I am willing to prove it in trial by combat.'

'But supposing the King will not allow it?' Anne said.

'Then I must take my chances,' Stefan said and smiled at her. 'Perhaps it will not come to a trial—there can be no proof since I killed no one that day.'

'But you must answer the charges,' Anne said. 'If you do not…' She caught back the sob of despair that rose to her lips. 'The punishment is death. You must know that.'

'I am aware that I could be beheaded for a crime I did not commit,' Stefan agreed. 'But I have proof that Cowper hath always been my enemy, and perhaps if there is any justice in Henry's England I shall be allowed to walk free, clear of the stain that Cowper has lodged against my character.'

Anne's eyes filled with tears despite her determination not to weep. 'What shall I do if you die?' she whispered. 'Do you not know that it will break my heart?'

'I am sorry for it,' Stefan said, his voice grating harshly. His face was stony, giving no sign of any inner turmoil. 'I beg your forgiveness if I have brought you pain, Anne. You are very young and beautiful. Other men, more worthy than I, will love you, and in time you will forget me and find happiness.'

'You must think me a shallow, silly girl, and therefore cannot love me,' Anne said and blinked back her tears as her pride came to the rescue. 'Forgive me, my lord. I shall go.'

'Yes, it is best that you do,' Stefan said. 'It would have been better if you had not come here.'

Anne turned and walked to the door, head high, shoulders squared. Well, she had had her answer from

Stefan's own lips. She had been a fool to come here! He did not love her enough.

Stefan turned away as the gaoler opened the cell door and let her out, the heavy door creaking and then clanking as it was firmly shut and locked. His body was stiff with tension as he sat down again, and only a little nerve at his temple gave any sign of the extreme emotion he was feeling. It had taken all his strength of will not to call her back, to take her in his arms and kiss her until she clung to him, yielding as he knew she would once their lips met.

He wanted her so much that it felt as if he were being ripped apart, but it was best that she should be angry with him. Anne must learn to forget him, forget anything she had ever felt for him, because he believed it was likely that he would die quite soon.

Cowper was a powerful enemy. Stefan had tried his best to bring him to justice in the lawful way, but it would have been better if he had simply killed him and returned to France. Henry's justice would not have followed him there, and he would have been free to live as he pleased.

Yet even as the bitter thoughts tumbled in his mind, Stefan knew that he would not have gone to Anne with blood on his hands. He had taken the way of law and justice because he loved her, and if it was his destiny to die for it, then he would do so—but she must be free of the stain. He loved her too much to take advantage of her generosity.

Anne was sitting with her sister and mother in the parlour when her father came in. She knew from his expression that he had news and her heart quickened.

Her sewing set aside, she got to her feet and stared at him, eyes wide and fearful.

'You have news?' she said.

'The trial is set for tomorrow,' Rob told her. 'Do not look so anxious, daughter. The outcome may be better than you think. A letter and some evidence that de Montfort may have been cheated of his birthright have come to light.'

'That would be justice,' Anne said. 'Yet it does not clear him of the charge of murder.'

'No, that is true,' Rob said. 'However, there is no proof that he did kill the lady Madeline or Sir Hugh either. Henry sent a letter commanding Lord Cowper to come to London and provide proof of the charges he laid, but he has not come. If he does not appear before the court, it will be up to the King to decide whether or not the charges are valid.'

'Will that help Stefan? He has been branded a mercenary and a murderer. Who will persuade the King to his cause? He has refused to do more than proclaim his innocence.'

'Has he told you what truly happened that day?' Rob's gaze arrowed on her face. 'If you know, you must tell me, Anne.'

'He was asked to help the lady Madeline, but when he went to her chamber she tore her gown and cried rape. Her uncle rushed in at once, for it was a trap. Stefan threw her towards Sir Hugh and he killed her. He would have killed Stefan, too, had not…someone else arrived. He killed Sir Hugh in fair fight and he gave Stefan his sword. Together they fought free of Sir Hugh's men.'

'Does he have a witness for this?'

'Not one he will call,' Anne said. 'He says that this

person would die in his stead and he might still be con-demned as an accessory, so he will not speak.'

Rob nodded and looked thoughtful. Anne's revelation brought new respect for Lord de Montfort. 'The man is proud and a fool, but honourable,' he said. 'Well, we must see what can be done. If Lord Cowper does not appear to put his charges in person, everything depends on the King.'

Anne's face was very pale. She had wept herself to sleep the night after her visit to the Tower, but since then she had been thinking hard and she had come to much the same decision as her father.

Stefan was proud, too proud to allow her to sacrifice herself for his sake, just as he refused to let Hassan testify. It must be for this reason that he had sent her away. His words denied her and yet something in his eyes had told her that he did not mean them. She clung to the thought that he loved her even though he would not say it.

'We are bidden to the court this evening,' Rob told his wife and daughters. 'I know that Anne is in no mood for merriment, but we must not offend his Majesty. Tomor-row, a man's life may hang on the whim of a King, and though I believe Henry a fair man, he can be stern. So we shall go to this masquerade this evening and smile— and that includes you, Anne.'

'Yes, Father, if it is your wish,' she replied.

She returned to her sewing, head bent as she con-centrated on her work. The knowledge that Stefan must stand his trial soon had hung over her like a dark cloud. She had no wish to dance or feast, but she knew that she had little choice. She must behave in a dignified way and keep her tears for the privacy of her bedchamber.

She loved Stefan, but he had rejected her love. He had sent her away and that hurt, but she would not lose all hope. She would pray for a miracle, and perhaps one day they would be together again.

'You look very beautiful this evening,' Comte De Vere said when they met that evening at the royal banquet. 'Indeed, you grow more lovely every time I see you, Mistress Anne. I hear there is to be dancing this evening. I hope that you will dance with me?'

'Thank you, you are kind, sir,' Anne said. 'But I am not sure that I wish to dance.'

Comte De Vere frowned. 'You must know that I have a great admiration for you, Mistress Anne. I had hoped that you felt something for me?'

'I am grateful for all that you did for me when I was ill,' Anne told him. 'I hope we may remain friends, sir, but…' She faltered, for she hardly knew how to answer him without offence.

'I suppose you imagine de Montfort still means to wed you. I should have thought your pride would forbid it, Anne. The man is nothing but an adventurer—a mercenary.'

'Whatever he is, I love him,' Anne said with a hint of defiance. 'Even if he dies, I shall always remember and love Stefan de Montfort.' She almost wished the words unsaid as she saw the flash of anger in his eyes. 'He plucked me from the sea and I should surely have died had he not found me, sir. I know you saved me, too, but…'

'I understand,' De Vere said with a stiff nod of his head. 'Well, you have made your choice, Anne. Please excuse me.'

Anne watched as he walked away. She felt a chill down her spine, because she knew he was angry. Her mother had warned her to be careful, but how could she have answered him otherwise? She had tried to answer him in a way that did not cause offence, but knew that he was offended. However, there was nothing she could do now to make things better. She had answered honestly, and she hoped he would appreciate her honesty when he had had time to think about it. Another woman might have chosen to flatter, even to wed for the wealth and consequence he could give her. Anne was not a dissembler, though when she caught him looking at her with cold eyes later that evening, she thought it might have been better had she answered in another way.

Watching Anne as she talked and laughed with her friends, Comte De Vere felt the anger fester inside him. Had she rejected him for someone worthy of her, he might not have resented her refusal to accept him as a suitor, but to be ignored in favour of de Montfort was an insult! If he did not end with his head on a block, something would be arranged. Cowper was a fool, and if what the man Marc had told him was true, a drunken sot. However, De Vere was a different man, and if de Montfort left the Tower alive, he would personally do what he could to see him dead!

He brooded over it for the rest of the evening, a malicious anger festering inside him. When he saw that Anne had joined her brother and his betrothed for a country dance where everyone joined hands, his anger intensified. She was a proud wanton and he was well rid of her! She would not be his wife, so be it!

However, he still wanted her and the desire to have

her—and to humiliate her—was strong. It was impossible to get near her for the moment, because she was surrounded by friends and family, but one of these times he would find her alone and then...

A smile touched his mouth as he thought of what he would like to do with the haughty Mistress Melford! He would teach her to mind her manners when she addressed her betters. By the time he had finished with her, no one would want her!

For the moment he had other business. He had come to England to discover what he could of certain matters relating to the King and Prince Harry's marriage negotiations, and would report what he suspected to his Spanish masters. The young prince was handsome, but arrogant. However, he should be encouraged to wed his late brother's wife.

As Comte De Vere left the main hall and walked towards the small courtyard where he had arranged to meet his spy, he was unaware that he was being followed.

Anne enjoyed her evening despite feeling uncomfortable every time the Comte De Vere's eyes were upon her. However, towards the end of the evening he disappeared. After he had gone, Anne felt at liberty to join in the dancing as she pleased. She had tried to refuse earlier, but Harry had insisted that she join him and Claire for the merry dance that everyone could take part in, whether they had a partner or not. Anne had found it impossible to refuse, for Harry had excellent news and his happiness was there for all to see. King Henry had given him permission to leave the court for four weeks so that he could marry and spend some time with his bride. That meant they would be leaving London on the day following Lord de Montfort's trial.

Anne wondered if Stefan would be free to accompany them to Melford. Would he wish to if he could? She was not certain, but her heart refused to accept that she meant nothing more to him than a life he had saved. She remembered their walks in the chateau gardens, and the way he had kissed her. When she thought of those kisses her whole body melted with longing and the desire to lie with him was strong. Surely he had felt something too! She could not believe that he was indifferent to her.

What would she do if the King's judgement went the wrong way and she was forced to live without him for the rest of her life? She tried not to think about it.

Anne spent a restless night tossing and turning in her bed, and when she did sleep her dreams were fretful and of Stefan.

She seemed to be running in a mist. Stefan was walking just ahead of her in the trees. The woods were dark and eerie and she was frightened, but for Stefan, not herself. She could see him and she called to him over and over again, but either he did not hear her cries or he would not listen. He just kept on walking, going further and further away from her.

She woke crying his name, to find her mother bending over her, the light of a candle falling on her face.

'You were crying out in your sleep, Anne,' Melissa said, looking at her in concern. 'Were you worrying about tomorrow?'

'Yes, for I do not know what I shall do if the King does not set Stefan free,' Anne said. 'I love him so,

Mother. I know he loves me, even if his pride will not let him admit it.'

'I do not know whether to love or hate him,' her mother said with a wry smile. 'If you love Stefan, I must welcome him to our family, but he has caused you so much pain, my dearest.'

'Is pain not a part of loving?'

'Yes, it is,' Melissa admitted. 'Your father and I suffered much for our love, and it has been the same for you, Anne. Perhaps because you are so like Rob. You have his pride, but also his spirit. I know that once you truly love, it will be for ever.'

'Yes, it will,' Anne told her and frowned. 'Comte De Vere made his intentions plain last night. I was obliged to tell him that I did not think of him in that way, and I fear it made him angry.'

'I am sorry for that,' Melissa told her. 'He is an arrogant man. I felt it at the start, even though it was because of him that we found you again. I know that we have much to thank him for as a family, but I should not have liked to think of you becoming his wife.'

'It will not happen,' Anne said. 'He looked at me coldly several times and it made me uncomfortable. I was pleased when he left.'

'I saw him just before we left,' Melissa said. 'He may have been absent for a while, but he did not leave the palace until after we did.'

'Oh…then he will have seen me dancing with others after I refused him.' Anne grimaced. 'I believed he had gone. He must think me ill mannered and be pleased that I refused to wed him.'

'We must hope that he feels that way,' her mother said. She smiled and pressed Anne's hand as it lay on the coverlet. 'It is good news that Harry has permission to come home for the wedding, it is not? He might have married here, of course, but I should like the wedding to be at home after all. Claire is so happy. She is a lovely girl and will make your brother a good wife.'

'Yes, she will,' Anne agreed. 'I love her as a sister and I am glad you will have her at home some of the time, Mother.'

'If you leave us to live in France, we shall miss you,' Melissa said. 'However, if it is for your happiness I shall not complain—and it will be a comfort to me to have Harry's wife, for I believe she may spend at least some of her time with us.'

'She will not wish to remain in London when Harry is on business for the King,' Anne said. 'If Stefan asks me to marry him and we go to France…I am sure that we can visit each other occasionally.'

'Yes, perhaps,' her mother said. 'Do you think you can rest now, dearest? Or shall I make you a tisane to help you sleep?'

'I think I shall rest easier for our talk,' Anne said. 'Father told me that things might turn out better than I hoped and I must pray that he is right.'

'You have three influential men willing to stand for Lord de Montfort in the court. If he is innocent of the charges, as you believe, then I am sure justice must prevail. I have found Henry fair, if a stern man and sometimes harsh.'

'Yes, I pray that justice will prevail,' Anne said and leaned forward to kiss her mother goodnight. 'I love you and my family, but Stefan means everything to me.'

'I understand,' Melissa said. 'Goodnight, dearest. Try not to worry too much.'

Anne nodded, lying back against her pillows with a sigh. There was no sense in worrying, for there was nothing she could do. She would not be present at the trial and would have to wait as best she could for her father to tell her the outcome when he returned.

Chapter Nine

Stefan woke as the first light began to filter in through the small grating that let air into his cell, but little daylight. He had put the finishing touches to the letters and papers he had prepared before he slept. He had written a letter to Anne, telling her that he loved her, and a will leaving much of what he owned to her. Chateau de Montifiori was to go to Hassan with the provision that he, Ali, Eric and Sulina had a home for life, as well as others he had taken into his service. He had also written down all the facts that he knew about his brother's murder and his father's humiliation at the hands of Lord Cowper.

If he was permitted, he would lay the evidence before the King. Hassan had the letter from Lord William de Montfort, and the papers that showed someone had tried to copy William de Montfort's signature. He knew that without a witness it was not proof, but surely he had enough to make the King doubt those false charges? If Cowper had been involved in the murder of Stefan's younger brother and had schemed to rob Lord William of his estate, it showed cause why he would conspire with Sir Hugh Grantham to have Stefan killed. And there were the other attempts made on his life. Of course, there were no independent witnesses of these things, and therefore no proof. If he were permitted, he would speak and the King would make his own conclusions.

Hassan had visited Stefan the previous day, begging him to allow him to testify that it was he who had killed Sir Hugh to prevent the man murdering Stefan. Stefan had refused, making him promise that he would not intervene in this way.

'I shall be judged by my peers,' he told Hassan. 'Let them believe my word or condemn me to a murderer's death. Even if they believed that you killed Sir Hugh, they might still blame me—and you would certainly hang, my friend.'

'Rather I than you,' Hassan said, a nerve flicking in his cheek. 'I owe my life to you, my lord.'

'And you will thank me by obeying me,' Stefan said, a look of steel in his eyes. 'If you try to speak, I shall deny you. I will stand or fall by the truth—or as much of it as I am prepared to tell.'

Hassan had gone away, looking grave. Stefan knew he thought the worst, and at times he felt close to despair, for his last attempt to gain a fair hearing had met with refusal. If the King believed Cowper's charges, he might be summarily dismissed. His expression hardened as the gaoler came to tell him it was time to leave.

He had donned an extra shirt—the wind was chill out and he would not wish to shiver and appear afraid if he were taken straight to the block. Stefan wished to live, but if he must die he would do so with honour and as bravely as he could.

One last thought of Anne almost unmanned him, but he put her from his thoughts. She was young and beautiful, and she would find another lover. Perhaps she already had, because she must hate him after the way he had dismissed her love.

'Lord Melford.' The page approached Rob as he stood waiting with the Earl of Gifford and Sir Harry in the outer chamber. 'There is someone who wishes for an audience with you.'

'I am busy for the moment.' Rob dismissed him impatiently with a wave of the hand. 'We shall be called to testify at any moment.'

'This…person says that his evidence has bearing on the case and that you should listen to him.'

Rob's eyes narrowed. 'Person—what manner of man is he that you describe him so?'

'There are three of them,' the page answered. 'One of them is dark skinned…like a Saracen, and one is an Arab doctor…'

'Indeed?' Rob frowned and turned to Andrew. 'Sir, I may be delayed for a few minutes. If the King should summon you, please go in without me. Say that I shall not be long delayed and beg his pardon.'

'Yes, of course,' Andrew said. 'Be careful, sir. This may be a trap.'

'I think I may know one of them and perhaps the doctor as well… He could be the one who treated Anne when she was ill. However, I have no idea why they have come or why they left it so late to present their evidence.'

'Go quickly, then,' Andrew said. 'We shall do our best to stall things and we must hope that you have not been waylaid for the wrong reasons.'

The pageboy led Rob from the room, indicating a small chamber where the men had been asked to wait. 'They are in there, sir. Do you wish me to wait? Or fetch an officer of the court?'

'No, I am in no danger,' Rob told him. 'Go about your duties, lad, for you may be needed.'

He hesitated, and then went into the small chamber where three men were gathered. He realised that he did indeed know two of them, though the third was a stranger.

'What may I do for you, sirs?' he asked. 'Speak swiftly, for I may be called at any time.'

Anne walked restlessly in the courtyard. The church bells had just tolled ten times and her stomach clenched with nerves. It must be almost time! They would be gathering in the King's council chamber for Stefan's trial at any moment now. Her mouth felt dry and she was racked with agony as she wondered what was going on.

She wished that she might have been there to hear the evidence, but it was a meeting that only nobles could attend. The King was supreme judge, and would decide whether Stefan was guilty of the crimes he stood accused of after hearing the evidence, though his peers might be called upon for their opinion of his innocence or guilt.

Would they find him guilty? Why would he not let Hassan tell them the truth? Why must he be so proud and so stubborn? If the King would not listen, Stefan could be executed this very day! Her thoughts were unbearable and the tears stung her eyes.

Anne shivered in the chill wind. The summer had fled and it was autumn now. She did not look forward to the winter ahead if the news were bad, for she did not know how she would face it.

'Anne, come in, my love,' Melissa called to her from the house. 'Catherine is here and we are about to have some refreshment. You do no good out there by yourself.'

Anne turned obediently and walked to the house. She was cold and would like some warm, mulled wine to sustain her while she waited. Her family were gathering, folding her into their embrace, and she knew that whatever happened, their love would always be there for her. She lifted her head, knowing that she must be brave, even though her heart cried out to Stefan.

'Come back to me, my love. Come back to me...'

'Stefan, Lord de Montfort, how do you plead to the charges against you? You are charged that you did wilfully murder the lady Madeline and Sir Hugh Grantham, and that your act was intentional and malicious.'

'No, sir, I did not kill either the lady or Sir Hugh,' Stefan replied. 'I am innocent of the charge and I would like to bring charges against Lord Cowper. He conspired with Sir Hugh to murder my brother and he robbed my father of his estate—'

'Silence! You are here to answer the charges against you and this other business hath naught to do with the murders of the lady Madeline and her uncle Sir Hugh Grantham.'

'I beg to differ,' Stefan said. 'These false charges have

been brought against me because Lord Cowper fears to be exposed as a murderer and a cheat. I challenged him to meet me in single combat so that we could prove by ancient law on whose side right lies—'

'You will be silent, sir!' The officer of the court was growing red-faced and indignant.

'I have the right to be heard, and my defence is that the charges are malicious and need no answer.'

King Henry held up his hand, as the officer would have begun again. 'The charges you bring against Lord Cowper may be heard at another time if it so pleases us, Lord de Montfort. You must answer to your peers for the charges today, and I am minded to be lenient, as I have heard good things of you—but you must answer the charge.'

'My answer is that I am innocent. The lady was killed by her uncle and that is all I am prepared to say on the matter.'

'That is insolence,' the court officer exclaimed angrily. 'You must tell the court all you know of the affair or be presumed guilty.'

'No, that is not the law.' The Earl of Gifford stepped forward. 'I have looked into this matter. Lord de Montfort left England under a cloud some years ago, but he was not guilty of the crime of which he was then accused. I have in my possession a letter from his late father exonerating him of all blame in the murder of his brother, and I have signed testaments to the good nature and honesty of Lord de Montfort.'

'We are not here to try Lord de Montfort on an old murder.'

'I am aware of that,' Andrew said. 'But there was a miscarriage of justice then and we must not allow it to happen again. This man was robbed of all that should have been his by an enemy. It may be that the same enemy is trying to destroy him again by bringing more false charges.'

The King held up his hand. 'Because I love you, Andrew, I shall allow your testimony to stand. We shall accept that Lord de Montfort is innocent of the earlier crime and that he is thought to be of good character, but we need him to tell us what happened that day.' Henry's piercing gaze travelled round the assembled courtiers. 'Is Lord Cowper in court? He may step forward and tell us of his proof. If he has witnesses, they must testify to what they saw.'

'Lord Cowper has not answered the summons to attend, Sire.'

'Indeed...' The King frowned. 'Do we have any witnesses in this case—anyone who is willing to say one way or the other what occurred on the day the lady Madeline was murdered?'

'Sire, I have a new witness in the case,' Rob said, his voice ringing through the chamber as he strode in, accompanied by three others. 'He swears that he was there that day and saw what happened.'

'No!' Stefan cried. 'I shall not allow it!' He had seen Hassan and feared the worst for his friend.

'You will be quiet, sir,' the King said. 'Or we shall try this case without you. You had your chance to speak and refused; now let us hear this new witness.'

Stefan looked and saw Hassan standing with Ali and a man he did not immediately recognise. He caught Hassan's eye and shook his head, but then saw that it was the stranger who was walking forward to take the Bible in his hand.

'By what name are you known, sir?'

'I am known as Fritz, my lord. I have none other, for I was a bastard born, and though I know the man who got me on my mother, he has never acknowledged it.' A Bible was held out to him and he took it in his right hand.

'Do you swear by this book and all you hold dear to speak the truth and only the truth, and may God strike you down if you lie?'

'I so swear,' Fritz said. 'I was in the service of Lord Cowper until recently. He sent me to witness what happened the day that it was planned to murder Lord de Montfort.'

'You say the plan was to murder Lord de Montfort—how is this?'

'The lady Madeline hated Lord de Montfort because she believed he had killed his younger brother. Her sister Anna was betrothed to Gervase de Montfort and when he was killed she drowned herself in the river. When it was suggested to the lady Madeline that she could lure Stefan de Montfort into a trap so that he could be killed, she agreed—she wanted revenge for her sister.'

'How do you know this?'

'I was there when they planned it between them, Sir Hugh and Lord Cowper. I have heard them plot many things over the years. They were wicked, evil men, sir. I saw them prey on an old man as his mind weakened and force him to sign his birthright away, and when he resisted they hit him until he lay unconscious. He would not sign and in the end Lord Cowper signed the deed himself. He made me witness it as well as Sir Hugh.'

'You saw him do it?'

'Yes, Sire.' Fritz looked at the King. 'He copied it out

many times before he was satisfied and discarded the wasted papers. I took them and kept them, and I took Lord William de Montfort's last letter to his son so that it should not be destroyed.'

'And where are they now?'

'Hassan has them, Sire.'

'I have them here, Sire,' Hassan said and stepped forward. 'I was there the day Sir Hugh killed the lady Madeline. He then tried to kill my lord, who was unarmed. I had followed them, because I suspected a trap. It was not the first time someone had tried to murder Lord de Montfort. He did not murder Sir Hugh, for he had gone there unarmed and had no sword until I took it to him. It was I who defeated Sir Hugh in a fair fight to protect the life of a good man.'

'Hassan! You fool!' Stefan cried. 'My best of friends…you had no need…'

'So you admit that you killed Sir Hugh.' The officer of the court beckoned to some palace guards, who started forwards, but stopped as the King stood. 'He has admitted his guilt, Sire.'

'If he speaks truly, he is guilty of a brave act to save a friend,' Henry said. 'If Lord de Montfort was lured by a foolish woman to his death, then he is the innocent party here. If Sir Hugh killed her by accident, it was unfortunate, but if he then tried to murder a fellow nobleman, he broke the law of this land. I do not approve of men settling their affairs by violence. I shall not have it, for it leads to division and weakness. England needs to be united and strong. We have enemies enough without squabbling amongst ourselves!'

'Your Majesty speaks truly. Shall I have the Saracen arrested?'

'He is free to leave this court, for it was not his quarrel. He fought to save a friend. However, my judgement is that he should leave England at once and return to his home, wherever that may be. If he returns, he may be arrested as an enemy of England. Please escort him from this court.'

'Go home, Hassan,' Stefan called. 'You have done all you can for me. Take care of the others.'

Hassan inclined his head, bowed to the King and then turned and walked from the court. The King turned to look at Stefan, an expectant hush falling over the assembled courtiers.

'It is our opinion that Lord Cowper maliciously lied. We shall study the papers placed as evidence and rule on the matter in due time. And Lord Cowper is to be arrested and brought before us here to answer various charges brought today. In the meantime, Lord de Montfort is cleared of the crime of murder—do all those gathered here agree?'

A chorus of 'Aye' rang out on all sides, for few would have thought of disagreeing even if they saw the matter differently.

'You will not be returned to the Tower, Lord de Montfort,' the King said. 'However, until I have had time to study the case further, I order you to remain in London. You will attend the court and I shall expect you to behave in a manner befitting an English gentleman. Until I give you leave, you may not leave this country. Do you give me your word that you will abide by my decision in these matters?'

Stefan hesitated, then bowed his head. 'I give you my word, Sire—and I thank you. May I be excused now? I would speak with Hassan before he leaves the palace.'

Henry waved his hand. 'Go, then. This council is dismissed until I summon you again.'

Stefan bowed and waited until the King had swept out. He then turned and hurried from the council chamber. He was afraid that Hassan would have left, but discovered him standing with the Earl of Gifford.

'I thank you, sir, for your good offices,' Stefan said and inclined his head to the Earl. 'I believe you have some influence with the King and he listened to you.'

Andrew smiled. 'I did what I could, but your own friends supplied the missing link. I am not sure that you would have been believed without the testimony of this man and Lord Cowper's man.'

'Hassan, you fool,' Stefan said and clapped him on the shoulder. 'You should not have spoken—but I do thank you for what you did.'

'It was no less than you would have done for me,' Hassan said, a slight smile on his disfigured mouth. 'When Ali told me that Fritz would testify against Lord Cowper, I knew that I must speak, too—even though you had forbidden it.'

'I thank God that Henry believed you both,' Stefan told him. 'You must go back to France. I need you there to take care of things. The others need you, Hassan.'

'We all need you,' Hassan replied and frowned. 'If the King returns your father's estate to you, will you stay here? It is your birthright and your home.'

'I am not certain,' Stefan said. 'That may depend on someone else. I have to speak to Anne as soon as I can. I do not deserve that she should love me, Hassan, but I believe she does. I sent her away when I thought I should die in disgrace, but if she will forgive me I shall ask her to be my wife. Where we live is for my wife to decide.

However, I shall not sell the chateau. It will always be your home—and the others may live there if they wish or join me. Perhaps in time Henry may relent and you could return, if Anne wishes to stay here.'

Hassan inclined his head. 'She loves you, and it is right that she should choose—but I could not live here. Men of my religion are not welcome in this country. In France they have left us alone thus far, but if you stay here I may go back where I came from.'

'That is your choice,' Stefan told him. 'We shall meet again before then, but I hope you will decide to stay with the others—they need you.'

Hassan inclined his head, but said no more. Stefan touched his shoulder once more, then watched as he walked away. He would be sorry if Hassan decided to return to the East, but he could not ask him to stay, for he did not know what the future held.

'Well, sir,' Andrew said, breaking the silence. 'Will you come back with me to Lord Melford's house? I know there are some ladies who are most anxious to hear the outcome of this trial.'

'Yes, thank you, I shall,' Stefan said, turning to him. 'I believe I owe my freedom to you and Lord Melford.'

'Anne's brother played his part, too. Henry is a busy man and he does not like nobles who break his laws. He will not have feuding, as it was in the old lawless days. He is right to break the power of the barons if he can, for otherwise they quarrel and make war upon each other instead of England's enemies. With the discovery of the New World, Spain grows more powerful. We are but a small island, though we hold our own amongst powerful neighbours. We cannot afford to have Englishman warring against Englishman.'

'You are right,' Stefan said. 'Cowper recently tried to capture and to kill us when we were out riding, and then his men broke into my home and stole something precious to me.' His expression darkened. 'I care not that he has wished me dead, and it is too late to right the wrongs done to my family—but for what he did to Anne I would like to see him dead.'

'Take care Henry does not hear you say that,' Andrew said. 'He would have you back in the Tower and keep you there until Cowper is brought to justice.'

'You need not fear,' Stefan said and smiled wryly. 'I had my chance to murder him if I wished. When it came I did not take it, because I thought of an innocent lady and did not wish to go to her with blood on my hands.'

Andrew smiled. 'You will have justice, de Montfort. Henry is no fool. Cowper will be brought to him and, if he is found guilty, he will die in the manner he had planned for you.'

'I can ask for no more, but even if he escapes I shall not spill his blood. I mean to ask Anne if she will marry me; if, as I hope, she says yes, I shall put the past behind me.'

Anne could not rest. She had put on her warmest cloak and gone out to the gardens once more, because she was too restless to stay indoors with her family. Her mother, sister and Claire were all excited about the wedding, which would take place in one week at Melford, the banns having been read in preparation some weeks earlier. They had done their best to temper their natural excitement, because they understood how Anne was suffering. Unable to sit with her needlework a moment longer, Anne had fetched her cloak and, refusing Claire's offer to accompany her, walked down to the river that wound its way past the garden.

She stood watching some swans swimming majestically on the brownish water. Overhead the skies were grey and threatening. There would likely be a storm before the day was out. Anne shivered, wrapping her cloak about her and feeling the chill of a bitter wind.

'Please let him come back to me,' she murmured to herself. Her eyes were gritty with the tears she had been holding back all day, because as the time went on she feared the news was bad. Feeling the first few drops of rain, she turned, knowing that she had been out here too long and her mother would be anxious.

As she walked towards the house, she saw a man emerge from the back entrance. He stood for a moment, as if searching for something, then began to stride in her direction. Anne's heart stood still before racing madly. She started to run to meet him.

'Stefan…' she cried, her throat catching with emotion. 'Stefan…'

He quickened his stride, breaking into a run at the last. As they came together, she stopped, breathing hard, staring at him uncertainly. What was he going to say to her? Oh, it did not matter! He was alive. He was free. Her heart swelled with happiness and she began to weep.

'Anne, my love,' Stefan said and reached out for her, catching her in his arms and holding her close. He looked down at her, the fire in his eyes making her tingle with anticipation as he bent his head to kiss her on the lips. 'My sweet Anne…can you forgive me for what I said to you when you came to the Tower?'

'There is nothing to forgive,' she said, her cheeks wet with the tears she allowed to trickle down her cheeks unashamedly. 'You sent me away because you thought you would die in that place, didn't you?'

'I believed I should be convicted of murder and executed as a common criminal,' Stefan said. He wiped the tears away with his fingers. 'I could not let you share my disgrace, Anne. Even now that I am cleared of all the crimes I was once accused of, I know that I am not worthy of you, my darling—but I am too selfish and I love you too much to give you up. I am asking you now if you will be my wife?'

'Yes...' Anne's breath expelled on a sigh. 'Oh, yes, Stefan. It is all I want. All I have ever wanted. You must know that I love you? I love you so much that I should have wanted to die had you not come back for me.' She smiled up at him, all her love and longing in her face. Her long golden hair tumbled about her shoulders, its fragrance wafting towards him, sensuous and enchanting. 'I will marry you as soon as it can be arranged.'

'I would that it could be immediately,' Stefan said and stroked her face with his hand. 'For me it cannot be soon enough, but my affairs are not yet settled, Anne. The King has cleared my name of the charge of murder, but he has not yet seen fit to return my father's estate to me. He wishes to consider the matter, and Lord Cowper is summoned to court to answer the charge of false accusation, murder and theft. I am to remain in London until his Majesty decides the matter and allows me to leave.'

'You must remain in London?' Anne's face clouded. 'We are leaving London in the morning. Harry and Claire want to be married at Melford now that he has been given leave of absence. I shall have to return home with them, Stefan.'

'Yes, of course, I understand that,' he said, and smiled as he saw her disappointment. He bent his head and kissed her softly on the lips. 'Do not let this temporary parting spoil your happiness, my love. We shall be together soon, and we have the rest of our lives to enjoy.'

'Yes, I know,' Anne said. She swallowed hard, knowing that she must be thankful for all she had been given. Stefan was alive. He was free and he loved her. She only had to wait a short time and they could marry.

'My sweet love. Forgive me. I would come with you if I could.'

'I know I must accept the King's will,' she told him. 'I shall go with my family and wait patiently, but every hour that we must be apart seems wasted, Stefan. Had I not been stolen away from you, we should already have been married.'

'I have not even laid that complaint against Cowper as yet,' Stefan said, 'though your father may have done so. I know that your father, and others of your family, have done much to help me and I am grateful to them.' He hesitated, then, 'If the King sees fit to restore my father's estate to me, would you wish to live there—or return to Chateau de Montifiori?'

'I want to be with you wherever you are,' Anne said. 'I shall live here if you wish it, but I was very happy at the chateau. I would ask only that something is done to make sure that no one can ever enter our gardens again without permission.'

'Hassan has ordered a wall built for this very purpose,' Stefan said. 'He has returned to France. The King banished him, because he killed Sir Hugh that day. It was not murder, for the fight was fair and he was protecting my life. However, the King has decreed that all such warring between the barons must cease. I believe that he has made progress in his aim to bring peace and that England is a safer place because of it.'

'But Normandy is warmer and I love your home,' Anne said. 'If your father's estate is restored to you, you must choose, my love. I shall be happy to live with you wherever you wish.'

'I wish our marriage could be at once,' Stefan said. 'I would relinquish all claim to my father's estate for the chance to be with you, Anne—but the King thinks I deserve some punishment for disobeying his law, even though the feud was not of my making. I must admit that I have wanted Cowper dead, and perhaps it was because he knew that I was bent on revenge that he tried to have me killed. For this crime I am kept kicking my heels at court.'

'I pray that the attempts on your life are over,' Anne said and smiled up at him. 'Kiss me again, Stefan. I have longed for this moment, and I can hardly believe that you are here with me.'

'I am here,' Stefan said. 'When his Majesty allows it I shall come to you and I promise we shall never be parted again.'

He bent his head, kissing her softly at first, the heat building between them as the kiss deepened and lengthened. Anne arched into him, feeling the burn of his desire, and the urgent need in him. She wanted so much to be his wife, to know the pleasure of lying close to him in their bed, but she knew that Stefan would never take advantage of her innocence. He would wait until his ring was on her finger. If only that could be tomorrow! She seemed destined to wait endlessly and that was hard for a girl of her quick, impatient nature.

A sigh left her as he released her. Stefan had no choice but to wait until the King gave permission for him to leave London. It might be only a few days or it might be some weeks. She would just have to wait as patiently as she could.

Stefan stayed with them that night, and Anne spent as much time with him as she could. Claire supervised the packing of her trunks so that she did not have to waste a moment of the precious time before they must part. They ate supper with Anne's family, but after that they were allowed to retire to a small parlour at the back of the house so that they could be alone to talk and plan their future.

Stefan had arranged that he would stay on in the house. He had some funds in England and he intended to visit the goldsmiths the next day and withdraw some of them so that he could purchase new clothes and gifts for his intended bride. He asked Anne what jewels she liked, but she smiled and shook her head, saying that she wanted only his love.

'You will be my wife, Anne,' he told her. 'I am a wealthy man whether or not the King restores my father's estate. When we are married, you will have all the clothes and trinkets you deserve.'

'You bought me cloth for gowns when we were at the chateau,' she reminded him. 'I did not even know my name, but you offered me yours. I was not sure then if you loved me—or if you offered because I had nowhere else to go?'

'I did offer because you had nowhere to go,' he replied and laughed as he saw her look of disappointment. 'But I loved you from the first time you woke up and looked at me. I wanted you then, and I was tempted to make you mine—but I loved you too much to ruin your chances of happiness. I did not think myself worthy of you, and I might not have offered for you had you not been alone in the world.'

'We should have lost so much if we had never met,' Anne said. 'I think it must be fate, as Ali says.'

'As Allah wills it,' Stefan said and laughed huskily. 'He told me that if you save a life, that life belongs to you and you must guard and protect that person all your life—and he was right.'

'He is a wise and clever man,' Anne said. 'We have much to thank him for, Stefan.'

'More than you know,' he replied. 'The man they found in the hut that you were taken to was near to death when my men brought him back to de Montifiori. Ali saved his life, and it was in gratitude for that that he gave evidence at my trial. We had some evidence, but without his word that Cowper and Sir Hugh had planned to murder me I might even now be back in the Tower, awaiting execution.'

'Then you must thank him properly,' Anne said. 'He may have been responsible for stealing me away, but he should be paid for his services to us.'

'And will be,' Stefan told her. 'I shall give him enough money to buy a house and land of his own.'

'Who is he?' Anne asked. 'What do you know of him?'

'He calls himself Fritz and gives no second name,

because he is a bastard—but Hassan told me he believes that he is the son of Lord Cowper.'

'Lord Cowper was his father—and yet he worked for him as a common soldier?'

'Yes, I believe that may be the case,' Stefan said. 'Cowper hath no legitimate son.'

'You would have thought he would acknowledge him and take him as family.'

'I dare say his mother was baseborn,' Stefan said. 'Cowper is arrogant and proud. He clearly thinks Fritz too low to be acknowledged as his son.'

'Yes,' Anne said thoughtfully. 'But it was as well for us that they fell out, was it not?'

'Yes, indeed,' Stefan replied. He smiled and kissed her once more. 'I think it is time you sought your bed, Anne. You have a long journey in the morning.'

'I suppose I must,' she said, still reluctant as she stood up. They faced each other, holding hands. 'You will come to me as soon as the King releases you?'

'The instant he releases me,' Stefan promised. He touched her cheek with his fingertips, both of them reluctant to say goodnight. 'Go now, my love. I would stay with you for ever, but we must part for a time.'

'Yes…' Anne sighed and then laughed at herself. 'I am greedy! Now I have so much, I want more.' She relinquished his hands and walked to the door, turning to look back at him once more. 'Until we meet again…'

'It will not be long,' Stefan said. 'Enjoy your brother's wedding, Anne. Very soon now it will be your own.'

'Yes.' She smiled at him. 'Very soon it will be our wedding.'

Anne had slept for a while, her mind content with dreams of the happiness that was to come in a few weeks, when the King allowed Stefan to leave court. However, she was up early and they had another short time together before they were forced to part.

Anne bore it as best she could, forcing herself to smile as she waved goodbye from the back of her palfrey. She knew that Harry's wedding to Claire was a joyous occasion for her family and she would not allow anyone to see how much it cost her to leave the man she loved behind. After all, she had been given much that she desired and it was only a matter of patience until she had all she could ever want.

Yet to ride away from Stefan was one of the hardest things she had ever done. It cut her to the heart, but she did not shed a tear, at least not while she was in company.

Anne was not alone in regretting the parting. Stefan had faced the truth when he was a prisoner in the Tower and uncertain of his future. He knew now that revenge meant nothing against the love he felt for Anne Melford. He no longer cared whether or not his father's estate was restored to him, and would have given it up willingly to be able to follow his love to her home immediately.

However, he understood that he had no choice but to obey the King. Henry was imposing this delay on him as a matter of obedience. He was being taught that he must not carry old quarrels into a feud that might end in bloodshed.

Stefan understood that he must attend court and play the part of a courtier, something that did not come easily to him. However, he would bend the knee and pledge allegiance if it were demanded of him in the hope that he would be given permission to leave and to go to Anne.

In the meantime, he would use his enforced stay in London to purchase the clothes he needed for court wear, and jewels for his bride.

'I know it is hard for you to leave Stefan so soon after his release,' Melissa told her daughter when they were home again. Anne had just come downstairs wearing her cloak, about to go for a walk to the village on an errand. 'I am proud of the way you have behaved, Anne. When you were younger you sometimes showed your displeasure too much, but you have learned to control that and I think it becomes the woman you are now.'

'Thank you, Mother,' Anne said and embraced her. 'It is true that I would not have left Stefan if it could be avoided, but I could not miss Harry's wedding. I do truly love Claire as a sister and I wanted to be here for the wedding.'

'Well, it is tomorrow,' Melissa said and smiled. 'We shall celebrate your brother's wedding for a few days, as is customary—but after that you could return to London with Catherine and Andrew.'

'Mother!' Anne stared at her in surprise, for she had not expected such an offer. 'How kind you are to offer it—but Stefan told me that I must wait here for him to come. He believed I should be safer here until he is able to arrange the wedding. I shall do as he asked; it is right and proper that I should.'

'Now I know that you do indeed love him!' Melissa teased, laughter in her eyes. 'He has achieved something I never could, for you were never as willing to oblige me.'

'Mother! I am sure I always did my best to obey you,' Anne said and then laughed as she saw the teasing expression in her mother's eyes. 'Well, perhaps not always. I may have been impatient and wilful as a girl…'

'But now you are a woman and I am proud of you,' her mother said. 'Go for your walk now, Anne. I have delayed you long enough.'

'Yes, I shall, for I promised to take this gown to a young mother in the village. She needs a new dress for her babe's christening and I thought she might have this one, for I do not wear it much.'

'It was one of your favourites once,' her mother said and nodded. 'But it was generous to think of her and you have my blessing.'

Anne smiled and went out. The air was chilly, but not yet bitter. She was happy to be walking in the fresh air, though she thought that she might prefer to be in Normandy before the worst of the winter snows began to fall. A little sigh escaped her, for she was not sure whether or not Stefan would have been released before then.

Anne was unaware of the eyes watching her or the jealous thoughts of the man who followed her as she walked as far as the village. It was an opportunity to take the revenge he craved and yet even as he hesitated, a horseman came trotting down the lane. He saw that it was the Earl of Gifford and drew back into the shelter of the hedgerows. It would be better to wait until the wedding was over, and then he would find a way to catch the haughty little bitch alone. He would teach her a lesson. By the time he'd finished with her she would be no use to any man.

He would have his way with the Melford witch and then make sure that de Montfort understood what had happened to her before he died. It would be sweet revenge. Once de Montfort was dead, he would make sure that the Chateau de Montifiori became his property.

Chapter Ten

'You look beautiful, Claire,' Anne said as she handed her a garter of blue silk. 'It is no surprise that Harry adores you. I am so pleased that you are to be my sister.'

'Thank you, dearest Anne,' Claire said and kissed her on the cheek. 'You have been kind to me from the first and I shall be happy when I can dance at your wedding, as you will at mine.'

'It should not be so very long,' Anne said and smiled, her eyes bright with excitement. 'I had a letter this very morning. Stefan says that the King's men have arrested Lord Cowper and he has been taken to the Tower to cool his heels for a few days before answering the charges against him. If things go well, it may only be a matter of weeks or even days before Stefan comes to me.'

'I pray that it is so,' Claire said and smiled, picking up the garland of flowers that her bridesmaids would use to lead her to the church. It was an ancient custom and a pleasant one. 'I think we should go down now, for I would not wish to keep Harry waiting at the church.'

'I think he would wait if it took you for ever to come,' Anne assured her. 'I have never seen Harry so happy, and it is all because of you, Claire.'

'Oh…do you truly think so?' Claire blushed, but looked pleased.

'Yes, I do,' Anne said firmly. She picked up the train of Claire's lovely gown, which was fashioned of dark cream silk embroidered with gold and suited her well. 'But you are right. We should not keep him waiting, for he will worry.'

Church bells rang out as the happy couple left the church, their family and friends following to shower them with dried rose petals. They ran laughing and trying to avoid the deluge. Everyone trooped behind as they made their way back to the house for the reception.

'Your sister-in-law looks very beautiful. She is a dutiful, pleasant girl and your brother will find her an obliging wife, I dare say.'

Anne turned to look at the gentleman who had addressed her, and a shiver ran down her spine as she saw the cold expression in his eyes. She wished he had not been invited to the wedding, but her father had thought it only right since he had been of such help to them.

'Yes, sir, I believe Claire is everything you say,' Anne said. 'However, she loves Harry and he loves her—that is what is important, is it not?'

'Is it?' The Comte De Vere's gaze hardened. 'I would have thought duty and breeding mattered more than love, which is hardly considered in most marriages. In France we do things in a more practical way.'

'Indeed?' Anne's eyebrows rose. 'I believe in this country, too, marriages are often a matter of property and family. However, my father would not have his children marry for such a reason, though of course Claire is an heiress.'

'I dare say your brother took that into account even if you did not,' the Comte said coldly.

'Perhaps, but I do not think it weighed with Harry,' Anne said. 'He might have married long ago had he thought only of wealth and consequence.' There was a hint of scorn in her tone, though she was not aware of it, but she saw the flash of anger in his eyes and knew that once again she had angered him. 'Forgive me, I must go to my mother. I think she needs me.'

Anne walked away, her head high. Comte De Vere's eyes followed her, glittering and dark with fury. The insolent chit would discover her mistake one of these days!

'And when do you return to France, sir?'

The Comte turned to glance at the man who had addressed him, his expression frozen as he saw that it was the Earl of Gifford. The interfering fool had robbed him of one chance to be rid of de Montfort!

'I believe my business here will be done in a few days,' he said. 'I have stayed longer than I intended already.'

'Anne is a beautiful girl,' Andrew replied. 'She knows her own mind and is not afraid to speak it. Her family hopes to see her wed soon—will you not stay for the wedding, sir? It is in part due to you that she is alive and able to marry.'

'Is it so certain that she is to marry?' the Comte asked.

'Yes, we believe it cannot be long delayed now. Lord de Montfort waits only for the trial of Lord Cowper and his release from the King.'

'Indeed? Then I wish her well, but I do not think I shall be here for the wedding.' If he had the chance, De Vere would see to it that Anne Melford never married!

'It is a shame that you must leave,' Andrew said and inclined his head before moving off.

Comte De Vere stood watching the merriment for a few minutes longer, then turned and left the house. He had put in an appearance, and when Anne met the fate he had in mind for her none would suspect him of being involved.

'I am sure you are wrong,' Rob said when Andrew finished telling him of his suspicions. 'He found her when she was ill that time and took her to his home. He allowed us to stay there and was everything that is generous.'

'I saw it in his eyes, in his manner as he watched her,' Andrew said. 'I believe he was minded to make an offer for her once, but something has changed. Now he hates her and will harm her if he gets the chance. Besides, I have heard things…' He shook his head as Rob looked at him questioningly. 'I am not certain yet. I am waiting confirmation before I speak—but in the matter of De Vere's intentions towards Anne, I am certain I am right.'

'She refused him when he offered for her,' Rob replied and frowned. 'Melissa warned her to be careful, for he is a proud man—but surely he would not bear a grudge against her for refusing his offer?'

'Some people harbour grudges,' Andrew said. 'I do not forget what happened to Catherine after we were wed. Lady Henrietta expected that I would make her an offer. When the King commanded that I marry Catherine, Henrietta assumed it was a marriage I did not want and that if my wife died I would turn to her. It was only vigilance and good fortune that saved Catherine from her spite.'

'She was deranged,' Rob protested. 'You are not suggesting that Comte De Vere would attempt to murder Anne?'

'I know that I saw him lurking yesterday as I met Anne on the way to the village, and I have sensed something in his manner. He is not a man I would trust, despite what he did to help Anne. If she hurt his pride...' Andrew shrugged. 'I believe he would bear watching, sir.'

'Yes, perhaps,' Rob said thoughtfully. 'I had hoped that she was out of danger now that Cowper has been arrested. I do not know what the King's judgement will be in the matter.'

'I have heard that Cowper is near to death,' Andrew said. 'I did not tell you earlier, for I did not wish to cast a cloud over the wedding, but he was not well when they arrested him...a matter of drink and neglect, I am told. When he was cast into the Tower, he fell in a gloomy state and developed some infection. It is doubtful that he will stand his trial.'

'I am not sorry for it,' Rob said. 'The sooner the whole regretful business is over the better. All I hope is that Henry will see fit to release de Montfort. It would be better if he were here to keep a watch over Anne. I cannot forbid her to leave the house and gardens, but, if you are right, she may be in danger.' He shook his head. 'I still find it difficult to believe that De Vere would do anything to harm her.'

'I may be wrong, of course,' Andrew said. 'I should have failed in my duty to you, as Anne's father, had I said nothing.'

'No, no, I am grateful to you,' Rob said. 'It is better to be forewarned. You may well be right. However, I believe De Vere returns to France soon and we shall be rid of him.'

'Yes.' Andrew looked thoughtful, but said no more. Rob was clearly sceptical about the suggestion that Comte De Vere bore Anne ill will, but Andrew felt it might be wiser to make certain arrangements with or without her father's knowledge. 'Yes, it would be a good thing if De Vere were to return to France.'

'I have learned that Lord Cowper has died of a fever in the night,' King Henry said, his expression giving nothing away. 'Without a trial, nothing can be proved either way. As he died intestate and has no issue, his estate and lands become the property of the Crown, and are in my gift.'

'Yes, Sire,' Stefan replied. 'I understand the law concerning this and I bow to your jurisdiction in the matter.'

'I have not yet decided what should be done with them,' the King said, eyes narrowed. 'I shall consult with others about the rights of this case and you will hear my decision in due course.'

'As your Majesty wishes,' Stefan said and inclined his head. 'Lord Cowper may have a bastard son, though I do not know if you would consider that he has a right to inherit a part of what his father owned. It is not my affair and I do not seek to influence your judgement. However, I would crave a boon of you in the meantime?'

'If it is reasonable, I see no reason why not.'

'I wish to leave the court and travel to the estate of Lord Melford on the borders of the Welsh Marches, where I would marry the lady Anne Melford, Sire.'

'You do not care for life at court?' Henry nodded. 'You have lived too long as an adventurer, I dare say. Well, sir, I trust that you have learned your lesson? I will not have petty quarrelling amongst my lords. Nor shall I allow disputes to be settled by the sword. If you have reason to fall out with your neighbour, you must settle within the law. If you must fight, contain it to the joust at feasting time. If you flout my wishes in this matter, you may discover that I am not so lenient next time.'

'I understand, sir,' Stefan said. 'Now that Lord Cowper is dead, I wish only to live in peace with my wife, here in England or in Normandy.'

Henry waved a hand in dismissal. 'You have my permission to leave the court, but not the country. You will remain in England until this matter is settled—do I have your word?'

'You have my word, Sire.'

'Go, then, and do not break it or you may feel my displeasure again.'

Stefan bowed and backed from the presence chamber. His heart was light as he left the palace. His arrangements were made and within hours he would be on his way to Anne…

The house felt empty now that all their guests had left. Ever since her return from France there had been several guests staying with them, but now they had gone and Anne felt restless. She had looked for a letter from Stefan, for she had heard that Lord Cowper had died in the Tower of a fever. Surely the King would release Stefan from his court duties now? He must know that the threat of a feud between them was at an end, and there could be no reason for more delay.

Anne would have liked to go riding or even walking, but the weather had been wet. Even had it been fine, there would have been no opportunity for her mother found her small tasks to do about the house every time she mentioned that she would like to go for a walk. She might have thought there was something odd about the way she was being kept at home, but her mind was pre-occupied with thoughts of Stefan.

However, on the fifth day after the wedding the rain stopped and the sun came out. Autumn had descended on them and the leaves were beginning to turn on the trees, but it was not truly cold as Anne put on her cloak and went downstairs.

'Are you going out, my love?' Melissa asked. 'I was thinking that you might help me make an inventory of the stores. We must start to make preparations for the winter.'

'Yes, of course,' Anne said. 'I shall be pleased to help you, but I have not been out for five days and, as it is fine, I thought I would like to walk for an hour or so.'

Her mother hesitated and then smiled. 'Yes, of course you may go out, but if I were you I should not leave the gardens, my love. I know it is fine now, but I think it may soon rain again.'

Anne wondered why her mother thought it might rain for there was not a cloud in sight as she left the house. However, since her mother seemed to need her, she decided to walk just as far as the wood that bordered their estate. She would be no more than an hour at most and then she could help with the inventory.

The air was fresh and the scent of the grass was strong after the rain of the past few days. Anne breathed deeply, feeling her spirits lift. She had needed this and she was smiling as she walked at a good pace. It was wrong of her to be impatient for Stefan's return, because she knew that he would come to her as soon as he could. Her mother had promised that there would be nothing to stop her marrying as soon as the banns were called and then…

'Good morning, Mistress Melford. I had almost given up hope of seeing you out walking.'

Anne caught her breath as the man stepped out in front of her. She had imagined that he would have returned to France long before this, and something warned her that she ought to be careful of him.

'Comte De Vere,' she said, her nails turning into the palms of her hands as she looked at him. His eyes glittered with something akin to hatred and she knew that he intended her harm. 'I am surprised to see you here, sir. We believed you had left us some days ago.'

'I have been waiting for you,' he said and smiled. His smile was menacing and sent shivers down her spine. 'I think we have a reckoning. You owe me something, mistress…'

'No!' Anne felt a thrill of horror shoot through her as she read his intentions in his eyes. 'Stay away from me! You will not touch me. I shall not allow it.' She instinctively understood what he intended and her heart raced as she looked frantically about her. She was too far from her home to call for help!

He made a move to grab her, but she dodged by him and began to run back in the direction of her home. She knew that he was pursuing her and her heart was racing. She ought to have stayed closer to the house as her mother bid her, but she had not dreamed that something like this might happen. She had been snatched from Stefan's home, but she was determined that nothing like that would happen again. She would try to outrun her pursuer if she could, but if he caught her… A little sob of fear escaped her. She would rather die than let him touch her!

If she could only reach her home she would be safe. Anne ran as fast as she could, but she knew that she had not shaken him off. He was close behind her and he would catch her if she stumbled, but she would not stumble. She would soon be near enough to call for help. One of the servants would see her and… She gave a scream as De Vere made a grab for her, catching her cloak. Anne struggled to free herself, but he had her fast. He grabbed her about the waist and pulled her close, his breath hot on her face. She struck out at him with her fists and he hit her across the face. She fought harder, scratching, kicking and biting him, and then he stuck out his leg, causing her to fall to the ground. In a second he was on her, clawing at her gown as he attempted to fumble beneath it.

Anne screamed for all she was worth, again and again as she clawed at his face with her nails, biting and scratching as she struggled against him. She was breathing hard, terrified, because she knew he must have his way in the end. He was too strong for her, and yet she continued to fight.

'Help me!' she screamed. 'Help me…'

From somewhere close by she heard an angry roaring sound. Even as she felt De Vere's hand thrusting between her thighs, she knew that someone was near. She heard a voice. Stefan's voice. And then the Comte was hauled off her and she heard shouting and grunts as the fight began. Pushing herself up from the hard ground, Anne saw the two men exchanging blows. She gave a sobbing cry as she watched them struggle, seeming equally matched for strength. She thought Stefan might have the upper hand. Then she saw something flash in the Comte's hand and realised that he had a dagger.

'He has a blade!' she cried. 'Stefan! Beware…'

She screamed as the Comte's knife struck home and blood spurted. Stefan had been wounded! Yelling, she scrambled to her feet and threw herself at the Comte's back in an effort to distract him, holding his arm with all her strength as he tried to strike Stefan again. He yelled and shrugged her off and she fell, screaming for help as she did so. Even as she tried to rise again, she saw men rushing towards them. At first she did not know who they were, and she thought they might be the Comte's men, but as they tried to pull him away from Stefan, she realised that they must be friends rather than enemies, though she did not know them by sight.

'Damn you!' The Comte was swearing, struggling and fighting like a madman, as they tried to disarm him. Then, as he continued to resist, something happened and his own knife was turned on him, sliding into his stomach. He screamed shrilly and sank to his knees, his hands covering the wound, and an oddly surprised look in his eyes as the blood trickled through his fingers. Then he fell forwards on his face, his body twitching for a few seconds before he lay still.

'Stefan!' Anne rushed to him as he rose to his feet. He had a wound to his side and he was unsteady as she reached him. Tears caught in her throat as she saw the crimson trickle through his fingers. 'Oh, Stefan, my love.'

'I am all right,' Stefan said, made a sighing sound and fainted into her arms. One of the other men rushed to help her support him and they lowered him carefully to the ground.

'It is a deep wound,' the man said, 'though I think not fatal. We shall carry him to your home, lady. I think he may be saved, but the other is dead.'

'He tried to…' Anne's breath caught on a sob. 'Stefan saved me, but he is hurt. We must get him home and then someone can fetch the Comte's body.'

Tears were streaming down her face as the men used their jerkins to form a kind of sling, each carrying a corner. They lifted Stefan and carried him, Anne flying in front of them to spread the news. Other servants were coming from the house, for the fight had been seen. Some added their hands to those already carrying the injured man so that the burden was eased. Others went to where the Comte's body lay slumped down on the ground. Anne was dimly aware that arrangements were being made to bring it back to the house, but her thoughts were only for Stefan. She was glad the Comte was dead! He had tried to murder Stefan and, because of it, she would have willingly struck the blow that killed him herself.

Her mother was in the hall as she entered. She saw Anne's distress and went to comfort her.

'Bring him this way,' Melissa said and then looked at the servants who had gathered in the hall to watch. 'Prepare the bed in the blue chamber, quickly! One of you must go for the doctor. There is no time to be lost.'

Anne ran on ahead of her mother. In the blue chamber, which was where Stefan was to have stayed when he came, the bed was made and ready. Anne threw back the sheets and turned to watch anxiously as the men carried Stefan in. His eyes were closed, but she heard a faint groan and knew he still lived. Her heart was aching and the tears burned behind her eyes, but she controlled her desire to weep and tried to remember what Ali had done for the wounded the day they were attacked by Lord Cowper's men.

'We must staunch the wound,' she said to her mother. 'I wish that Ali was here, for he is a wonderful physician, but we must do what we can for him.'

'It will be hard for you to watch. Are you strong enough to help me?' Melissa asked. Anne inclined her head. 'Very well, I shall cleanse the wound and we shall discover how bad it is. If it is deep, it must be cauterised. It is the only way, otherwise there will be infection.'

'I saw Ali do that to one of Stefan's men who was badly wounded,' Anne said. Her face was pale for she knew that the man had screamed in agony, and had suffered a great deal in the days that followed. 'If it is the only way, we must do it, Mother.'

'Do not despair, my love,' Melissa said. 'I do not have all the arts your Arab physician has, but I am skilled in the arts of nursing, for I have learned that the physicians are not always to be trusted and I care for most of our people myself.'

'I know you will do what you can for him, Mother,' Anne said and smothered a sob. 'I do love him so. I could not bear to lose him now.'

'We shall both nurse him,' Melissa said. 'If God is good to us, he will recover.'

'As Allah wills it,' Anne said and tears caught at her throat. She did so wish that Ali were with them so that he could advise her mother, but she knew that he had returned to France with Hassan. 'I pray that Stefan is strong enough to stand what he must.'

'He is a strong man, and has been wounded before,' Melissa said, as she drew away the bloodstained cloth that had covered the wound, revealing old scars. She glanced round at the silent servants. 'Fetch boiling water and clean linen—and my salves. And put the cauterising iron to heat…'

Anne sat by Stefan's bedside. It was late in the evening now and he was sleeping, for the physician had given her mother some strong medicine to help him fight the pain. However, after examining the patient, he said that he could not have done better if he had been there from the start. He commended Lady Melford on her work, left a tincture of poppy juice and departed, telling them that they must call him if the wound turned bad.

'I doubt we shall trouble him,' Melissa told her daughter after he had departed. 'I trust my instincts better than his for all his learning. He would tell us to bleed Stefan and after so much loss of blood I think it the last thing he needs. What he will need is patient nursing, my love—but I do not think you will shirk the task.'

'I shall sit with him for as long as he needs me,' Anne

said. Her eyes felt hot with tears, but she refused to let them fall. Stefan was everything to her and he needed her to be strong. It had hurt her to watch him writhe in pain as the white-hot iron seared his flesh, but she had not run from the room. Now all she could do was to watch over Stefan and pray.

He was tossing restlessly as the fever gained on him. Anne fetched cool water and bathed his forehead. He felt very hot, so she smoothed her cool cloth over his arms and chest, and he quietened a little, a sighing sound issuing from his lips.

'Father…forgive me for failing you…' he said, and then he gave a cry of distress, half-starting up from his pillows. 'Anne…Anne…where are you? Anne…'

Anne bent down and kissed him on the mouth. She smiled as she stroked his hair from his forehead. 'I am here, Stefan. I am with you. I shall always be with you, my dearest. I love you so…'

Her voice seemed to ease him, for he quietened, lying easily for a while until once again the fever gripped him. Anne fetched some of the mixture her mother had left for the fever, and managed to pour a little into his mouth. He fell into a deep slumber, and she felt the heat gradually leaving his body. After an hour or so he started to shiver. Anne touched him and discovered that he was very cold. She hesitated and then slipped under the covers with him, putting her arms about him and holding him close. His body became warmer and his restlessness ceased. She lay beside him, her face against his head, whispering words of love, kissing him and stroking him.

She was there, fast asleep, when her mother came in and found them some hours later. Melissa watched for a few minutes and saw that both her daughter and Stefan were sound asleep. She smiled and went away, leaving them undisturbed.

'How is the patient?' Rob asked as she crawled back to the warmth of their bed and snuggled into his body. 'Did you tell Anne she should rest? If she does not get some sleep, she will be ill herself.'

'Stop worrying, my dearest,' Melissa said and kissed him. 'Anne will do very well as she is, believe me—and as for our patient, I imagine he is already well on the way to recovery.'

Stefan lay with his eyes closed; he frowned as he became aware of the pain in his side. He put out a hand to explore what had happened and discovered the warmth of a soft body next to his, turning his head to look. A breath of surprise left his lips as he saw Anne's sweet face on the pillow beside him, her long lashes soft on cheeks that were flushed with sleep.

What had happened here? Were they married? Suddenly, the memory of her screams as that devil attacked her swept back and he remembered the fight that had ended with him being stabbed...in exactly the same place as he had been wounded some months earlier. It was no wonder that he had bled a great deal, though the thick scarring from the earlier wound might have deflected the blade and thus protected vital organs. He wondered what had made the pain so bad this time, and then remembered the hot iron being applied to his flesh. He had fought against it, and the doctor had given him some foul stuff that had rendered him unconscious.

Why was Anne in bed with him? Had she crept in to comfort him? He knew that he must have been restless in his drugged sleep, for he had dreamed vividly. A smile touched his lips, and he leaned towards her, brushing his lips over hers as she slept. Her eyes opened and she looked at him. Surprise, shyness, and then pleasure flickered across her face as she put out a hand to touch him.

'You are awake,' she said softly. 'Last night you were hot and I bathed you to cool you, but then you turned cold so I wanted to keep you warm but I must have fallen asleep.'

'You looked so lovely, but I should have left you to sleep,' he said. 'I thank you for your good care of me, my darling, but perhaps you should not be seen here. People may think ill of you, Anne. You are not yet my wife, though I hope you will be very soon.'

'I shall be your wife as soon as you are well. Besides, I do not care what others think,' she said. 'But I shall get up, because I am supposed to be nursing you, not sleeping in your bed.'

'If my side did not feel so sore, I would not allow you to sleep long,' Stefan said huskily and edged a little closer to her. His eyes caressed her as she sat up and bent over him, her long hair hanging down and brushing over his face. She kissed him sweetly. Her perfume was subtle, but enticing. Stefan reached up, his hand caressing her breast beneath the thin silk of her gown. Anne took his hand and slipped it inside the bodice of her gown, shivering with pleasure as his thumb smoothed over her nipple. 'Temptress, go now or I may risk opening my wound and ruining your reputation.'

Anne laughed, for she knew that he was past the time of danger. It was as her mother said—he had been wounded many times before and he was strong. The fear had been of infection, but the iron had burned that away and with good fortune he would not now suffer a fever.

'The sooner you are better and we can marry, the happier I shall be,' she said and threw back the covers. She had left the bed and was fetching him a glass of water when the door opened and one of the menservants entered with a tray of what smelled like her mother's good broth.

'Lady Melford sent me with some food, my lord,' Ian said. 'She says that if you eat your broth I am to return and help you wash and shave later—and she said that she wished to see you, Mistress Anne.'

'Yes, of course, I shall go to her,' Anne said. She smiled at Stefan. 'I shall return later to see how you are, my love.'

'Only if your mother permits it,' Stefan told her. 'I shall be well in a few days. Please tell your father that there is nothing to delay our wedding any longer. As soon as I can walk down the aisle, we shall be married.'

'I looked in at you in the early hours,' Melissa told her daughter in the privacy of her solar. 'I saw what you did, Anne, and I do not censure you—but you must leave most of the nursing to others now that Stefan is recovering. I shall not ban you from his chamber, for you have been apart too long, but you must be a little more careful, my love.'

'Stefan said much the same thing,' Anne said and smiled at her mother. 'Perhaps I was reckless, but he was so cold, and when I held him he slept so peacefully.'

'I shall say no more of it,' Melissa told her. 'I do not

forget what I felt when I was young and first in love with your father. Besides, you will marry soon.'

'Stefan says that he will be well in a few days, and I believe him. It is as you said, Mother—he is strong and has recovered from worse wounds before this, even though there was much blood loss.'

'Your father will see to the arrangements and you will be wed as soon as the banns are called. You must not be tied to the house, Anne. I tried to keep you indoors, because Andrew warned your father that that wicked man might try to harm you. It was Andrew's men that arrived and stopped De Vere from finishing what he had begun after Stefan was wounded. You have much to thank your brother-in-law for, Anne. Your father doubted the Comte De Vere would do anything unlawful, but it seems that Andrew was right.'

'The Comte was angry because he thought I had slighted him,' Anne said. 'I tried to be polite when I refused him, but he was jealous and sought to punish me. If Stefan had not come when he did, he would have raped me.'

'Stefan arrived soon after you left the house. I told him the direction you had taken and he came after you. I thank God he did! Andrew's men might not have been there in time, for he had told them to be discreet. We did not wish to frighten you.'

'I had no idea they were following me,' Anne told her. 'I shall write to my sister and ask her to thank Andrew for me.'

'I am sure they will come for your wedding, my love,' Melissa said. 'You must thank him properly then, but you may write and invite them to your wedding just the same.'

Anne kissed her mother, thanking her warmly for all she had done for Stefan. She asked if there was anything her mother wished her to do in the house, and was given several small tasks to keep her busy.

When she went to visit Stefan later, she discovered that he had been shaved and was sitting up against the pillows, reading one of her father's precious books. It was a privilege that Anne had seldom been allowed herself, for they were very expensive and as a child she had been forbidden to touch them.

'I thought your mother had warned you not to visit me here,' Stefan said and smiled. 'I was about to see if I was strong enough to rise and come in search of you.'

'Mama is not as strict as you were when I was ill and you stayed away from my chamber. She said that I may visit sometimes, providing I am discreet.'

'Then she saw you last night,' Stefan said. He smiled. 'You thought I stayed away from your room, but I came sometimes as you slept, just to see that you were safe and resting.'

'I thought once that I heard the door close and it made me restless. That was the first time I went down to the pool.'

'I saw you bathing,' Stefan told her. 'When we are home again I shall teach you to swim so that we may swim together in the river.'

'Yes, I should like that,' Anne replied. 'When the nights are hot, it is so good to bathe in the pool.' She looked at him thoughtfully. 'Have you decided that we shall go back to Chateau de Montifiori?'

'At least for a time, though we may visit England

sometimes to see your family,' Stefan told her. 'From what I have heard, Cowper destroyed my father's house and disposed of its treasures. It would need restoring before we could live there. I think I might sell it if it were returned to me, and buy something nearer to your father's home…if that would please you?'

'Yes, I should like to stay sometimes in the summer,' Anne said. 'Yet I love your home in Normandy, Stefan, and I shall be content there. Shall we go there as soon as we are wed?'

'No, for the King ordered that I should not leave England until he gave me leave.' Stefan frowned. 'Henry bid me keep his peace. I think he may not be pleased when he learns that Comte De Vere is dead, for he may have to answer to King Louis of France for it.'

'You were not to blame,' Anne said and looked anxious. 'He will not blame you? All you did was stop that man attacking me.'

'Your father has written to the King, telling him what occurred here,' Stefan replied. 'I do not fear that I shall be blamed, for I did not kill De Vere, but I may be kept kicking my heels here for longer than I wish—and we may be summoned to court. We shall not go until we are wed. Lord Melford has arranged for a special dispensation and we shall be wed next week, my love.'

'Are you sure you will be well enough?'

'I shall walk down the church aisle and be there when you come to join me,' Stefan told her. 'I may not have the strength for much else, but I am determined we shall be wed as soon as I can get out of this bed and walk the length of the aisle!'

'Yes,' Anne said and smiled at him. 'If I am honest, that cannot be soon enough for me, my love.'

* * *

'You are beautiful,' Catherine said as she placed a coronet of white flowers on Anne's head and attached some veiling to her hair at the back. 'I am glad that you will be happy at last, dearest.'

'If I am, it is in part due to your husband,' Anne told her. 'Andrew's instinct to protect me from the Comte De Vere was a good one.'

'Yes, he told me what he had done,' Catherine said. 'I believe it was because of what happened to me when we were first married. The lady Henrietta tried to murder me in my own chamber. None of us could believe it at first, and Andrew has never forgotten it, even though she has been dead three years or more.'

'I am very grateful to him. I had hoped that he would be here for the wedding, Catherine.'

'His Majesty summoned him to court,' Catherine said. 'When the King sends an order like that, there is no choice but to obey. Andrew hopes that he may be here in time for the celebrations. However, he insisted that I came and sent you his good wishes.'

'Your gift was generous,' Anne said. 'Such beautiful cloth is expensive, I know, and there is enough for both Stefan and I to have clothes made—and the fur to line my cloak is beautiful and soft.'

'We were not sure what to give you, Anne. Lord de Montfort is a wealthy man and we thought he would have silver and jewels, but cloth is always useful. I am pleased we decided as we did—having seen the jewels he has given you as a wedding gift, I do not know how we should have matched them. I have never seen rubies as fine as the necklace you are wearing.'

'They are beautiful,' Anne said. 'I believe they came

from an eastern prince's treasure chest, as payment for some boon that Stefan performed. He said they were uncut and he had them polished and mounted for me.'

'They are certainly lovely,' Catherine said. 'You will be spoiled and adored, Anne—and that is as it should be. Andrew tells me that Lord de Montfort is richer than anyone might have guessed.'

'He has many treasures at the chateau, and many trunks that still remain to be unpacked,' Anne told her. 'I had just begun the work when I was stolen from the gardens.'

'I know what it is to be abducted,' Catherine said. 'I was fortunate for Andrew found me within hours, but you were separated from Stefan for nearly two months.'

'I have been on thorns lest something should occur and prevent the wedding,' Anne confessed. 'So much has happened to me this past year, Catherine. I am afraid that something will occur to prevent our marriage.'

'You must not be afraid,' Catherine said and kissed her. 'Stefan's enemy is dead and so is the Comte De Vere—nothing else will go wrong, my dear sister. I am sure of it.'

'I pray that you are right,' Anne said, but a little shiver went through her and she felt suddenly cold. 'If anything should part us now, I do not know how I could bear it.'

Anne was nervous until she saw Stefan waiting for her at the end of the long aisle, but as he turned his head and smiled at her, her anxiety melted. Her love welled up inside her and she seemed to float towards him, almost as if she walked on air and were in a dream—a dream from which she prayed she would never wake.

Anne answered her vows in a clear voice, her heart racing as the priest asked if any dissented or could show good cause why they should not be joined as man and wife. No one spoke and the ceremony was completed as Stefan turned, looking down at her with love. He bent his head and kissed her so sweetly that she felt the heat radiating through her body like the rays of the sun, and suddenly she was filled with happiness.

They left church to the sound of bells and the cheers of their friends and family. Showers of dried rose petals were thrown over them, and they ran hand in hand towards the house, followed by their friends and family.

The banquet was soon underway, and Anne led the dancing with Stefan. It was a slow, graceful dance and she saw that every movement caused him pain still, though he did his best to hide it from her. However, he was white from the effort when they sat down and she refused when there were calls for her to dance again.

'You may dance with others,' Stefan whispered to her. His eyes caressed her, thrilled her, warmed her. 'I shall not be jealous, my love. This is your wedding and I want you to be happy.'

'I am happy,' she said, and her face was bright with happiness. 'I have all that I need, and I shall dance with you at home when we have guests and you are truly well again.'

Stefan lifted her hand and kissed the palm. 'I shall be well enough to show you how much I love you later,' he promised, and Anne trembled with delight. It seemed that all her dreams had come true at last.

* * *

The evening wore on and she began to feel a little nervous again, for the guests had drunk deeply of her father's good wine and had begun to make ribald jests. The bedding ceremony was something that must be endured, though she hoped the guests would accompany Stefan to the door of their chamber and then leave them in peace. Catherine had been spared this ceremony since her marriage took place at court and she left immediately afterwards to journey to her husband's home, but Anne and Stefan were to stay here for the time being.

The hour was late when her mother beckoned to her. 'I think you should slip away now, dearest,' she said. 'Catherine will come up with you and help you to—'

She broke off as there was a disturbance at the far end of the hall and then someone came in. Anne saw that it was her brother-in-law, the Earl of Gifford, and as she saw his face she sensed that something was wrong. Catherine had gone to greet him, and whatever she said made her look grave. She spoke to him again and then came hurriedly to Anne's side.

'Shall we go up, sister? I have something to tell you and it is best said in private.'

'Yes, of course…' Anne glanced over her shoulder and saw that the Earl was speaking with Stefan and both men looked grave. 'What has happened?'

'I shall tell you when we are alone,' Catherine said. 'There is news—though Andrew was not sure whether it was good or bad.'

Anne looked at her impatiently, but Catherine said nothing more until they were in the bridal chamber and she had sent the maidservants away.

'I told you that Andrew was summoned to court to explain what had happened to the Comte De Vere?'

'Yes.' Anne looked at her fearfully, for she had had an odd feeling at the back of her mind the whole day. 'Please tell me at once!'

'Lord de Montfort is summoned to court immediately. He will have to leave here at first light.'

'Then I shall go with him,' Anne said. She saw the doubt in Catherine's face, but refused to be swayed. 'Do you think I could sit here while Stefan may be in danger? If he is to be cast in the Tower again, I shall ask to be imprisoned with him.'

'Anne! You could not possibly share his cell. It would not be right, my love. You would sicken and die in that dread place.'

'Stefan's wound has not healed properly yet. I shall claim my right as his wife to be with him. I would not be the first woman to be imprisoned in such a place, nor the first wife to share her husband's punishment.'

'Anne—' Catherine broke off as the door opened and Stefan entered. 'I shall leave you alone together. You have a few hours before you must leave.'

'Stefan!' Anne said as her sister went out, closing the heavy door behind her. 'Is it true that the King has summoned you to London?'

'Yes, my love,' Stefan said, looking grave. 'It seems that Henry was not pleased by the news about Comte De Vere. He says that he may be called to answer to France and would have me explain myself.'

'I shall come with you,' Anne said. 'I was there. I saw what happened. You are innocent of any crime—and if they shut you in that terrible place, I shall come with you. I refuse to be parted from you again.'

'How fierce and brave you are, my love,' Stefan said and touched his fingers to her lips as she would have gone on. 'Hush, my sweet Anne. I agree that you shall come with me to London, but not to the Tower. If Henry wishes to punish me, he must do so, but not you. I will not have you suffer in that place. I love you too much, my darling.' He hushed her with a kiss as she would have spoken, then took her hand and led her to the bed. His eyes caressed her, heating her with their fire, driving all else but the need to be with him from her mind. 'You heard what Catherine said, Anne—we have a few hours. We must make the most of them and they will have to sustain us in the days ahead.'

Anne smiled up at him, her eyes bright with love and longing as he helped her to unfasten her gown and remove the under-dress. He dropped a kiss on her satin-smooth shoulder and then pulled the chemise to one side, letting it slither down over her hips so that her soft, naked flesh was exposed to his view.

'You are so lovely, my darling,' he breathed, his hand caressing the side of her face, travelling down her throat and stroking her shoulder. He bent his head, flicking at her breasts delicately with his tongue, the sensation so sweet that Anne arched her body, trembling with this new wonder. 'I want you so very much…'

'Are you sure you are well enough?' Anne asked, for she knew his side was still painful. She saw the answer in his eyes. He wanted her and he would lie with her no matter what the cost. She felt the heat pooling at the inner core of her and shivered in delightful anticipation. She offered her hand, leading him to the bed, and then lay down, looking up at him with perfect trust. His clothes were soon discarded and he joined her on the bed. For a while they savoured the pleasure of being together, gazing at each other, touching, kissing softly, but the passion mounted swiftly.

Anne gasped with pleasure as Stefan bent over her, his kisses inflaming her senses past the point of reason. She clung to him, moaning as his hands and lips caressed her, seeking out all the secret places of her body, rousing such hot desire that she writhed with pleasure. As his body covered hers, she felt the hot, hard length of his manhood against her thigh and melted into tingling desire. She cried out once in pain as he thrust into her, but his kisses took the momentary pain away, and she moved to meet him as he plunged deeper and deeper into her welcoming warmth. Moaning, she bucked and arched beneath him, crying out again and again as the wonderful feeling burst through her and she felt almost as if she had died.

Her tears were wet against his shoulder. He eased to one side, looking at her anxiously.

'You weep, Anne?'

'Tears of happiness,' she said and snuggled closer to the warmth of his body, her lips tasting the salt of his sweat as she kissed him, burrowing into him like a little kitten. 'I love you so much, Stefan. I shall love you all my life and no one else...'

'That is as well,' he said, a fierce glint in his eyes. 'For if another man tried to take you from me now, I should kill him. You are mine and mine alone.'

'It is all I want of life,' Anne told him and gasped as he pulled her against him and she felt the burn of his manhood. He wanted her again already, and she knew that after the exquisite pleasure she had found in his arms the first time, she would always be ready for him, always want this wonderful closeness, this content that came from loving. 'You…only you, Stefan.'

Anne woke with a start as she felt a hand shaking her shoulder. She looked up at Stefan and saw that he had already dressed. She had not meant to sleep all night, but after their last incredible loving she had fallen into a deep sleep.

'I hate to wake you, my love,' Stefan said. 'But we must leave soon. I shall go down and prepare the men your father is sending with us. Get dressed and come down as soon as you are ready.'

'Yes, of course,' Anne said and smiled as he bent to kiss her. She felt so warm and comfortable in their bed, and she wished that she might pull him down to join her. After their loving of the night before, she would have stayed here for ever if she could, but she knew they had no choice but to leave at once for London. They would be at least three days on the road, and perhaps they could spend those nights wrapped in each other's arms, but she knew that whatever happened in the future, she would never forget her wedding night.

Dressing hurriedly in gown a maid had put ready for her the previous night, she was soon ready to join her husband down in the hall. A maid had brought a cup of ale and a pastry to her while she was dressing, but she had eaten no more than a few morsels and taken but a sip of the ale. They would stop on the road and she might feel like eating then, but for the moment she was too nervous.

Melissa was waiting down in the hall for her. She embraced her and looked at her for a moment, smiling as she saw her eyes.

'You are happy, my love. I have packed food for the first part of your journey, and you must try to eat. I know you are anxious, but Andrew has decided to come with you. He will speak to the King on Stefan's behalf if necessary—and you know you are always welcome to come to us should you need to, my love.'

Anne thanked her mother and hugged her, then went out into the courtyard where perhaps twenty-odd men-at-arms were waiting together with another group of servants. They were a mixture of her father's retainers and the Earl of Gifford's train, and they would make a stir as they passed through the countryside.

Anne went to her husband. He smiled at her and gave her his hand, helping her to mount her palfrey. She saw her father and brother amongst those who had gathered to see them off and she waved, a brave smile on her face.

'Are you ready, Anne?' Stefan asked and she inclined her head. 'Then we should leave.'

Chapter Eleven

'**Y**ou must wait here,' Stefan said, a determined glint in his eyes as he saw the wild look on his wife's face. 'You have not been bidden to the hearing and you may not attend.'

'I should be there,' Anne said, her eyes blazing with passion. 'It is unfair that I must remain here and have no say in what happens at your hearing.'

'You know I would take you if it were possible,' Stefan told her. 'I cannot allow it, my love.'

'But…' Anne protested. She was silenced by a kiss that sent her senses swirling. 'Stefan…' She saw the anguish in his eyes and said no more. 'Forgive me. This is as hard for you as it is for me.'

'I would never leave your side again if it were my choice,' he told her harshly. 'The King commands and I must obey, Anne. Wait here and Andrew will come to tell you what has happened if I cannot.' A cry reached her lips but did not leave them—she could not bear to think that he might be returned to the Tower or worse.

Her heart felt as if a giant hand had squeezed it, but she stood back and allowed him to leave her. To make a scene would cause him pain and avail her nothing. She must wait in patience, hard as that might be.

'I am sorry that you have been summoned here when you should have been with Anne,' Andrew said as they waited in the antechamber. 'I pleaded your case with Henry but he was adamant that you should put your case yourself.'

'You have done all you could, Gifford,' Stefan said, 'and I am grateful for it. All I ask is that, if the worst happens, you will make sure that Anne is safe. She has some idea of sharing my imprisonment, and I know she would do it—but it cannot be allowed to make such a sacrifice.'

'She would do it, too,' Andrew said. 'Anne has courage and she is stubborn—very like her father. However, I shall make sure she returns home to wait for you there should Henry see fit to punish you with another sojourn in the Tower, though I hope he will not.' He turned his head as a page came to the door to summon them. 'It is time, my friend. Be of good heart. Henry Tudor is a harsh man, but fair.'

Anne could not rest in the house. After wandering about like a lost soul for what seemed like hours, she donned her cloak and went out to the garden. She walked to the river's edge, standing in contemplation of the dark waters. If Stefan were lost to her, she thought that she would prefer to cast herself into the river rather than live on in a world that was empty because it did not contain him.

She stayed in the garden for almost an hour, and then, driven by the cold, went in to sit by the fire, but she was too restless to work at her sewing or read from her Bible, though it might have given comfort to a less rebellious soul. Anne was ready to rage against the world and God, for it was cruel to give so much and then take it away almost as soon as it was given.

The day had gone and it was growing dusk when at last she heard the sound of voices. Jumping to her feet, she rushed into the hall, tears springing to her eyes as she saw both Andrew and Stefan.

'Oh, thank God!' she cried. 'I have been so afraid…'

She rushed at Stefan. He caught her in his arms, laughing down at her, his eyes filled with such love and pride that her heart leapt for joy.

'I should have sent word,' he said. 'Forgive me, my love, but the King kept me with him the whole day and I have not had a moment to call my own.'

'Well, Anne, you have your husband back,' Andrew said and grinned, looking very pleased with himself. 'I shall leave you to tell her your news, Stefan. Catherine will be waiting for me and I shall return to Melford with the glad tidings. Then we shall go home.'

'Goodbye,' Anne cried. 'I forgot my manners, Andrew. Thank you so much for all you have done for us.'

'I did very little,' Andrew said. 'It appears your husband hath done the King a service…but he will tell you himself.'

Anne looked at Stefan as the Earl left. He smiled, took her hand and led her into the chamber where a fire had been lit to drive away the chill of a November evening.

'It seems that I have rid Henry of an enemy,' Stefan said as he drew her near to the fire. He stood gazing down at her face. 'At least, you were the reason he was dealt with—by Andrew's men, as it happens. However, since I was the first on the scene, his Majesty chose to reward me. I have been made Earl Montifiori, and Henry's ambassador to France, if I choose to take the honour. Do not look alarmed, for it is a post I declined. However, I have agreed that I will take a message to his brother monarch in France.'

'I do not understand.' Anne was bewildered. 'Are you saying that Comte De Vere was an enemy of the King?'

'Henry believes that he came to court to spy for Spain. His Majesty was not deceived, for he had his suspicions some time ago. England has many enemies, though some disguise themselves as friends. He was not sure whether I might also be involved in the plot, but apparently the fact that he was willing to kill me has convinced Henry that I was blameless. I am free to return home when I choose…and my father's estate is mine to do with as I please.'

'Oh, Stefan…' Anne's face lit up. 'That is so wonderful. I spent the day thinking the worst and now…' She fell silent as he bent his head and kissed her. 'We are so lucky…so very fortunate.'

'I am fortunate to have found you,' Stefan told her. He smiled, touching her cheek with the tips of her fingers. 'So, my love, do we stay here or do we go to Normandy?'

'We go home,' Anne told him. 'We shall visit your

home here when you wish, but I would choose to live at the chateau, because it is where we first fell in love.'

'So romantic,' Stefan said and laughed huskily. 'It is my choice, too. I have asked Fritz if he will be my steward and live in my father's house as the master, caring for the house and lands as if they were his own. For that he will receive one half of all the rents and tithes. The house will be there if we wish to visit and as an inheritance for one of our children one day.'

'Yes, that is a good solution,' Anne said. She smiled at him. 'So, my lord—when do we go home?'

Anne had been busy all day, supervising the unpacking of the trunks that had come with her from England. There were many wedding presents, which would add to the store of treasures the chateau already possessed. In the past few days since their return from England, she had gradually brought out many of the fine artefacts that Stefan had collected over the years, arranging them in an eclectic mix that gave the house a charm and mystery all its own.

The house had become a home, warm and comfortable, scented with the perfume of flowers and exotic spices that added to the atmosphere. They had not yet held a banquet to celebrate their wedding with friends, but Stefan had issued invitations for a few days' time and she was looking forward to meeting the friends she had met when she had stayed here before, but this time as Stefan's much loved wife.

She had wondered what kind of reception the French King would give them when they visited the court, but they had been welcomed and received warmly. It seemed that King Louis had also known that De Vere was a traitor both to France and England, for his loyalty lay with Spain. As he died without issue, his estate was forfeit to his king, and therefore Louis had no reason to regret his passing. His lands and house would be sold or given to one of the King's favourites, and they would have a new neighbour.

Anne looked about her, feeling pleased with the atmosphere that now prevailed in her home. It was ready for visitors, and her brother Harry and his wife would be amongst the first when they visited Claire's father at Christmastide. However, Catherine and Andrew had also promised to visit, and Anne's mother might be persuaded to make the journey in the New Year.

Her heart quickened with joy as she heard footsteps and then her husband walked in, accompanied by Hassan. They were laughing together, at ease and happy in each other's company. Stefan saw her, his face lighting up as he came to greet her. She went to meet him, lifting her face for his kiss.

'You are home,' she said and smiled. Love flowed from her, wrapping about him like a warm, scented cloud of silk.

'Yes, I am home, my love.' His eyes were as blue as the summer sky and reflected their love for one another. 'For wherever you are is my home…'

* * * * *

MILLS & BOON®

are proud to present our...

Book of the Month

Sins of the Flesh
by Eve Silver

from Mills & Boon® Nocturne™

Calliope and soul reaper Mal are enemies, but as
they unravel a tangle of clues, their attraction grows.
Now they must choose between loyalty to those
they love, or loyalty to each other—to the one
they each call enemy.

Available 4th March

Something to say about our Book of the Month?
Tell us what you think!

millsandboon.co.uk/community
facebook.com/romancehq
twitter.com/millsandboonuk

HISTORICAL

Regency

MISS IN A MAN'S WORLD
by Anne Ashley

With her beloved godfather's death shrouded in scandal, the impetuous Miss Georgiana Grey disguises herself as a boy and heads to London to discover the truth. Being hired as the notorious Viscount Fincham's page helps Georgie's investigations, but plays havoc with her heart...

Regency

CAPTAIN CORCORAN'S HOYDEN BRIDE
by Annie Burrows

After her father scandalously auctions off her virginity, Miss Aimée Peters flees London to become a governess in remote Yorkshire. But her new employer, the piratical Captain Corcoran, never sought a governess—he wants a bride!

Regency

HIS COUNTERFEIT CONDESA
by Joanna Fulford

Major Robert Falconbridge and English rose Sabrina Huntley must pose as the Conde and Condesa de Ordoñez on a perilous mission. Soon Falconbridge doesn't know what is more dangerous—his enemies or the torment of sharing a room with this tantalising beauty...

On sale from 1st April 2011
Don't miss out!

Available at WHSmith, Tesco, ASDA, Eason and all good bookshops

www.millsandboon.co.uk

0311/04a

HISTORICAL

Regency

REBELLIOUS RAKE, INNOCENT GOVERNESS
by Elizabeth Beacon

Notorious rake Benedict Shaw can have his pick of *ton* heiresses, but one woman has caught his experienced eye... governess Miss Charlotte Wells! And he isn't used to taking no for an answer...

WANTED IN ALASKA
by Kate Bridges

Outlaw Quinn can't risk doctor's visits—kidnapping a nurse is the only answer. But Autumn MacNeil is only dressed as a nurse for a costume ball, Still, there's no way he can let her go now...

TAMING HER IRISH WARRIOR
by Michelle Willingham

Widow Honora St Leger knows there is little pleasure in the marriage bed, so why should she care that the disturbingly sexy Ewan MacEgan is to wed her sister? Ewan finds himself drawn to the forbidden Honora—one touch and he is longing to awaken her sensuality...

On sale from 1st April 2011
Don't miss out!

Available at WHSmith, Tesco, ASDA, Eason
and all good bookshops

www.millsandboon.co.uk

She was his last chance for a future of happiness

Fortune-teller Jenny can make even the greatest sceptic believe her predictions just by batting her eyelashes. Until she meets her match in Gareth Carhart, the Marquess of Blakely, a sworn bachelor and scientist.

Broodingly handsome Gareth vows to prove Jenny a fraud. But his unexpected attraction to the enchantress defies logic. Engaging in a passionate battle of wills, they must choose between everything they know…and the endless possibilities of love.

REGENCY

Collection

Let these sparklingly seductive delights whirl you away to the ballrooms—and bedrooms—of Polite Society!

Volume 1 – 4th February 2011
Regency Pleasures by Louise Allen

Volume 2 – 4th March 2011
Regency Secrets by Julia Justiss

Volume 3 – 1st April 2011
Regency Rumours by Juliet Landon

Volume 4 – 6th May 2011
Regency Redemption by Christine Merrill

Volume 5 – 3rd June 2011
Regency Debutantes by Margaret McPhee

Volume 6 – 1st July 2011
Regency Improprieties by Diane Gaston

12 volumes in all to collect!

MILLS & BOON

www.millsandboon.co.uk

2 FREE BOOKS
AND A SURPRISE GIFT

We would like to take this opportunity to thank you for reading this Mills & Boon® book by offering you the chance to take TWO more specially selected books from the Historical series absolutely FREE. We're also making this offer to introduce you to the benefits of the Mills & Boon® Book Club™—

- **FREE home delivery**
- **FREE gifts and competitions**
- **FREE monthly Newsletter**
- **Exclusive Mills & Boon Book Club offers**
- **Books available before they're in the shops**

Accepting these FREE books and gift places you under no obligation to buy, you may cancel at any time, even after receiving your free books. Simply complete your details below and return the entire page to the address below. You don't even need a stamp!

YES Please send me 2 free Historical books and a surprise gift. I understand that unless you hear from me, I will receive 4 superb new books every month for just £3.99 each, postage and packing free. I am under no obligation to purchase any books and may cancel my subscription at any time. The free books and gift will be mine to keep in any case.

Ms/Mrs/Miss/Mr ——————— Initials ———————

Surname ————————————————————

Address ————————————————————

————————————————————————

——————————————— Postcode ———————

E-mail ————————————————————

Send this whole page to: Mills & Boon Book Club, Free Book Offer, FREEPOST NAT 10298, Richmond, TW9 1BR